Published by Autumn Day Publishing
Copyright 2015
Cover by Toby Gray
Other works by L.S. Gagnon,
Witch: A New Beginning
Witch: The Secret of the Leaves
Original release, 2013
ISBN 978-0-9962305-3-7
All characters in this book are fiction
and figments of the author's imagination.
If you want to receive our monthly newsletter, text the word
'witch' to 42828 to sign up.

WITCH: THE SPELL WITHIN

by L.S. Gagnon
Facebook/TheWitchSeries

Table of Contents

Prologue

Someone once said that misery lives in darkness, thrives in sadness, and grows in evil. But the only misery I know lives in my heart, thrives in my tears, and grows in my soul.

Today my misery would end. I would set James free. With a single wave of my hand, I would erase James' memory of our love, of our wedding day. After this moment, he would never remember me. My only way out was to give him up forever.

James held onto my hand as his feet slid closer to the edge of the cliff. I looked down and hoped the jagged rocks below would kill me instantly. We were up too high for me to survive if he lost his grip. He fought the spell's power with everything he had, resisting the urge to let go of my hand as the spell implored him to do. He wanted to pull me up and save me, but the spell was telling him to let me fall.

How I wished this were a dream, one I would wake up from any minute. But a happy ending wasn't in the cards for me. I looked into my husband's eyes one last time. "I love you," I whispered. I let my hand slip from his and began to fall to my death.

Chapter 1
The Burial

Crisp autumn air caressed my face and leaves crackled under my feet as I sprinted through the woods. This was the most beautiful fall yet, and Salem's trees were alive with color. When the town swarmed with tourists, I sought solace in the woods. At times, the lake felt like my only friend. The silence I found there gave me peace when nothing else could.

I ran faster, trying not to think, knowing that a single thought could bring the pain rushing back in an instant. The events of the past few days haunted me. So much had happened. If only I could turn back time to when my life was still boring and dull, before *he* had walked into my life.

James had turned my life upside down, jumped out of those books and changed my world. The news that he was my husband had shocked me more than the discovery that I was a witch. And not just any witch: I was half wizard. Unlike my half-human, half-witch friends, I possessed pure witch and wizard blood. No one else had the powers I had. My friends could employ their magic only through the casting of spells. I was much more dangerous than that; even warlocks feared me. Warlocks could throw spells, but only I could destroy whatever I wished with a mere wave of my hand.

As my feet carried me faster along the trail, the memory of the battle roared in my mind: the fire burning beneath me, my skin melting away. But my friends had saved me, had broken the hourglass and released my spell. They knew the time had come for me to remember who I was, to summon the memories that I myself had them erase.

But that was not the end of my nightmare. Simon had cast a spell on James, his own son. Soon James would grow to hate me. Simon was also determined to get his hands on the crystal my father had given me. He knew I had hidden something important inside it, but for some reason, I couldn't remember what that was. I knew only that I had to keep it out of Simon's clutches.

I noticed I was starting to forget things. When my best friend Delia and the boys brought up things that had happened, I struggled to recall the details. It terrified me, and I feared telling my father and friends about it.

The only thing I seemed able to think clearly about anymore was James. But thoughts of him were not good ones. The boys told me they had seen Helena in James' car, and that he was kissing her. I waited up for him that night with the intention of confronting him, but my father insisted that I not speak to him about it. That had me more confused than ever. Everyone went back to asking if I was okay. I must have heard that question a dozen times over dinner that night. Without a word, I had left the table, locked myself in my room, and sat staring out the window for countless hours.

A dark mood had fallen over me, one I couldn't shake. I often snapped at the boys and Delia for no good reason. Even my father got a taste of my bad mood. Fury burned inside me when I heard him defending James at every turn. There were so many things to be worried about, yet I couldn't get James' betrayal out of my mind. I had accepted that Simon's spell was poisoning James against me, but why was he turning to Helena?

Soon I would see him with her at Amanda's burial. He had been helping her with the arrangements. I was more worried about my temper. Seeing them together might well strip me of whatever shred of sanity I had left.

Only Cory seemed able to calm me. We had grown up together, so he knew me best. He stayed glued to my side anytime James was around. The spell was changing James, making him hate me more with each passing day. Cory seemed determined to soften the blows any way he could. Fish, Joshua, Javier, and Samuel seemed decidedly unworried about any of it. They had given up the job of protecting me the moment I regained my powers.

Delia spent hours talking to my father, peppering him with questions about his life. She was fascinated, seemingly obsessed, with learning every single detail about his world—the wizard world. She anxiously awaited the return of his powers, hoping to bear witness to all the amazing things she'd heard he could do.

I picked up my pace, the sting of James' betrayal still fresh in my mind. I jumped over tall maples as though they were bushes, slowing only as the lake came into view. At the water's edge, I sat and stared out into the water.

"One more day," I whispered. Tomorrow we would leave for my father's world to bring back the white energy he needed to regain his powers and break Simon's spell. My nightmare would finally come to an end. But first I had to get through this day, and I wasn't altogether sure I could.

Helena had arranged a human burial for her sister Amanda, who had died fighting in the battle against Simon and his warlocks. James would no doubt be standing by Helena's side during the ceremony today. He appeared to be attending to Helena's every need these days, and I was growing sick of it. I wanted to hurt them both, make them pay for my pain. It was getting harder to fight the urge to fly right into her house and break her neck. Sometimes I even felt like hurting James. His interest in that witch made no sense to me. Then again, I was starting to see James in a whole new light.

My heart still raced when I saw him, but I was no longer sure if it was from love or anger. His beauty still overwhelmed me, but the blue of his eyes had begun to fade. It was something that happened to male witches. When male witches fell in love, their eyes turned blue, but only for their beloveds to see. When female witches fell in love, our hair transformed into a tangled mass of curls, nearly unmanageable without magic. I had always thought this was unfair. No matter how angry James made me or how far down I buried my feelings, the unruly mats on top of my head wouldn't let me forget my love for him.

I rose from the edge of the lake and broke into a run, trying desperately to clear my head. I didn't stop until I reached James' house. The mansion had lost some of its former beauty to me. The tall iron gate now looked more like a jail cell, holding my heart prisoner. James had intended for this mansion to be our home, but it seemed out of place in my life now. All of his money couldn't fix what I felt. The thought of him falling out of love with me was more than I could stand, and it scared me to think I might be falling out of love with him, too. I couldn't understand the change in either of us.

Cory was waiting outside when I stepped through the gate. He was dressed for the burial, and I couldn't help but notice how handsome he looked in all black. His muscles showed despite the clothes. With every move he made, I saw how beautiful he was. His green eyes, his perfect smile, caused me to notice him each day. Cory had loved me once, but I had chosen James— a choice that now felt like a big mistake.

"James already left," Cory said, eyeing me worriedly. "We're going to be late."

"I'll shower fast," I replied. "I won't be long." I dashed into the house and started for the stairs.

"There you are," my father said when I passed the kitchen. "You are going to be late."

My father was always in the kitchen these days, no doubt making more potion to slow down Simon's spell. But I had already given up on that. No matter how much James drank, it didn't seem to do any good. His mood grew darker by the day.

I didn't bother hiding my anguish from my father. What was the use? He could read my mind and always knew how I felt.

I walked into the kitchen, I spied a pot on the stove. "More potion for James?"

He nodded. "Ten times stronger than the last batch. I believe this will slow down the spell."

"Is there a potion to make him stop seeing

Helena?" I asked angrily.

His shoulders drooped. "Do not start, Thea."

"Just let him hate me, Father. I don't care anymore."

He crossed the kitchen and reached for my hand. "You understand that it's the spell that poisons his mind against you, don't you? You must never turn your back on him."

I pulled my arm away. "I'm going up to shower." I hated feeling angry with my father, but I was tired of him defending James. I felt his eyes on me as I climbed the stairs to my room.

Delia and the boys, all dressed in black, were waiting by the door when I came back down. Delia looked radiant in her tight dress, her long black hair pinned up in a bun, and her dark eyes more beautiful than ever. Fish couldn't take his eyes off her. His boyish face couldn't hide the lustful thoughts stirring in his blond head.

Javier stood in front of the mirror to the right of the door, making sure not one hair was out of place. His Mohawk, he believed, was what made the ladies look his way. Joshua, my red-headed teddy bear, was standing by the door. He was nearly as tall as the doorway. Samuel was being his usual impatient self, pacing the foyer and periodically glancing down at his watch. He was tall and muscular like Cory.

The people standing before me were my reasons for living, my guards and friends. I loved them deeply and hoped to one-day give them back the time I had taken from them. They had spent hundreds of years protecting me, watching over me when I didn't know who I was. Spells and potions had kept them young, and years of training kept them looking like gods.

I wore my usual dark colors and flowing fabrics. I could never pull off a dress like Delia's. Even now, as a powerful witch, I still had issues with my body. Hiding my larger build inside loose clothing offered a sense of comfort I wasn't willing to give up.

As I walked down the stairs, Cory stepped forward. "You sure you want to do this?" he asked. I knew he feared what I might do to Helena.

I sighed. "No, but I owe it to Amanda."

We left the mansion and made it to the burial on time. I couldn't help but notice James and Helena under the tent at the gravesite. They sat in front, his arm around her back, her head resting on his shoulder. When my eyes met hers, she drew nearer to him and broke into a sob. James responded by pulling her closer.

We took our seats directly across from the loving couple. I swallowed down my anger as James stroked her long blond hair. Several times during the service, Helena glanced at me from the corner of her eye, smiled, and nestled closer to James. I trembled with rage. Cory's grip tightened around my hand. I had to stop myself from jumping over the coffin and breaking her neck. When the service ended and the rest of the mourners stood to leave, I remained glued to my chair, trying to reclaim my sanity.

A man's voice came from behind me. "Thea, is that you?"

I turned to see an old friend I had known long before my memory was erased. "John-John?" I asked. "How are you?" I stood and wrapped my arms around him.

He chuckled quietly, returning my embrace. "Only you call me that, Thea."

"That's because your name is so sweet, I have to

say it twice." I pushed away and smiled up at him.

"It's good to see you," he said. "I was glad to hear that your memory returned."

"Last time I talked with your mother," I said, placing my hand on his cheek, "she was very worried about you. You've been gone so long."

John-John was a dear friend. Our mothers had served on the council together. As children, he and I had been hide-and-seek buddies. He was my first real friend. But my father was strongly protective of me back then, and careful about whom I talked to. I cried for days when John-John's mother sent him away out of the blue. He was her only son. It never made any sense to me. After my mother died, many of the witches sent their sons away from Salem.

John-John had grown into a handsome gentleman with shining brown eyes and light brown hair. He wasn't muscular like the boys, but lean and sturdy. His radiant smile rarely left his face.

"How's Donna?" I asked. "I haven't been to her shop in a while."

"Mom's good." His eyes drifted to Delia, who stood behind me, talking with the boys. "She's glad to have me back."

I reached for him again. "That makes two of us."

"So, who are your friends?" he asked, looking at Delia

"Oh, of course." I extended my arm toward the group. "Do you remember Cory?"

"No, I don't think so." John extended his hand. "Nice to meet you."

He shook hands with the rest of the boys, but John's smile widened when the introductions came around to Delia. "It's more than nice to meet you," he said, mesmerized.

Fish rolled his eyes and gave John a dirty look.

Delia smiled back. "Nice to meet you, too."

"What a pretty name you have," John said. I don't think I've ever heard it before."

"Do you like *my* name?" Fish hissed. "They call me Killer."

As the boys laughed, I stole a glance at James, who was still holding the sobbing Helena. I could feel my temper getting the best of me.

John smiled and looked at Delia. "I hope I see you again."

Fish stepped in front of her. "You know what I hope for—"

"Fish, stop," Cory cut in, pulling Fish toward him.

John looked amused. "I think your little brother needs a nap," he said to Delia. He flashed her another of his winning smiles before turning to leave.

Javier stepped in to help hold back Fish, who was fuming.

Cory chuckled quietly and reached for my hand. "Come on, let's go pay our respects and get out of here."

We got in the line that was forming in front of Helena. It seemed as though every witch in Salem had come out for the service. There were corsets and velvet dresses everywhere—fitting attire for this time of year.

Humans didn't think twice about our usual October apparel. This was Salem, after all. We called it our "normal" time of year, when we could be out and about, minus the strange looks. We blended in with the humans and openly referred to ourselves as witches. Some went as far as telling fortunes and selling potions and spells, passing as mere shopkeepers making the most of the season. We amused ourselves with stories about rash outbreaks and spells gone awry. I could always pick out Delia's spells. They were the ones that had people scratching incessantly as they walked the streets. Hives were her way of getting back at people who laughed at us during other times of the year.

We inched forward in the line. Helena didn't want me there, but I owed it to Amanda. She had died fighting to save me; it was the right thing to do. When I reached the front of the line, Helena stood abruptly.

"I have nothing to say to you, witch," she hissed.

I wanted to slap her, but James was sitting right there. Surely he would jump to her defense.

"I didn't come to talk," I replied. "I only wanted to tell you that I'm very sorry for your loss. I wish things had been different."

Helena's eyes narrowed. I wanted to yank her pretty blond hair out by the roots.

"Oh, things are going to be different, witch," she said. "In fact, I believe things are changing already—returning to their proper place." She looked at James and back at me, a snide smile spreading across her face.

I stepped closer until our faces were only inches apart. "And I think we could be going to another funeral . . . real soon."

Her smile disappeared. She backed away, sat down, and looked at James. I glared at him. Despite my rage, his beauty set my heart pounding. His thick, dark eyebrows indicated his mood: he was angry, now more than ever. The scar on his nose had vanished, fixed by Helena, no doubt. His gray eyes showed no trace of the blue I had once cherished.

I inhaled his scent, wishing for it to calm me. I had marked him with this wonderful scent so I would know he was near, even when my memory was gone.

"When you're done being a shoulder sponge to this witch," I said, "William needs to speak with you."

James stood, and Cory stepped in front of me. He was tall, but James towered over him.

"Are you kidding me?" Cory said. "You really want to do this here?"

They stared at each other for a long, tension-filled moment before Cory grabbed my hand. "Come on, Thea," he said. "Let's get the hell out of here."

I glanced over my shoulder as we walked away. Helena tugged at James' arm, and he sat back down.

"Was he going to hit you?" Sammy asked me as we rejoined the group.

His question stopped me cold. I didn't want the boys to ever have to fight James. My heart would break if any of them got hurt because of me. "Listen, you guys," I said, "if James ever tries something like that again, let me handle it."

Cory shook his head and looked toward James.

"Cory, promise me you won't get between us if something like that happens again." I looked into his eyes. "I can take care of myself."

When he didn't answer, I put my hands on his shoulders. "Cory, promise me."

He exhaled. "I promise."

I shot James one last glance before ducking into the car. My heart sank when I spied him kissing Helena on the head. It was more than I could take. I wanted to run back to them and rip his head off, but I wouldn't let my temper get the best of me. "Take me to the lake," I ordered.

"Why?" Cory asked.

He was angry with James. Like me, he couldn't

understand why James had taken up with Helena.

I stared straight ahead. "Just take me there—now."

Without asking another question, he stepped on the gas and headed in the direction of the lake. I sat in the back seat with the boys, oddly happy in my pain. I had been driving myself crazy wondering if I still loved James, but my broken heart was proof that I still loved him, now more than ever.

Helena, on the other hand, I hated with a passion.

Sharron had told her about the spell Simon cast on James, and now Helena was using it to her advantage. She called James with any excuse to ask for his help, and he was always more than happy to oblige. I had planned on telling Helena to back off, but had waited because she was in mourning. Now the gloves were coming off.

But I had to calm down first. If I approached her now, I'd likely cast a horrible spell on her—or worse, kill her. I knew that would only make James' hatred for me grow faster. I had to compose myself before I told her she was making things harder for me. Of course, that's exactly what she wanted.

She seemed to take pleasure in my pain. I wasn't sure if she was lashing out because of the pain of losing her sister or losing James. The battle to save me had resulted in her sister's death, but she'd also lost James when I came into the picture. Whatever Helena's reasons, she wasn't hiding the fact that she despised me.

I pictured Helena's slender frame and her long, neat hair. She really was a beautiful woman. She didn't wear loose clothes; she dressed elegantly, often in designer fashions. With my "full-figured frame," as Delia called it, and the unruly mop atop my head,

Helena and I couldn't be more different.

Regaining my powers had given me back some of my previous confidence, but it had done nothing to change my feelings about the rest of me. I still hated my body, hated the shape of my thighs. I wasn't sure why I had become so insecure.

Delia constantly tried to convince me that I was beautiful. She said most women would love to have my curves. But I didn't believe her for a minute. Helena looked like a goddess standing next to James. I shook my head and tried not to think of her.

When we pulled up to the lake, I threw open the car door and jumped out. I was so angry. I wanted to run fast, release my frustration. How could he kiss Helena on the head like that when he knew how special that gesture was to me?

I ran up a tree trunk to escape my thoughts. I no longer needed Sammy's shoe spells; my mind knew what to do. When I reached the top of the big maple, I let out a loud scream. With a wave of my hand, I tore several branches from the tree and sent them plummeting to the ground. I wanted something to hurt as much as I did.

Suddenly exhausted, I lowered myself to one of the branches and sat. What good were my powers if I couldn't break Simon's spell? If I broke it, James would die—something Simon had made sure of before he went into hiding.

"Thea?" Cory called. "Where are you?"

He looked up after a cluster of brilliant red leaves fell onto his head. He sighed and made his way up the tree. "We have to tell James about the spell," he said when he reached the top. "It could make things easier."

"No," I snapped. "You know James would kill himself if he knew about the spell. I'd rather him hate me than take his own life. I forbid you to tell him."

"He's making me want to kick his ass." Cory balled his fists. "I can't stand the way he talks to you."

"It's the spell," I said, reaching for his arm. "It's not James. You know that."

"I know it's not him, but do you? Because it doesn't seem like it right now."

I had to stop reacting to the situation; I was making them hate James. "Don't hate him, Cory. No matter what happens, please don't ever hate him."

He sat down next to me on the branch. "I'm trying," he said, sounding frustrated. "But you need to stay away from him until your father breaks the spell. Seeing him with Helena only makes everything harder."

"I can't leave that house." I looked away. "I have to keep an eye on him."

"Okay, but if he so much as lays a hand on you, all bets are off."

I turned back to him. "Don't say that. I can stop him if I need to."

He sighed. "Man, things could have been so different."

"You mean, between us?"

"Yeah." He averted his eyes. "You'd love me the way you love him."

I wondered if he was right. So many times I had been tempted to tell Cory how much I cared for him, how as a kid I'd had a huge crush on him. But he was always too busy running around with human girls. I didn't understand that he had feelings for me, much less the depth of those feelings. It had broken my heart to watch him disappear into the woods with his conquests. I had buried my feelings and eventually given up on him, thinking of him more like a brother than a potential lover.

"I never knew you felt that way about me," I said, affectionately bumping my shoulder into his arm. "You never told me."

"And if I had, what then?" He looked down. "Would you have loved me back?"

I thought for a moment before saying, "Yes."

His head shot up. "What do you mean, yes?"

I smiled. "I had feelings for you, Cory. But you were always going after the human girls. I had no idea how you felt about me, so I forced myself to get over you."

He seemed shocked. "Why didn't you tell me how you felt? I had no idea you had feelings for me. I only went out with those girls because I was lonely, because I'm a man, because I needed the warmth of a woman. Because I loved you and thought you didn't love me back—at least, not that way." He pushed my hand away and shook his head. "I was going to ask you to marry me, did you know that? Right before *he* came into the picture. I even had a ring."

I didn't know what to say. I gazed out at the lake. A ring? It was the last thing I expected to hear.

After a moment, he grasped my hand again. "If James hadn't come into the picture, what would you have said if I had asked you to marry me?"

I looked into his eyes. "If I had never met James, and it was just me and you . . ." I sighed. "I would have said yes."

We stared into each other's eyes. After a moment, Cory laughed.

"What?" I asked.

"I was hoping the answer was no. That would have been a lot easier to live with." He paused. "Can we use Delia's memory box to visit one of my memories?"

I shot him a curious glance. "Why?"

"Because I want to go back and slap myself."

I chuckled and leaned my head on his shoulder. "Things are the way they should be, Cory. We were meant to be friends—good friends. I think that's why I was able to get over you. You never lose your real friends."

"Yeah, I suppose you're right." He rested his head on mine. After a moment, he squeezed my hand. "Come on, let's get out of here."

Once again, Cory had managed to calm me. We climbed down the tree and returned to the car. We saw Delia and the boys sitting by the lake.

"Come on, " Cory called. "Let's get out of here!"

But Delia and Fish were arguing. Fish waved his hands as he carried on, while Delia, arms crossed, rolled her eyes and tapped her foot on the ground.

"What's going on?" Cory asked, as we approached the group.

"It's her," Fish replied. "She thinks I'm just some stupid kid, that I'm not man enough for her. Just because I'm younger than her, she thinks I'm not good enough. I bet she thinks that John dude is man enough for her."

"It's not my fault he smiled at me!" Delia said.

"Oh, please." Fish's voice was laced with contempt. "You loved every minute of it. I bet you even think he's your type. You must have loved that he liked your name, too."

Delia dropped her arms to her sides. "You have no idea what I think. You know, it's seriously annoying when you presume to know how I feel."

"Now *I'm* annoying?" Fish shot back.

"What do you care, anyway?" Delia asked. "I'm just some stupid crush to you."

"You want me to tell you what you really are to me right now?"

"Enough, you two!" Cory stepped between them. "You're acting like children. You guys never treated each other like this before. Maybe you ought to go back to just being friends."

"I have a better idea," Fish said. "Maybe I should find myself a witch who doesn't think I'm just a stupid kid. I bet I can be plenty man enough for her." He stormed off toward the car.

Delia stared at him, her mouth agape and hands on her hips. "Fine by me!" she shouted. "You just made my day, you stupid kid!"

Cory and I exchanged glances as Delia took off after Fish. The boys shrugged and followed her.

"What the hell is going on?" Cory asked. "It's not like them to fight like that."

"She's scared," I said. "She's frightened out of her mind to be in love."

Cory looked at me, incredulous. "That was Delia in love?"

"No, that was Delia afraid of love."

When we reached the station wagon, Fish was sitting in the far-back compartment. Delia sat in the front seat, arms folded across her chest. From the middle ground of the backseat, I tried to get them to talk to each other on the way home. Delia looked over her shoulder, rolled her eyes, and turned back around. Fish ignored me altogether. I caught Cory's eye in the rearview mirror and shrugged.

Seconds after Cory brought the wagon to a stop in the driveway, Fish stormed out of the car and into the house. My father stood in the foyer and eyed Delia curiously as she breezed by him, rolling her eyes. Cory and I lingered in the entryway as she and the boys made their way up the stairs.

"Is everything okay?" my father asked.

"They'll be fine," Cory answered. He looked up the stairs, concern on his face. "At least, I hope they will."

My father nodded. "James is home. He's drinking the potion," he said to me.

"You should really give that news to Helena, Father," I replied curtly. "She's the woman in his life now."

"Excuse me," Cory said. He gave us a short nod and disappeared upstairs.

"Why don't you try talking to James?" my father said. "He seems calm."

I crossed my arms. "Well, I'm not. I've got nothing to say to him."

He looked into my eyes, as if waiting for a different answer. "Do you want him to die?"

"What? How can you ask me that?"

"Then go in there and talk to him." He pointed to James' study. "If you do nothing to fight this spell, his death will be on your hands."

It was as though all the air went out of the room. My mood changed instantly. What was I thinking? I should be storming into James' office, begging him to keep loving me. None of this was his fault. It was Simon's spell. What I couldn't understand was why it was changing me.

"I'm sorry, Father," I replied, bowing my head.

"I'll go talk to him."

"Good." He lifted my chin. "And please, try to be nice."

I drew a deep breath, walked across the foyer, and knocked on James' office door.

"Who is it?" he called out.

"It's Thea."

My heart leaped when he opened the door. He was smiling, and his eyes were blue. I wanted to jump into his arms and let his scent fill my head. He was the most beautiful man I'd ever seen, with his wavy brown hair and perfect, rugged face. My breath caught when my eyes met his. I always felt safe when I was near him.

"Am I interrupting?" I asked, trying to compose myself.

"Not at all." He opened the door wide. "Please come in. I was just having some tea William made to treat my headache." He rubbed his temples. "I've been getting more than my fair share lately."

So that was how Father was getting him to drink the potion.

"Are you okay?" I asked, stepping into his office. I looked around at the hundreds of books that filled the shelves and the old-fashioned typewriter sitting on his desk. I wondered why he didn't have a computer; he could certainly afford one. It looked as though he was in the middle of writing something.

He closed the door and walked behind his enormous desk. I saw two cigar ends in the ashtray next to the typewriter. I had never known James to smoke.

"I'm fine," he answered. "What can I do for you?"

His tone was cold. My heart sank. I remembered my father's words and did my best not to let it bother me. I swallowed down the anger rising inside me and tried to ignore the smell of Helena's perfume on his clothing. "I was wondering if you wanted to have dinner tonight . . . just the two of us."

He started shuffling papers around his desk. "I thought you were mad at me."

I am! I thought. "Why would you think that?"

"Uh, I believe the term you used was 'shoulder sponge'. I assumed you were upset."

I wanted to tell him he was right, that it killed me to see him with Helena.

"I'm sorry for saying that."

He looked up at me.

"But I wasn't mad," I lied.

"Good. But I already have plans for dinner."

My temper flared. "What do you mean you already have plans?"

He went back to shuffling his papers. "After what happened at Amanda's service, I didn't presume you'd want to have dinner with me. I promised Helena I'd help her with Amanda's will."

"Since when do witches have wills?" I asked. "We have nothing to pass on but spells."

"Maybe you don't. Not everyone can make money with the wave of a hand. Some of us have to work for it."

My anger was getting harder to control. "Since when? Those witches have never hesitated to use spells to make their lives easier. I didn't know Helena even knew what work was."

His eyes narrowed. "Why don't you like her?"

I leaned over his desk. "Why didn't you ever tell me about her, or that you and she had a romance?"

"Is that what this is about?" He stood, resting his

hands on the desk. "You're jealous?"

"Answer the question!" I hadn't planned on arguing with him, but I also hadn't expected him to tell me he was having dinner with Helena.

He glared at me. "I never told you because I knew you'd treat her cruelly."

His answer stunned me.

"I wanted to protect her from you," he continued. "I knew you would have made her life a living hell if you knew we'd dated."

I didn't know what to say. I was hurt and couldn't believe James thought this of me. "You were protecting her . . . from me?"

"Yes, and I have a feeling I still need to," he said, his voice rising. "It doesn't look like things have changed that much."

I had to stop myself from waving my hand at him to cast a spell. "When have I ever given you reason to believe I could be cruel? I've never bothered that witch."

"Let's keep it that way, shall we?" He returned to his papers.

I shoved his precious papers aside. "That won't be a problem," I said, "as long as you remember that you're married—and bonded—to me!"

"I'd never forget that!"

"Let's keep it that way, shall we?"

I stormed out of his study, slamming the door behind me as I stepped back into the foyer. I wanted to wring his neck and drag him across a field of sharp stones. I reminded myself that it was the spell at work. This was not my James, not my husband. It wasn't his

fault. But his demeanor toward me was making it very hard to stay calm.

Helena, on the other hand, knew all about the spell. She knew exactly what she was doing. It was time to deal with her and her smug little glances, which I planned to slap right off her face.

Chapter 2
The Muddy Sand

My eyes burned as I hurried up the stairs, blinking back tears the whole way. "No more tears, witch," I said to myself. I had to find a way to numb the pain. I knew my temper; I'd do something stupid if I couldn't control myself. Before I'd regained my memory, I would run off at every little upset. But this version of me didn't run. Now I only knew how to retaliate.

I was different now. That Thea had been timid and insecure, and that wasn't me. I wanted to keep a part of her alive, but I detested how weak she was. She had made me soft and emotional, and now I was allowing pain to break through into my heart.

It was time to put a stop to it. I needed to be my old self again—strong and cold. I couldn't allow her to break me down any more than she already had. She had never dealt with the things I had. She'd always had the good James, the James who loved her and would do anything for her. She never had people counting on her like I did.

Others looked to me to solve their problems. They looked to the cold-hearted witch I had become. I was bringing her back. The responsibility was on my shoulders. It all fell to me, the witch with the unrivaled powers.

I'd had very few friends because of who I was and what I could do, and even fewer suitors. Then James had come along. He was the only one who treated me like a woman and was never intimidated by my power. He looked at me with tender eyes. But that was starting to change.

I reached the boys' room and threw open the door. They were playing a video game. "What are you guys doing tonight?"

Cory looked up. "Why? What's up?"

"I need to get out of this house. You guys want to come with?"

Fish tossed the controller onto the floor. "Yeah, and I don't even care where we go. I'm sick to death of being stuck in this house."

Delia appeared in the doorway. "Let's drive into Boston," she suggested.

"Like your piece-of-junk car could even make it that far," Fish jabbed.

Delia flashed him a dirty look. "I thought you were ignoring me?"

"Oh, I'm sorry," he said. "Maybe we should ask John-John where he wants to go."

"Stop it—both of you!" I'd had enough of their bickering. "We can go anywhere you want," I said, striding out of the room. "Right after we stop at Helena's."

Cory followed quick on my heels. "Why are we going there?"

"No questions," I said. "Let's just go."

We met James coming out of his study. His eyes appeared blue at first, but rapidly turned gray when he looked at me. He waved to the boys and Delia as he passed.

"Let me tell my father we're leaving," I said over my shoulder. I walked into the kitchen, where my father sat in front of an enormous book.

"Catching up on some reading?" I asked.

He looked up and smiled. My father exuded confidence. His face suggested that he had all the answers. His gray hairs were like strands of wisdom, making him appear wiser than anyone else I knew.

"I'm getting some spells ready for when you leave for my world," he said.

"Spells? What kind of spells?"

He closed the book and poured himself some tea. "I will explain everything tomorrow."

I nodded and told him we were going out. He asked where to, but I glossed over the specifics. I knew he wouldn't approve.

"How did it go with James?" he asked.

"I don't want to talk about it," I said as I walked out of the kitchen. "You'll have to ask James."

I rejoined my friends, and we drove to Helena's shabby little house. It stood out from the others on the street, which were neat and impeccably maintained. The faded blue paint was peeling from the siding, and the yard was filled with dried-up bushes and plants that had never been tended to.

As we pulled up to the curb, I told the others to wait in the car. This was between Helena and me. "Look out for James," I ordered.

I made my way up the short walk and knocked on the door. I was surprised by who answered. "Pam?"

"Thea!" Pam hugged me and kissed my cheek.

"I didn't even know you were alive," I said, pulling away from her.

Pam laughed. "Alive and well, and glad to see that your memory is back."

"I haven't seen you since you got married." I couldn't help but wonder why she was here. And why now?

She sighed. "He passed away, Thea—twenty years after we moved."

Pam had married a human and moved away. He never knew she was a witch, and she never wanted him to find out. She and I had met before Delia and the boys were even born. My father had already stopped my aging by then, but Pam, of course, continued to grow up. She was my best friend and I was glad to see her, but I would have expected her to die of old age by now. She had obviously started taking an anti-aging potion like the one used by Delia, the boys, and many other witches I knew. I was surprised. Not all witches wanted to stay young forever, and I'd always assumed Pam was among them.

A number of years had managed to get by her; she was clearly much older than me. She could have passed for my mother. Nevertheless, she still had her signature red hair, and her eyes hadn't lost one bit of their shine. Her body was still curvy and her skin milky white.

"He was a good man," I said. "I'm very sorry for your loss."

"Thank you. He was everything to me."

"How did he die?"

"Cancer. I tried spells, but none of them worked."

I nodded knowingly. "Humans never do well with our spells."

"I know, but I had to try something." She smiled and shrugged.

"Of course. What brings you back? The funeral?"

The smile disappeared from her face. "Yes, and Sharron called me. She said my cousin needed some sense knocked into her. She told me about Simon's spell, and about what Helena's been doing." She offered me an apologetic look.

I closed my eyes and sighed in relief. *Thank you, Sharron.* Pam and Helena had always been close. If Helena would listen to anyone, it was Pam.

"So you know she's after my husband?" I asked.

Pam fiddled nervously with the talisman that hung from the chain around her neck. "Yes, but it's only fair that you know: James is the one who's been coming here looking for her. It's not all Helena's fault."

"And what about the twenty phone calls a day she makes to him?" I asked. "I suppose that's not her fault either. He's a married man, Pam."

"But he comes even when she doesn't call. I've tried to make him leave."

"Enough!" I snapped.

Pam jumped, her eyes wide.

"He's bonded to me. I don't care how many times he comes here, she needs to stop calling him."

"I'll talk to her," Pam answered, her voice quavering. "I promise."

"Please do. And if you don't, the next time I come, I won't bother to knock."

"I can't make any promises, Thea, but I'll try to

make her understand."

Pam's revelation stunned me. Why would James come looking for Helena even when she hadn't reached out to him? I wondered if his real feelings for her had resurfaced. Maybe he really had loved her once.

"If she calls him again," I added, "I'll be back."

Pam nodded, and we said our goodbyes. As I started back down the path, I was suddenly hit with a rancid odor. I halted in my tracks. I knew that smell. I had marked Simon with a stench so powerful it made my eyes water when I came into contact with it.

I turned on my heel, catching Pam just before the door closed.

"Who's here?" I leaned in and sniffed her. She was clean.

"Thea, what are—?"

I pushed her aside and barged into the house. Moments later, I heard Delia's heels clicking up the path.

She slipped through the door behind me. "What's going on?" she asked.

I ignored her and started inspecting the house. Simon was everywhere. "Bring me my stick, Delia," I ordered, my eyes still darting from room to room.

She dashed from the house.

I heard the boys pile in through the door. "What's going on?" Cory asked.

Delia arrived just behind them and handed me my stick. I snatched it from her and pointed it toward a wall in the living room. "He was here."

"Who was here?" Cory asked.

"Simon." I handed him my stick, ran toward the wall, and broke through it feet first. Muddy sand oozed from the wall as it came crashing down.

"Thea, what's going on?" Pam asked, frightened.

I stood and waded into the pile of sand. "Put Pam to sleep," I told Delia.

Seconds later, I heard Delia wrestling with Pam, and the boys stepping in to help.

"What is that stuff?" Cory asked as he stared down at the sludgy mound.

"He's trying to hide his scent from me, but I can smell him." I watched as the boys laid Pam on the sofa. "Put her in the car. I'm checking her memories. I want to know why she really came back."

With a wave of my hand, I set the wall back in place, sand and all. I wanted to leave everything the way it had been. I didn't want Simon finding out I was onto him.

We left Helena's and headed back to the house. After spotting James' car in the drive, we decided it was best to sneak in the back door.

"Keep him busy, Sammy," I whispered, "while we get Pam up the stairs."

We watched from a distance as Sammy approached James' study and knocked on the door. Then Sammy waved to us discreetly and walked into James' office. Joshua threw Pam, who was still asleep, over his shoulder.

"Let's take her into our room," Cory whispered.

Joshua trotted up the stairs as easily as if he were holding a feather. The rest of us followed into the boys' room and closed the door. Delia handed me the memory box. Although my father had given me the box when I was a little girl, he left it in the care of Delia, who would one day need its magic to save my memories.

"Lock the door," I ordered.

I knelt on the floor next to the bed where Pam lay

and pulled her recent memories, checking for Simon. I found nothing. I went back several more years. Still nothing, only sad memories of tears cried and countless worries.

"Thea, who is she?" Delia asked.

"She was my best friend until she outgrew me and moved away. I assumed she died of old age."

"She looks like she stopped her aging around forty or so. Why would she wait that long?"

"I think because that's around the time her human husband died."

Delia's eyes widened with surprise. "She married a human?"

I nodded and continued sifting through Pam's memories. "I've gone back quite a few years now, and I can't find anything."

I searched for a while longer, but Pam's memories gave no hint of Simon's presence. I was about to give up when one memory caught my attention. It was of James and Helena, from just yesterday. I hastily snatched the memory bubble and went in.

James and Helena were seated side by side on the sofa, his arm around her as they laughed and talked in whispers.

Pam was watching the happy couple from the kitchen as she made dinner. *"Are you not expected home for dinner, James?"* Pam asked.

"He's having dinner with us," Helena replied.

"Well, I'm sure his wife will want to join us," Pam said, reaching for the phone. *"I'll call and ask if she can make it."*

Helena stormed into the kitchen, yanked the phone out of Pam's hand, and slammed it down on the receiver. *"Why are you doing this?"* she hissed. *"He doesn't want to go home. He hates her."*

"Yeah," Pam said. *"And you know why."*

Helena seized Pam's arm and dragged her across the kitchen out of James' earshot. *"That witch took him from me,"* Helena said. *"If he wants to be here, I'm not sending him away. He loved me first, and he's going to love me again."*

Pam pulled her arm from Helena's grasp. *"He left you, Helena. He picked her, and you're just angry because she didn't have to use a love spell on him."*

Helena stumbled back, her eyes widening in shock.

"Yes, cousin," Pam said, *"I know all about it. Sharron told me everything. James never loved you, only her."*

"Well, I'm not using a love spell this time," Helena replied, attempting to compose herself. *"He wants to be here. He has feelings for me."*

Pam grabbed her cousin by the arm. *"Don't be a fool, Helena. He's already bonded. He'll never be able to give you what you want."*

A sinister smile spread across Helena's face. *"Death breaks that bond, cousin,"* she said. *"It's just a matter of waiting."*

Pam shook her head as Helena breezed out of the kitchen and took her seat again next to James.

But Helena's secret was out. She had used a love spell on James when she first met him, a spell that no doubt had been broken by Simon when he saw that James was getting close to her. Simon needed James to love me. Helena's spell would have only made things difficult for him.

Surely Helena had to be lying about not using a

love spell on James now. It was obvious she'd cast another to trap him in his vulnerable state. What she didn't count on was my finding out about it. I smiled to myself as a feeling of satisfaction settled in. I could easily break the spell of a mere witch.

I pulled myself from the memory. "She's clean. She doesn't know anything."

I was glad to be able to say that. I really liked Pam. She had been a good friend to me, and from what I saw, she still was.

"What about Helena?" Cory asked.

"I'm going to check her memories next, but not here. It's too risky with James around."

"How about our apartment?" Cory suggested.

"No. I'll think of something." I looked at Delia. "Erase tonight's activities from Pam's memory, and you and Joshua take her home."

I handed Delia the box and left to find my father. I needed to tell him about what I'd found at Helena's house. I also wanted to break Helena's spell before James left to have dinner with her. No way was I going to let that witch get her paws on my husband again.

I went to the kitchen, but hesitated before going in. James and my father were talking on the other side of the door. I leaned in close to listen.

"It's happening so fast, William," James said. "I'm getting nervous."

"I know," my father replied. "It's getting harder to keep her calm. I do not like how things are going."

"Why don't we just tell her?"

"No, James. It would change everything."

"Yes, of course. I'm sorry."

I heard someone pacing the floor—my father, most likely.

James spoke up again. "I wish you would just kill me. It would solve everything."

"I can't do that, son. She would never forgive me."

"Then I'll find another way."

"Please give up on that plan, James. I told you, I will find a way. We'll get through this."

I stepped back from the door in disbelief. Why would James ask my father to kill him? Did James know about the spell, about what it was doing to him? I waited for more, but their conversation had apparently run its course. I took a deep breath and stepped into the kitchen.

"Thea!" my father said, startled. "I didn't know you were home."

James glanced over his shoulder and stood up from the table. He, too, seemed surprised by my presence. "I'll speak to you later, William," he said. "Samuel is waiting in my study."

"No, wait." I blocked his way to the door.

I noticed fresh bandages around James' lower arm, and he hastily yanked down his shirts sleeve. I knew what those bandages meant; my father had shown him something. But it didn't make any sense. Everyone knew about my vision. What else could my father possibly be showing him?

"I need to ask you something," I said to James.

"What is it? I'm running late."

"The guest house—does anyone live there?"

He regarded me curiously. "No, why?"

"It's the boys. I heard them talking. They're going crazy being stuck in this house. I thought maybe the guest house would serve them better, give them more of a feeling of freedom."

"Why don't they just go home?" James asked.

I didn't want to tell him about my fears. Simon knew what they looked like now. He would have them killed if they were alone.

"They like being here," I lied. "They could just use a little more space, is all."

A hint of a smile tugged at his lips. "Then please, insist that they take it."

"Thank you."

When our eyes met, a feeling of repulsion shot through me. His eyes turned from blue to gray in an instant.

He looked away. "I'll go ahead and tell them now." He went to the door.

The feeling of disgust was overwhelming. I was horrified and couldn't shake it. In that moment I wanted to kill James—kill my beloved husband.

"Maybe you should finish your tea first, James," Father suggested. "Thea, go upstairs and give the boys the good news yourself. I'm sure they are waiting on you."

But I couldn't tear my eyes away from James. I wanted to rip him apart as he passed me and returned to the table.

"Thea!"

My father's voice jolted me from my violent reverie. "Go and give the boys the good news," he told me. He said it slowly, carefully, as though he wasn't sure he'd be able to get through.

After one last glance at James, I darted from the kitchen and hurried up the stairs, feeling confused. I was upset because of Helena, but this was different. What I felt in that kitchen was pure hatred. I stopped halfway up the stairs and ran my hand through my hair, trying to regain my sense of composure. There were other issues at hand. I had to get Pam out of here before James saw her.

I was relieved that James had consented regarding the guest house. Now I could take Helena there and search her thoughts, perhaps even take James there and find out what my father had shown him.

I walked into the boys' room as Delia was closing the memory box.

"We need to get her out of here," I said. "Are you done?"

"She's all set," Delia replied.

"Good. You and Joshua get her home." I turned to Cory. "I found a safe place. You guys are moving to the guest house. Get the keys from James. He's waiting for you."

"Are you in a hurry?" Cory asked.

"I just don't want James coming up here. He might see Pam."

"I'll help Joshua get her out," Cory said as he lifted Pam from the bed.

I ran out of the room and sped down the stairs. I still had to break Helena's spell before James left the house. That witch wasn't going to get near him again.

"They're delighted," I said, breezing back into the kitchen.

James flashed me a hateful look over his shoulder and continued talking to my father. "Maybe I'll let them use one of the cars in the garage," he said. "I don't even drive half of them. I'm sure they're growing tired of Delia's wagon."

"That would be very generous of you," my father said. "I am quite sure the boys will be more than grateful."

I concentrated on James, closed my eyes, and broke Helena's spell. When I opened my eyes, my father was watching me with a look of suspicion across his face. I avoided his gaze and held my breath.

James got up from the table as Cory walked in. "Cory, let's go so I can show you and the boys the guest house. I'm happy it's finally going to be of some use."

As soon as Cory and James were out of earshot, I felt my father's forceful hand seizing my arm. "We need to talk," he said, practically dragging me up the stairs. When we reached my father's room, he pushed me in before him and slammed the door. I'd never seen his temper get the best of him. I swallowed thickly. Despite all my years in the world, my father still had the power to make me feel like a child.

"Why did you go to that woman's house today?" he asked. "I ordered you to leave things alone. You need only concentrate on bringing back the energy so I can break Simon's spell. You need to put those two out of your head."

I stepped back. "I can't. It's Simon. I smelled him today in her house. I found muddy sand inside Helena's walls that he used to mask his scent. He's been there, Father. I'm sure of it."

"Yes, I know about that."

I sat down, trying to make sense of what I'd just heard. "What are you not telling me?"

He clenched his jaw and closed his eyes. For the first time, I saw just how worried he was.

My heart raced. "Father?"

"I promise, I will tell you soon," he answered. "Please be patient with me, and more importantly with James."

"Be patient while I watch him fall in love with

another woman?" I ask. "Is that what you're asking me to do?"

"Yes."

I couldn't believe what I was hearing. "How can you ask that of me?"

"I'm asking for time," he replied. "I'm begging you to leave things alone."

I could tell he was hiding something. "He's going to die, isn't he?"

He looked at me intently. "I give you my word, I will not let him die."

Yelling in the hallway interrupted our conversation. It was James, and he sounded furious. "Thea! Where are you?"

I rushed to the door and opened it. "Over here."

He stormed out of our bedroom and walked down the hall toward me. "Why did you go to Helena's house today?" he asked, his eyes full of rage.

I shut the door behind me. Where was Cory? I needed him to keep me calm. "I heard Pam was there," I lied. "I went to say hello."

"Lies!" He roughly grabbed my arm. "I'm warning you, Thea, stay away from her."

I tried pulling my arm away, but his grip was too strong.

"She's frightened out of her mind because of you." He dug his fingers deep into my skin. "What did you say to her?"

"I didn't even talk to her," I said, still struggling to yank my arm away. "I told you, I wanted to say hello to Pam."

"Helena just called me. You sent Delia over there to scare her. Why would you do that?"

"Let go of me!" Finally, I was able to push him

away. "I didn't send Delia to do anything. That hag lied to you."

He grabbed my arm again, nearly breaking it.

I struggled to free myself. "You're hurting me."

"Get your hands off of her!" Cory appeared suddenly and punched James square in the face.

My father's door opened.

"Cory, don't!" I shouted, pulling him away from James. "You promised!"

James lunged at Cory, but I jumped between them. "James, don't!"

He shoved me out of the way. I slammed into the wall and fell to the floor.

"James!" my father shouted.

Cory ran to help me. "Thea, you're bleeding." He helped me up, then turned to James and flicked his arms, readying his blades.

"Cory, no!" I reached for his shoulder.

He dodged my hand and glared at James. "If you ever touch her like that again, I'll kill you."

James stood stock still, as shocked by his actions as everyone else. I attempted to move closer to him.

"You're not going near him," Cory said, blocking my way.

My father approached James. "Cory, take Thea to the guest house. I need a moment with James."

I tried again to step closer to James, but he backed away from me. Cory flicked his arms again, and his blades disappeared. He grabbed my hand and led me away.

I watched over my shoulder as my father herded James into his room.

Chapter 3
Great, Now We're Aliens

Cory was still fuming when we walked into the guest house. "You're not staying in that house," he said, pulling me in behind him.

I jerked my hand away. "I can take care of myself. That wouldn't have happened if you hadn't punched him."

"He's going to hurt you." He stopped to face me. "Look at you. You're already hurt."

I folded my arms across my chest. "Are you forgetting who I am?"

"You shouldn't be in the same house with him. Soon, he'll want to kill you."

"You promised you would stay out of it."

Cory threw his hands up and stormed off into one of the bedrooms, muttering under his breath.

I looked out the window and up toward my father's window. I could feel James' pain. I had seen the look in his eyes when he realized what he'd done. He had come back to me in that moment, as if the spell had been lifted for a split second. I knew for certain that he was hating himself right now.

I stepped out into the garden and sat on a bench. Something was bothering me, and I didn't like it. When Cory was holding me back, I hadn't wanted to run to James to comfort him. I had wanted to kill him. I was able to fight the impulse, but my heart had raced with excitement at the thought of finishing him off.

I pushed the troubling thought aside when I noticed blood running down my cheek. I had hit that wall harder than I thought. As I wiped at the blood, an odor hit me. It wasn't strong, but was enough for me to know that Simon's men were nearby.

It was starting to get dark. I strained to see across the massive yard. I noticed movement from the corner of my eye and spotted three men looking through the first-floor windows. I quietly got to my feet and made my way toward them. Their scent suggested they were human. They were so busy looking inside, they didn't notice me standing behind them.

"Looking for me?" I asked.

Before they could turn around, I waved my hand and sent their weapons flying across the yard. They tried running, but I sent them slamming into the trees. I waved my hand at some branches, which came to life and grabbed each of the men. By the time I made my way across the garden, the men were hanging upside down. Upon closer inspection, I realized they were just boys—eleven, maybe twelve—and they were scared out of their minds. Why would Simon send humans, boys no less, to do his bidding?

"Who are you, and why are you here?" I asked.

The one wearing a green jacket and baggy jeans spoke up. "Please don't hurt us!" he begged.

The boy with spiked blond hair asked, "What the hell *are* you?"

I reached out and touched his face. "Your worst nightmare, if you don't tell me who, or what, you came looking for."

"James," Spike replied. "We're looking for James."

I eyed the boy curiously. I had assumed they were looking for me. "Why James?"

The third boy, with shaggy brown hair and a backpack dangling from his shoulders, finally spoke. "What the hell did you get us into?" he asked Spike.

"Silence," I commanded. "Why are you looking for James?"

My boys arrived on the scene. Cory already had his blades deployed. He was about to plunge right in when I stopped him.

"Wait! Only kill them if they don't answer my questions," I said.

"I'll check the house," Sammy said, and ran toward the back door. Meanwhile, Fish checked the yard for more intruders.

"Oh my god," Spike said tearfully. "Please don't kill us."

"What the hell *are* you guys?" asked Shaggy.

Cory strode over to me. "Thea, I think they're human."

I continued staring at the three partners in crime. "Yes, I can see that."

Green Jacket spilled the beans. "A man gave us money to bring James to him."

"What was the man's name?" Cory asked.

"Simon," the boy cried.

"And where did this Simon want you to bring James?" I asked.

"This crappy blue house in our neighborhood, the one my mom always complains is driving down our property value—whatever that means."

Cory and I exchanged a glance. "I knew it," I said. "I'm going to kill that witch."

Green Jacket started praying.

"You really don't know who I am?" I asked.

They shook their heads.

Shaggy spoke up: "We promise not to tell anyone what we saw. Just please don't take us to your planet."

Cory and I looked at each other again and erupted in laughter. I waved my hand, and the boys fell into a deep sleep.

Cory shook his head as he cut the boys down from their restraints. "Great," he said, chuckling. "Now we're aliens."

"So, Simon's using humans now," I said. "He must not have any friends left."

"Now what?" Cory asked.

"I'm going to Helena's house. If Simon sent them to bring James, then he must be there waiting."

A look of concern washed over Cory's face. "You sent Delia and Joshua to Helena's. They're still not back yet."

Fish walked up. "The yard's clear." He looked from Cory to me. "What's going on?"

Cory pointed to the boys. "Simon sent these kids to lure James to him. He's waiting at Helena's."

It took mere seconds for Fish to put two and two together. "Delia!"

Cory and I followed as Fish ran to the front of the house, pushed open the gates, and started down the street on foot. I waved my hand toward a tree, and a branch tore off and fell into my hand.

"I'm going with you," Cory said.

"No. Go tell Sammy to make sure James stays here, and tell my father what happened." I mounted the branch. "And get rid of these boys."

I flew off and quickly spotted Fish. I swooped down, grabbed him by his shirt, and pulled him aboard.

"Hurry!" he shouted as we flew through the darkness.

When we neared the house, Fish dismounted from the branch. He sprinted to the front window as I hovered above him. "They're having dinner," he whispered. "I don't see Delia or Josh anywhere."

I flew to the back of the house, landed the branch, and peeked inside. Pam and Helena appeared to be alone. I walked to the door and knocked, not sure what I was going to say. I was relieved when Pam answered and not Helena.

"Thea?" Pam said as she opened the door. "What are you doing here?"

"Hi, Pam. I'm sorry to bother you, but have you seen my friend Delia?"

"Delia?" she asked. "You mean the witch from the stand? Why would she be here?"

Helena came to the door. "What the hell do you want?"

And that was all it took. I barged into the house and struck Helena across the face. I grabbed a fistful of her hair and dragged her across the floor.

I threw Helena against a wall and wrapped my hand around her throat. "Why did you lie to James?"

When she didn't answer, I leaned in until my face was inches from hers. "If you go anywhere near James again, I promise you will die a horrible death. This is your only warning. The next time you see me, you will die."

Helena burst into tears.

Pam rushed in. "Thea, you're hurting her."

I ignored Pam and tightened my grip around Helena's throat. "If you tell James I was here, I will skin you alive and not let you die until you have suffered. Do you understand?"

She swallowed hard and nodded.

"Where's Delia?" I asked.

"I . . . I don't know."

"Don't lie to me, witch," I said, slamming her head against the wall. I wanted to kill her, but I had to know what connection Simon had made with her. I was about to strike her again when I heard Fish whistling for me to come outside. I released Helena and waved my hand. She flew across the room and slammed into a wall. Her body collapsed on the floor.

"Please, stop!" Pam begged, and ran to Helena's side.

I walked out the door and spotted Fish on his cell phone. "What's going on?" I asked.

"James is gone," he said, holding up his hand. He continued his conversation.

"What do you mean?" I snatched the phone from him.

"Thea, don't!"

"Hello, Cory?"

The phone blew up in my hand, startling me and sending pieces flying. My eyes scanned the yard, trying to see who had thrown a spell.

~ 45 ~

"Aw, man," Fish whined. "I really liked that phone, too."

I looked at him, exasperated. "What the hell is going on?"

He leaned down to pick up the remnants of his destroyed phone. "Delia and Josh are home. They're safe."

"And what about James? Where is he?"

"I don't know, but your father said to get back home right away." He slipped the broken pieces into his pocket, and we left.

Back at the house, the others were waiting for us. Fish ran up to Delia, who was sitting on the sofa. "Don't ever do that to me again!" he said. "Where were you?"

Delia got to her feet. "We were hungry after dropping off Pam, so we got something to eat." She smiled. "You were actually worried about me."

Fish looked into her eyes, took a step forward, and began to kiss her. Delia was stunned at first, but slowly wrapped her arms around him and kissed him back.

"I love you," Fish whispered between kisses.

"You'd better," she replied, finding his lips again.

They were still kissing when I felt my father's hand on my shoulder. "A word with you, if I may."

I followed him into the kitchen. Now what had I done?

"Sit down," he ordered.

"Where's James?" I demanded.

"Sit," he repeated sternly, pointing to a chair.

I did as he ordered. "Did you send him to look for Helena?"

He pounded his fist on the table, startling me.

"What did I tell you?" he shouted. "I warned you not to worry yourself about that girl, pleaded with you to leave it alone. Why will you not listen to me? Put those two out of your head!"

"He's my husband! How dare you tell me to step aside?"

My father sighed and closed his eyes. "You are testing my patience, Thea."

"And you are testing mine." I stood.

"Sit down! I am not one of your underlings. I am your father, and you will treat me as such. I am tired of your nonsense and your attitude. You will change your tone and show some respect."

I dropped back down into the chair, my eyes fixed on his. "Father, what did I do?"

"Why did you remove the love spell that was on James?"

Was he serious? "How can you ask me that? He's my husband."

"Exactly. Nothing will ever change that."

I looked away. Of course he defended James. "He looks for her, did you know that? How do you think that makes me feel?"

"He's bonded to you," my father said, banging the table again. "You have nothing to worry about. We have other matters at hand."

"How can you keep saying that to me?" I stood again. "Why does this not bother you? Can't you see it's killing me?"

He looked at me silently for a long moment. "It is necessary."

"Breaking my heart is necessary? Allowing my husband to cheat on me is necessary?"

"He's not cheating on you. James is not that kind

of man."

I turned my back to him. "It seems your precious James has changed."

"Thea," he said, his voice softening, "you know it's the spell."

"No," I said, facing him. "The spell makes him hate me, not fall madly in love with another woman."

At that moment, James strode into the kitchen through the back door. Without hesitation, my father crossed the room and tapped him on the forehead. James closed his eyes and bowed his head.

"Why did you do that?" I asked.

My father hurried back to me and seized my shoulders. "You foolish girl," he said. "James is not falling in love with Helena. Simon put a love spell on him."

"What?"

"Simon needs James to stop loving you. He's using Helena to fortify the spell."

"I thought Helena cast the love spell on James."

"No."

"You should be glad I broke it then."

He sighed heavily. "Thea, Simon doesn't realize that I'm making Helena look like you."

I gasped. "What?"

"In his mind, James knows it is Helena, but his heart only sees you. Simon needs James to stop loving you. It is the only way he will ever get to your mother's heart. Don't you see?" He dropped his hands to his sides. "The love spell will give you time to bring back the energy to me so I can break Simon's spell."

I glanced at James, who continued to sleep. "Why didn't you tell me, Father? Why would you keep something like this from me?"

My father turned and ripped open James' shirt.
I was stunned. His chest was covered in bruises.
"What happened to him?" I asked.

"Before Simon can get to your mother's heart, he
must first cut out his son's heart. As you can see, he has
not yet been able to pierce the skin. James' love for you
is still strong enough to protect it."

As I bent over my husband, tears welled in my
eyes. I ran my hands over his battered skin, touched the
rough edges of the scars Simon had left behind. My
hand trembled as I reached toward James' face and
brushed my fingers across his cheek. My father stepped
up beside me and raised his arms as if trying to stop me.
Did he think I would hurt James?

I lowered my hand. "How could you allow Simon
near him?"

"I'm buying time," he said. "I do not wish for
Simon to learn that his spell can be broken."

"Does this mean Helena is helping Simon?"

He shook his head. "No, she truly believes James
is falling in love with her. She has no sense of Simon's
presence when he sleeps them both to examine James."

"He's going to hate me soon. Simon will be able
to get to his heart."

"Not if he loves Helena," my father said. "Not if
his heart believes that she is you."

What a horrible mistake I'd made by removing
the love spell under the assumption it was Helena's
work. "Oh, Father! What have I done?"

"You can fix this by recasting the spell."

I nodded and looked at James. "Does he know?
About the spell, I mean?"

"No," he said, looking away.

He was lying to me—about what, I wasn't sure.

"I wonder why Simon used humans to lure James to him?" I said.

"When you ended the love spell, James broke his date with Helena. That's why Simon sent those innocent boys to the house. They were probably just a means to an end, the first people he came across to do his bidding." The tension showed in my father's face. He was uncomfortable with me being near James. When I moved so much as an inch toward my husband, my father's jaw tensed and his arms rose again. He relaxed when I backed away. "Now, stop bothering that girl," he said, closing James' shirt. "And go fix your mistake."

My eyes remained fixed on my father. *What am I missing?* "I'm sorry, Father. I didn't realize . . ."

"Never mind that. Just go and reverse what you did tonight."

I waved my hand and recast the spell.

I had to get to Helena before she left town. My anger at her had transformed into pity. She actually believed James was falling in love with her, but once again he was going to break her heart. At least now I understood why James was being so protective of her. No matter how difficult, I would have to learn to look the other way whenever I saw them together.

I hurried to the guest house in search of Cory, anxious to tell him what I'd learned. Laughter filled the place as I walked in. The spacious living room was bigger than my entire apartment and was tastefully decorated with white leather furniture. Even here, James had hung expensive pieces of art on the walls. Two French doors opened onto the back garden. A breakfast bar large enough to seat ten people surrounded the open kitchen.

Fish was sitting on one of the sofas with his arm around Delia.

"We'll buy you a new one tomorrow," Cory called to Fish from the kitchen.

"A new what?" I asked.

"Cell phone," Delia replied, holding up her own phone.

I was reminded of the evening's events. "Oh yeah, why did his phone—" I paused as another thought occurred to me. "Hey, why don't I have a cell phone?"

They all erupted in laughter, much to my confusion.

"You've had about twenty of them," Delia answered.

"I have? Well, where are they, then?"

Fish held out his hand and dangled what was left of his phone. "You killed them," he said. "Just like this one. The moment you place one against your ear, it blows up."

"That's ridiculous." I extended my open hand toward Delia. "Let me see that."

"No way!" she said, clutching her phone tightly. "I just learned how to use this one."

"Here," Cory said, handing over his phone. "I want a new one, anyway."

I snatched the device from Cory's hand and held it up to my ear. In an instant, it blew apart, scattering pieces across the floor. I jumped back, shocked by the jolt. "What the . . ."

"Told you," Delia said, rolling her eyes.

"Why would that happen?"

Cory gathered up the pieces from the living room floor. "I think your wizard energy is too strong, even for modern-day technology."

"But I've never seen that happen with my father."

"Ah, but remember, your father is weak right now," Cory said. "Oh, and don't go near any computers, either."

I placed my hands on my hips. "Why?"

"The minute your fingers touch the keys—boom!"

"That's why your apartment has a rotary phone. James had them installed here, too."

Delia looked at me and tilted her head. "You don't remember any of this?"

"Should I?"

"Um, yes. I erased those memories from your head at one time, but I've since given them all back to you."

My failing memory concerned me, but there were other more pressing things to attend to at the moment. "What did you say to Helena?" I asked Delia. "Things got ugly between me and James."

"I didn't say a word to her. I promise."

"It's true," Joshua added. "I was there."

I looked at Cory. "Want to come on a ride with me?"

He regarded me suspiciously. "You're not going down there to hurt her again, are you?"

"No. I'll explain on the way."

"We can take one of James' trucks," Cory suggested. "He said we could use them."

I nodded, and we took off toward the garage.

Chapter 4
I Thought I Could Handle It

We climbed into one of James' trucks. "Okay, what's going on?" asked Cory.

I told him everything my father had told me.

"So you broke the spell, thinking it was Helena who had put it on James?"

"Yes, but I've recast it."

Cory started the truck. "Man, I'm so glad I'm not a wizard."

A mild feeling of annoyance rose inside me. "Why would you say that?"

"Because having all those powers only seems to bring misery."

I had to admit, Cory had a point. "And yet, so many want them."

"I'm happy just the way I am," he said, smiling.

"That's one of the things I love most about you, Cory. You're happy with whatever life gives you."

He glanced at me. "Not always."

I searched the inside the truck as we drove—so many gauges, buttons, and lights. I had no idea what any of them were for. "How many of these things does James own?" I asked.

"Cars or trucks?"

"He has more than one car, too?"

He laughed. "I'm not sure why, but yes."

I breathed in the pungent yet pleasant scent of leather. The vehicle appeared to have never been driven before; it was immaculately clean. "Why don't you have one of these?"

"I just use Delia's wagon. That's all the car I need."

"Is it for lack of money?"

"What would we do with money?" he said, chuckling. "Spells provide us with everything we need."

"Why do you suppose James has so much of it, then?"

He shrugged. "I don't know. I think because of you."

"Because of me?" This surprised me. "Why would you say that?"

"I suppose it's because he wants to give you the best of everything. You know, because he never could before."

"You know I don't care about those things, Cory."

"But maybe James does. Maybe it's the only way for him to feel powerful."

"He's not like that. You know that."

"Okay then, why? Why the big house? Why all the cars?"

"I don't know," I said, looking out the window. It was a valid question. James was never one to brag about his lifestyle. He didn't wear expensive clothes. Most of the time he wore jeans and T-shirts. He carried himself like a down-to-earth man. If you saw him walking down the street, you would never assume he was rich. But he *was* rich—very rich, in fact. It bothered me that he felt the need for so much money. In our world, money had no real value.

I was tired of rolling it over in my head and decided to change the subject. "Did you have any problems with the kids—the humans?"

"Nope, none at all. Delia took care of it." He chuckled. "She practically cried laughing when I told her the boys thought we wanted to take them back to our planet."

Despite my inner turmoil, I couldn't help but smile. "She erased their memories, then?"

"It's all set," he said. "Don't give it another thought."

When we got to Helena's, the lights in the house were still on. "They're awake," I said. "I'm going in the back door."

"Be careful," Cory said, placing his hand on my arm. "I'll be right outside if you need me."

I crept into the backyard and peeked through Helena's bedroom window. Just as I thought: she was packing. Pam stood in her doorway, seemingly trying to talk her out of it.

I tapped the kitchen door to unlock it. As I entered, I waved my hand, putting them both to sleep. I retrieved their memories of my earlier visit. Because I didn't plan on saving them, there was no need for Delia's memory box. Once inside Helena's room, I commanded the clothes out of her suitcase. I cringed when I saw her cheek, badly bruised from where I had hit her. With a wave of my hand, the bruise faded, and with it the memory of how it got there.

I was finishing up when I heard Cory whistle. I sat Pam down on a chair in the living room and erased her memory, as well. One last wave before walking out the door woke them up. I took off in search of Cory but stopped short when I heard James' voice at the front door.

"Helena," James called. "Are you still up?"

I tiptoed back to the window in time to catch Helena shaking off my spell. She stood, smoothed her hair, and walked out of the bedroom. I scrambled to the kitchen window, hoping it would afford me a better view of the main part of the house. I wasn't disappointed. As she passed the living room, Helena shrugged and smiled. I commanded to hear.

"Helena, it's late," Pam said. "He shouldn't be here."

Helena ignored her cousin and swung open the front door. "James!" She practically fell into his arms.

James lifted her up. I felt my heart explode when he began to kiss her.

I stumbled back as pain filled every part of my body. I could barely breathe. I couldn't move. He held her like he used to hold me, giving her the kisses that belonged to me. I told myself to look the other way, but I couldn't tear my eyes off the two of them.

"Why are you doing this to yourself?" Cory whispered, stepping up beside me.

Jolted from my trance, I looked at him, but had no words. I looked back at James and Helena. They were still kissing.

"Why is the bond not stopping him?" I asked.

"Don't worry," Cory said. "It will." He pulled me

away from the window.

I climbed back into the truck, overcome with shock. I felt my heart dying as the image of their kiss replayed in my mind. It caused me more pain than any of Simon's needles ever could. I was too numb to cry. I looked out into the night as Cory drove. I had thought I could handle it, but I was wrong.

Moments later, I became vaguely aware of blue lights flashing behind us.

"Thea, snap out of it," Cory said, pulling over. "It's the police."

I continued to sit, dazed, too emotionless to care.

I heard the officer say to Cory, "May I see your license and registration, please?"

Cory cleared his throat and searched the glove box. "Thea," he hissed, reaching in front of me, "you need to wake up and get us out of this!"

"Is this your vehicle, sir?" the officer asked.

"No, Officer," Cory replied, gesturing toward me. "It belongs to her husband."

The officer pointed the flashlight into the car. "What's your husband's name, ma'am?"

I turned my head slowly toward him. "His name is *traitor*." The words came seemingly from nowhere. I was no longer in control of my actions.

Cory cleared his throat again and smiled nervously. "She's just a little tired, Officer. Her husband's name is James Ethan Wade."

"And does he know you're driving his vehicle?" he asked.

"Yes, he does." Cory finally located the registration and handed it to the officer, along with what looked to be a driver's license.

"Hang tight, folks." The officer nodded and walked back to his car.

"Thea!" Cory said, nudging me. "Snap out of it!"

I understood what Cory needed me to do, but I didn't feel right. An ugly rage was rising inside me, and I didn't seem to have any control over it.

"Thea, hurry! Wave your hand or something." Cory was starting to sound desperate. "He's not going to find me on that computer of his."

When I failed to answer him, Cory ran his hand through his hair and said, "Fine, then. I guess I have no choice." He swung open the car door.

"Stay in the car," the officer shouted.

Cory jumped from the vehicle and tossed powder at the officer, freezing him in place. He then chanted a few lines and, moments later, was back in the truck with the items he'd handed to the officer. He pulled away from the curb and drove home.

When we got to the house, Cory opened my door and extended his hand. "It's late," he said. "Go and get some rest."

But I couldn't move, couldn't even look at him. I stared out through the windshield with tears rolling down my face. I couldn't shake the image of James and Helena together, and it was killing me.

"Come on, sweetie," Cory soothed, gently reaching for my arm. "Let's go inside."

But still I sat, paralyzed by my pain.

"It's only the spell, remember?" he urged.

"Tell that to my heart," I said, my voice barely a whisper.

Cory reached his other arm under my legs and lifted me out of the truck. "Like I said," he replied, kicking the door shut, "nothing but misery."

I rested my head on his shoulder as he carried me inside. My father greeted us from the door of the kitchen. "What happened?"

"She saw James kissing Helena."

"She was still there?" he asked. "I never would have allowed James to leave for Helena's if I'd known." He looked at me with pity in his eyes. "I'm sorry, Thea."

Cory started up the stairs. My father followed.

"Did she . . ." He seemed to be searching for the right words. "She didn't try to . . ."

Cory gave a slight shake of his head. "No," he said quietly.

Their voices faded as I withdrew into myself. I didn't know whether it was the bond or simply that my heart was breaking, but I was helpless against my feelings. My world was crashing down. There was also something else, something shifting inside me: a sense that my love for James was slipping away. "Make it stop," I whispered.

"What was that, sweetie?" Cory asked. He laid me gently on my bed. "What did you say?"

I felt my father's touch and looked up at him. "Make it go away." I hoped he understood that I was no longer in control of my actions. I wanted to kill James, run to him and end his life. It took all the strength I had to stop myself from following through.

Despite what my father had told me, I felt betrayed. How could James kiss her like that? I kept telling myself it was just the spell, but pain prevented my heart from understanding. I grabbed my father's hand and tried to sit up. "You have to stop me."

My father gently pushed me back down and placed his hands on my head. Their voices faded as I began to drift away.

"What are you doing to her?" Cory asked.

"Giving her mind a rest," my father replied. "I need to take away her anger before she kills James."

I had odd dreams that night. I was alive and happy as James' bloodied body lay at my feet. I had taken his life with my bare hands. His death had given me pleasure. With every dream, I felt only the satisfaction of having his blood on my hands.

When I woke up in the morning, the feeling of rage was gone. There was only emptiness in my heart. My love for James seemed far away, like it had vanished overnight. But it couldn't have entirely disappeared. Why else would I be so jealous of James and Helena? Strangely, the misery of the situation kept me clinging to the one thread of hope I had: that beneath the surface, James and I still shared great love for one another.

I sat up when someone knocked on my door. "Who is it?"

"It's me, sister," said Steven. "Can I come in?"

I perked up. "Of course!"

Steven was a boy I had rescued during the battle. Although I only made him *believe* he was my little brother, I truly did love him as a brother. He had such a tender way about him that one couldn't help but love him. He had dark, silky skin and sad eyes that made me concede to him time and time again.

Steven peeked around the door and smiled. "You feeling better?"

I held out my arms. "Was I sick?"

He jumped onto the bed and hugged me. "I heard you crying last night and thought you might be."

"Ah, that," I said, squeezing him. "I feel better now." I looked at him and smiled. "You've been

~ 60 ~

keeping yourself scarce lately."

"Just trying to keep up on my studies like you told me."

I nodded approvingly.

"Where is Auntie Delia?" he asked. "I haven't seen her since the day before yesterday."

"She's not in her room?"

"No, and the guys are gone, too."

"Oh, right. The boys moved to the guest house, and I'll bet that's where you'll find Delia."

He gave me a kiss on the cheek and hurried out of the room. I heard him say hello to my father in the hall.

"He's a good boy," my father said as he walked in.

I nodded. "A gentle soul."

"You did good bringing him here." He sat next to me on the bed.

I reached for his hand. "Thank you for helping me sleep."

"How are you feeling this morning?"

"Honestly, I'm not sure—but I don't want to kill him anymore. That's good, right?"

"You're not mad at him, then?"

I wanted to shout, "Yes!" and tell him how much I hated James. "I don't know how I feel right now, Father."

"Do you still love him?" he asked, lifting my chin.

I bit my lip and looked away. "I can't love him. Look at what it's doing to me."

He scooted over and placed his hand on mine. "Thea, it's a spell," he said. "Only a spell. Don't make him pay for something he has no control over."

"I'll be fine. I don't plan on going there again, so they can see each other all they want." I looked down. "I don't care."

I felt my father's eyes studying me closely. "Don't say that, Thea. He's your husband."

"Oh, now he's my husband? I don't think James cares about that anymore."

"Thea," he said, placing his hands on my shoulders.

I sighed. "Please, Father. I don't want to talk about him." My father's constant lecturing was causing more tension than I could stand. He kept trying to look into my eyes. I was starting to feel violated by his attempts to read my mind.

"You must find the part of you that makes you strong," he said, getting to his feet. "Then you will see. Seek the wizard in you; it will help you see more clearly."

"I can see just fine." I swung my legs over the side of the bed. "Now please give me a minute to get dressed."

Chapter 5
My Father's Pain

    I dragged myself to the shower and allowed the steaming hot water to hit my face. I was so angry with myself for allowing the pain to control me. What kind of blubbering idiot had I turned into? I leaned against the shower wall. "Get a hold of yourself, witch."

    I stepped out, dried off, and quickly got dressed. As I was slipping my feet into my shoes, I heard someone coming down the hall. A moment later there was a soft tap on my door.

    I walked over and opened it. "Pam?"

    "May I speak to you?" She looked nervous. Her hands were trembling.

"Of course. Please, come in."

She turned to her right. "Wait right here."

"Is someone with you?"

Pam smiled sheepishly. "My daughter."

"You have a daughter?"

"Yes," she said, stepping into the room. "She's been very sick."

I closed the door. "What's wrong with her?"

"That's why I'm here. I need your help."

My heart went out to her. "What can I do?"

She looked down. I noticed a tear land on the floor.

"I've used spells and potions, but nothing works." She looked up, glassy-eyed. "She's dying, Thea," Pam cried. "She's dying."

"What are you talking about?"

"When your memory and powers were gone, I understood that you couldn't help. But now . . . I know you can help her. That's why I came back, so you can help my daughter."

I offered Pam a seat and knelt on the floor in front of her. "What's wrong with her, Pam?"

"A warlock cast a spell on her," she sobbed, "and I can't break it."

My eyes narrowed. "Which warlock?"

She tried to catch her breath. "He and I had been courting around the time I met my husband. He became very angry when I married a human—called me a *human lover*." She pulled a tissue from her purse and dabbed at her eyes. "When he found out I was with child, he put a spell on the baby—my daughter—and no matter what I do, how hard I try, I can't break it."

I knew warlocks hated humans, but I never imagined they would go so far as to hurt a child. "Why didn't you tell me this before?"

"I thought you'd be mad because I didn't come and fight. I figured you'd say no. I wanted to see if you still had any good feelings left for me."

Now I understood why all of her memories were so sad. I had thought it was because of her husband, but now I could see her real pain.

I smiled. "Pam, I have no reason to hate you. It wasn't your battle to fight, it was mine."

"I've waited so long, Thea," she said, choking up again, "waited for your powers to return. I've been keeping her alive with spells, but nothing helps now."

"Why hasn't anyone else helped you?" I asked.

"Sharron and Donna came to help. Someone taught them a spell they thought might work. It helped at first, but it wasn't strong enough to actually break the warlock's spell. Later they called and told me that your powers were back. But I wasn't sure you would help me." She reached for my hand.

At that moment I realized that my father had tried to help her, but his powers were barely strong enough to keep Pam's daughter alive. I straightened and looked toward the door. "Bring her in."

Pam stood and rushed to open the door. "Come on in, honey."

A sunken-eyed teenaged girl shuffled into the room. She seemed to be using most of her energy just to remain upright. Her face was pale, her lips white and cracked. She had golden hair and big brown eyes, but she looked tired and worn, as though she hadn't slept in weeks. Her frame was rail thin. I couldn't believe she was still alive.

"Meaghan," Pam said, "this is Thea. She is my oldest friend in the world."

The girl looked at me with fear in her eyes.

I smiled and held out my hand. "Hello, Meaghan. It's nice to meet you."

She didn't respond, but instead looked at her mother.

"Give me your hand, Meaghan," I whispered.

"Do as she says," Pam ordered gently.

Meaghan slowly extended her hand. I smiled and reached for the tips of her fingers. When our fingers touched, the spell was broken.

"You'll be feeling better from now on," I said.

Pam threw her arms around me, nearly knocking me off balance. "Thank you, my old friend. Thank you."

"You're welcome." I could smell Simon on her. He had been near her again. A thought occurred to me: Where was Meaghan the night Fish and I had gone looking for Delia? I hadn't seen her at the house. "I must have missed you the other day when I stopped by." I looked at Meaghan. The dark circles under her eyes were already fading, and her lips were turning a soft pink color. Her previously dull, scraggly hair shone.

"She's been staying with Sharron," Pam answered.

"With Sharron?" I asked, confused. I could see Pam didn't want to talk about it in front of her daughter, so I let it go. "It was very nice meeting you, Meaghan. I hope you feel better soon."

"Thank you," she said, smiling shyly.

Pam reached for my hand. "Thank you again, old friend. I owe you everything."

"You owe me nothing," I replied. "Come on, I'll walk you down."

When we reached the bottom of the stairs, James was leaving his study. He seemed surprised to see Pam.

"What are you doing here?"

"I was talking to your wife," Pam said, her tone taking on a distinct edge. "Remember her?"

James looked at me nervously, made his way to the door, and slipped out.

Pam leaned closer to me. "I'm sorry about my cousin."

"It's okay, Pam. I'm over it."

She thanked me again and opened the door.

Joshua came in as Pam and Meaghan were leaving. "Oh, hello," Joshua said, staring at Meaghan.

The three exchanged polite hellos, and Pam and Meaghan left.

"Who was *that*?" Joshua asked, stepping over to the window to peek out. "She's pretty."

"That's Pam's daughter," I said. "Her name is Meaghan."

"Meaghan," he whispered, mostly to himself.

I stifled a giggle and walked into the kitchen to find my father—not surprisingly—standing over the stove.

"Why are you always in the kitchen?" I asked.

He flashed me a smile. "That would be your mother's fault. She loved to cook. I suppose I feel closer to her in here."

I sat down at the table and watched him. I had never noticed before how handsome my father was, with his salt-and-pepper hair and sparkling green eyes.

He cracked some eggs into a bowl. "I knew you would help that girl."

"Well, of course," I replied. "It was silly of Pam to think I'd be angry with her."

"Pam is a devoted mother. You did well, Thea."

"Why don't you ever talk about my mother?"

He stopped for a moment and went back to whisking his eggs. "What do you want to know?"

"I want to know why you never talk about her."

He hesitated again. "It's true, I do not talk about her, but I think of her every single day—of how I could never stay mad at her. One smile, and I was putty in her hands. That woman was my whole life, but I suppose my pain prohibits me from speaking her name." He paused, gazing into space dreamily. "But that smile of hers shall forever remain in my heart."

"At least you can think of her, Father. I can hardly bring myself to do that."

He looked genuinely concerned. "Why is that?"

I tried to find the words to explain. I wanted to tell him that I missed her so much that it caused me too much pain to think about her, that her passing was the one pain I still couldn't get over. I remembered her scent, her smile, her touch. I was so young when she died, but I remembered every single day I spent with her.

Her love was like no other love I'd ever known. Just thinking of her sent me to a dark place. The pain of losing her hurt just as much today—maybe more—as it did when I lost her. At the time, it was more than I could take, so I had learned to put her out of my head.

My thoughts sometimes drifted back to how my father reacted when she died. It had taken Sharron and the other witches three days to pull my mother's body away from him. The others tried to keep me away from him, but I made my way through the trees and found him. He was holding my dead mother in his arms; her heart had been cut out. His eyes filled with tears as he rocked her, telling her how sorry he was, that he didn't know this would happen.

I had watched mutely as he stroked her face and kissed her gently. "Emma," he cried, "my beautiful Emma." I sat for hours watching him, listening to the beautiful words he said to her. On the third day, I finally had to help the others pull her away. Sharron always said how my eyes should have never seen that. But I was numb to it all. I could only see my father's pain. He was a broken man. I'd never seen someone hurting so much.

After the funeral, he went missing for months. I knew he was searching for Simon. Hunting Simon down and killing him were the only things my father could think of anymore. Several of the witches stayed with me. Sharron never left my side for a moment. She was always trying to get me to cry. "Let it out, dear," she would say. But I never cried, only waited by the window for my father's return. When he finally reappeared, he was suddenly in a hurry to teach me all sorts of new spells.

From that day forward, my father acted strangely. He allowed me to age again for a while, but then reversed his thinking when Simon resurfaced. He prepared a special potion and instructed Sharron to begin administering it to me when I turned eighteen. He and I would go for long walks and talk about so many things. I knew he was trying to fill my head with as much information as he could. He would leave me again, and this time I wouldn't see him for hundreds of years.

When he left months later, I kicked everyone out of the house. I wanted only to be alone. I always thought my father had passed away from sadness and that I would soon follow. But that little boy next door wouldn't leave me alone, not for one moment. Cory came over every single day. He ate breakfast, lunch, and sometimes even dinner with me. He added a much-needed sparkle to my life. I grew into a woman with Cory at my side. For so long, he was my only family. My father became a distant memory, confined to the back of my mind, along with my mother.

"Thea?" My father's voice jolted me from my reverie. "Did you ever grieve your mother's death?"

"What do you mean?"

"You never cried when she died. That has always bothered me."

"I had to be strong for you, Father."

He looked at me, sighed, and reached for more eggs. "I should have been there for you. I abandoned you because of my own pain."

"Your heart was broken," I said. "I understood."

"I will see to it that your heart never suffers through that kind of heartbreak again, my child."

"What are you saying?"

He poured the eggs into a hot skillet and grabbed a spatula. "Nothing," he replied. "What else would you like to know about your mother?"

I thought for a moment. "Why didn't you ever take her to live with you in your world?"

"Because my world enchants, it changes people—not for the better. I planned on easing your mother into my world slowly, but then you were born."

"So you never took her there?"

"No," he said, a hint of a smile appearing on his face. "But I took you."

"Me?"

"Yes, when you were a little girl."

"Why don't I remember?"

"Because it's not time for you to remember." He ladled some pancake batter onto the griddle.

I looked at him and wondered why he was always saying things like that. He spoke in riddles, rarely making sense—not any sense I could see anyway. "Father, why do you keep so much from me?"

"I keep nothing from you," he said. "You simply have yet to find the part of you that understands."

"What is that supposed to mean?"

"It means you will find things out as you need to."

"Why don't you just tell me?"

"Because I can't. It doesn't work that way."

I was about to question him further when Cory, Javier, Sammy, and Joshua piled into the kitchen. "Good morning," they greeted in unison.

"Just in time," my father said.

"Where's Delia?" I asked.

"She's in the guest house with Steven and Fish," Cory said.

My father set out five plates and the boys joined me at the table.

"What's the plan today?" Cory asked.

"We're leaving tomorrow," I replied. "My father's going to brief us tonight."

My father gently placed platters of scrambled eggs and pancakes on the table.

"Thanks, William," Javier said. "This looks and smells amazing."

"Well, eat up," my father said. "You're set to leave in three hours."

We all turned and stared at him.

"In three hours?" I asked, eyeing him curiously.

He nodded.

"But—"

"Yes, three hours," he repeated, smiling impishly.

I stood up from the table. "Really, Father? We can leave today?"

"As soon as I inform you of all the details, you can leave."

My heart filled with joy. At last, we were on the road to ending this nightmare. "How long do you think it will take us?"

He put his hand up. "No questions. I will tell you everything you need to know in a bit." He gestured toward the food. "Now, eat."

Chapter 6
Delia's Memory Box

I left the boys to finish their breakfast and ran to the guest house in search of Delia. I knew she was dying to go home. She hated being stuck here, just like the boys did.

The guest house was quiet. "Delia, where are you?" I called.

I heard the shower running. I walked to the bathroom door and knocked.

"Yeah?" Fish yelled through the closed door.

"Is Delia in there with you?" I asked.

"I wish!"

I giggled. "Well, do you know where she is?"

"She's watching a movie with Steven."

I searched the house again, but couldn't find either one of them. I walked out into the garden and spotted Delia—covered in powder, clothes torn—lying at the base of the large oak at the far end of the yard. I ran to her and shook her. "Delia! What happened? Who did this?" I waved my hand, trying to wake her, but she wouldn't come around. I gently released her and ran to Steven, who was lying just a few feet away. He, too, was unresponsive to my magic.

I whistled loudly toward the mansion and ran back inside the guest house. "Fish, get out here!"

I rushed back to Delia's side, repeatedly waving my hand in an attempt to wake her, but she remained still. I was beginning to panic when I heard a rustling behind me. When I glanced back over my shoulder, I received a warlock's foot in my face. The kick sent me flying across the yard. I crashed against the iron gate and fell to the ground. When I tried to rise, one of his spells hit me in the chest and knocked me back down.

He threw spell after spell, none of which truly hurt me, only slowed me down. I was finally able to wave my hand and sent the warlock flying. He slammed against the house and landed on the ground with a thud.

"You filthy witch!" he yelled. He picked himself up and started toward me.

I waved my hand and sent him straight back against the house. "Stay!" I commanded.

He kicked and flailed, trying to free himself.

I approached, my eyes narrowing. "What did you do to them?"

"Go to hell, witch!"

Fish appeared at my side. "Who are you yelling at?" He turned and spotted Delia on the ground. "Delia!" He stumbled to her, trying desperately to wake her, but she was still unresponsive. Fish turned, walked over to the warlock, and flicked his arms.

"Move out of the way, Thea," he said, his hooks ready to strike.

"Hold on, Fish." I said. "I need to know what he did to them. I can't wake Delia."

But Fish just stood and glared. "When she's done with you," Fish told the man, "you're going to die a horrible death."

The boys ran outside and, seeing Fish with his hooks at the ready, immediately brandished their weapons.

"He's mine!" Fish shouted, his eyes fixed on the warlock. "Do what you need to, Thea. I'm tired of waiting."

Cory carried Delia into the house. Sammy grabbed Steven.

"That your girlfriend?" the warlock asked Fish. "Because she felt real good."

Before I could stop him, Fish threw one of his hooks, hitting the man in the eye. "That felt real good, too," Fish answered.

Cory ran back outside and joined us. "What the hell happened?"

"I don't know," I replied. "I found them like that."

Again, Fish pitched his hooks at the man.

"Cool it, Fish," I yelled. I waved my hand and blocked the weapons from making contact. "I need to find out what he did to them."

The man tried to pull himself away from the side of the house.

Fish threw another hook, piercing the warlock's arm and nailing him to the surface. "She said stay."

The man stared Fish down as a wicked smiled spread across his face. "Thinking your girlfriend may not want you anymore, man. She kept begging me for more."

~ 75 ~

Fish lashed out again, but a wave of my hand stopped the hook in motion. "Grab Fish," I told Cory. "Don't let him do anything else until I'm done."

I tugged at my hair, pulling out several strands. I held them out and spit into them. The hairs writhed snake-like on my palm, and I held them up to the man's face.

"What are you doing?" he asked, his eyes filling with fear.

I smiled. "I'm going to make you talk."

I grabbed him by the neck and held the hair to his nose. His eyes rolled back as the strands worked their way into his nostrils and coiled inside his eye sockets. Soon he began to shake. This warlock was not going to talk on his own; this was the only way. He closed his eyes as the trembling intensified.

"What's happening to him?" Cory asked.

"The hairs are destroying the part of his brain that lies," I replied. I waited until the man opened his eyes, which were now glazed over and bloodshot. "Why did you come here?" I asked.

"Simon sent me."

"Why?"

"He wants the memory box that belongs to the witch Delia."

"What does he want it for?" I asked, stepping closer.

"I don't know, witch. And I don't care."

"What kind of spell did you put on my friends?"

"Simon's sleeping spell. He said you would never be able to break it."

Simon was wrong. I knew exactly how to break it. "If I let you live, will you come back here again?"

"Yes," he replied. "I'll come back as many times

as it takes."

"We have to kill him," Cory said.

I continued my line of questioning. "Are you the only one helping Simon?"

"Not even close," he replied. "There are many. Simon's training us to fight the ones like you. If we don't help him, we die."

Cory and I exchanged glances. "What do you mean?" I asked.

"He has promised us the reverse spell if we help him."

"What reverse spell?"

He looked into my eyes and smiled. "Now it is you who lies, witch."

I didn't have time to ask him what he meant. Sammy ran outside and announced that Steven wasn't breathing.

"Quick, Cory," I ordered. "Get me a knife."

"What about him?" Fish yelled, gesturing a hook toward the warlock.

I stopped at the door of the guest house. "Fish, he only put her to sleep. He didn't rape her."

A hint of relief crept onto Fish's face, but he was resolute. "When do I get to kill him?"

I looked to the warlock and back to Fish. "He's all yours." As I hurried into the house, I heard the warlock scream.

Steven was laid out on the couch in the main room. "Get me a knife!" I said.

"What for?" Cory asked.

"I need it to break the spell," I said. "I need wizard blood."

Javier dashed back with a small steak knife from the kitchen. "It's the only one I could find," he said, offering it to me.

Cory rolled his eyes and flicked his arm. When the blade appeared, he grabbed my hand. "How deep?" he asked.

"Just enough to make me bleed."

After Cory made the cut, I held my arm over Steven, allowing the blood to drip onto his head. I reached down to Delia, who lay on the floor below the couch, and did the same. Within seconds, they stirred and came to.

"Where's Auntie Delia?" Steven said, sitting up. "He's hurting her."

"Delia's fine," Cory said. "The man's gone now."

Fish stormed in, covered in the warlock's dust. The warlocks had been mixing their anti-aging potion wrong; when they died, they turned to dust.

Fish ran to Delia, lifted her up off the floor and sat on the sofa, holding her close. "Are you hurt, baby?"

"Someone is here," she whispered.

Fish held her tighter. "I know, baby. I took care of him."

"Let's get them to the house," I said.

Cory nodded and offered to help Fish with Delia.

"No, I've got her," Fish said, standing with Delia in his arms.

I headed toward the back door.

"Where are you going?" Cory asked, grabbing my arm.

"To make sure no one else ever gets through that gate."

He nodded and lifted Steven off the couch.

I walked outside and held up my hands. "Chains of metal, ropes of steel, surround this house with an iron seal." I waved my hand toward the gate, and there was a single powerful jolt. I waved again, using my magic to test whether all was secure. I watched as my spell bounced off the gate and flew back to me. I caught it in my hand and blew it into the air. If my magic couldn't get through those gates, nothing could.

I headed for the house. When I got there, Fish still held Delia as though both their lives depended on it. Steven seemed dazed as my father examined him.

"Father, how are they?"

"They're fine," he replied. "He only put them to sleep. But Delia put up quite a fight. He struck her more than a few times."

Fish kissed Delia on the head. "Don't worry, baby. I struck him a few times, too."

Delia smiled weakly.

"What does Simon want with the memory box?" Cory asked.

"I don't know," I said. "I don't even know how he found out about it."

My father looked at Cory. "Simon came looking for Delia's memory box?"

Cory nodded. "Yeah. The question is, why?"

My father seemed nervous. "What else did you find out?"

I told him about the reverse spell the warlock mentioned.

"Reverse spell?" my father asked. "To fix what?"

"I don't know, but the man said he would die without it. He also said he was training to fight the 'ones like me.'"

My father's eyes widened.

"Father, what is it? Do you know something?"

"You must leave to my world, right away." He

raised his hand before I could ask questions. "Take the boys up to my room. You can leave after we talk. We must hurry, Thea."

"What's going on, Father?" I asked. "Does this have something to do with James?"

He looked at me intently. "Thea, something has changed. Do you understand? Something took another path. I can't explain it to you—you just have to trust me."

He ascended the stairs two at a time, with four of the boys close behind. Fish stayed behind with Delia. I slipped into James' office to make a phone call. I couldn't leave my family unprotected after what had happened today, and I knew someone who could help.

Ciro was James' good friend, and he and his brothers were there for us in the battle against Simon. I dialed his number.

Ciro picked up on the first ring. "Bueno!"

"Ciro, it's me, Thea."

"Thea, is everything okay?"

"No, I need your help. My family is in danger."

"Say no more," he said. "We will be there in the morning."

"Thank you. I knew I could count on you."

"I am at your service, Thea."

We talked for a few moments more and said our goodbyes. After hanging up the phone, I turned to leave but was startled by James, who was standing behind me. "Oh, you scared me."

"Who can you count on?" he asked.

I didn't like his tone and found myself suddenly angry.

He pressed on. "Who were you talking to?"

I looked away. Why was I getting so upset? "If

you must know, I was talking to Ciro. He's coming to visit."

"Well then," he said, skirting around me. "I'll ask William to prepare some rooms for Ciro and his brothers."

I closed my eyes as he passed me. The need to lash out and hurt him was so intense that it gave me pleasure just to think of it. I had to get out there before he said another word. I opened my eyes and made for the door.

"You in a hurry?" he asked.

I stopped and closed my eyes again. The mere sound of his voice agitated me. "What do you care?" I asked through clenched teeth. I heard him approaching me from behind. Slowly I turned to face him. "Why don't you stick to pestering Helena with your questions? I don't owe you any explanations."

He smirked. "There are a lot of things I'll stick to doing with Helena. Don't you worry about that, witch."

"Is dying with her one of those things?" I asked.

He slapped my face. I responded with a kick that sent him flying across the room. I scanned the room, searching his office for something to thrust into his heart.

Fish threw open the door. "What the hell is going on in here?"

"Get her out of here!" James shouted.

Fish reached for my arm but I pushed him away. I stormed out of James' office and hurried up the stairs and into my father's room, slamming the door behind me. "What the hell is wrong with me?" I asked him.

My father glanced in my direction and quickly looked away; he was blocking his thoughts from me.

"Stop doing that!" I shouted. I tried to tamp down the panic rising inside me. The murderous anger I felt toward my husband scared me more than all the other horrors I had faced in my long life.

"What's wrong?" Cory asked.

My breaths were coming in short rasps, and my heart pounded in my chest. "Something is wrong with me, Cory."

"What do you mean?"

I shot my father a knowing look. "Tell me why I want to kill James, Father."

His eyes widened in alarm. "Did you hurt him?"

"Why? Are you expecting me to?"

"Yes."

Collectively stunned, we all stared at my father.

"Father, what the hell is going on?"

"Sit down, Thea," he said. "The journey is more important right now."

I didn't move. I continued searching his eyes for answers. Why would he expect me to hurt James? "Please, Father," I pleaded, "talk to me."

He turned his back to me and pounded on the table, his frustration clearly growing. He sighed and turned to face me. "I can't tell you."

"You must!"

"Just tell her, William," Cory said.

"Thea," my father said, stepping toward me, "after today, you will understand why I can't tell you. I give you my word that it will make sense to you. You just have to trust me."

Cory grabbed my shoulders. "Come on, Thea," he said. "The sooner we leave, the sooner we can come back and end this."

I looked away as the feeling of rage subsided. I

sighed and sat next to Cory. I had such a bad feeling about this. What was my father keeping from me?

He seemed more at ease when he started talking to the boys. "The world you are about to enter is like nothing you have ever seen," he began. "Nothing in this world can prepare you for what your eyes will behold. It is very important that you do exactly as I say, because your very lives depend on it."

The boys nodded.

"My world changes people," my father continued. "It makes them feel like they never want to leave. If any of you start to have those kinds of feelings, you must tell Thea immediately, and she will bring you back at once."

"What do you mean?" Javier asked. "What will we feel exactly?"

"You may feel like hiding from her so you can stay behind. If you feel like you'd do anything to stay, particularly if you're willing to avoid or deceive Thea to do so, you must tell her right away before the pull becomes too strong."

"Why?" Joshua asked. "What's the big deal?"

My father leaned in. "If you stay, you will end up like Simon—enchanted by my world and willing to do anything to go back."

Cory looked around at the others, concerned. "Then why are we going?"

"Thea will need you by her side. You will soon see why."

Cory gave a short nod. "What do you need us to do?"

"I need you to keep her safe," my father answered.

The boys exchanged glances.

"What do you mean?" I asked.

~ 83 ~

"Like I said, you will see things you never imagined. But they will not harm you if you do as I say."

"*They* who?'" Cory asked, worry creeping onto his face.

"You will soon see, my son. You will soon see."

"Will the boys be in danger?" I asked.

My father walked over to his desk and opened a box. He pulled out some gold leaves and held them up. "You must each eat one of these leaves before setting off on the journey. These leaves will give you a distinct scent, a scent that is sweet to them. No harm will come to you if they smell the scent of this leaf."

"And who exactly are *they*?" Sammy asked.

"Let me finish," my father replied. "You will understand the moment you arrive." He handed each of the boys a leaf. "Please, eat it now."

"What about Thea?" Sammy asked. "Doesn't she get one?"

"These will not work for her; she needs to prove herself to them."

"How do I do that?" I asked, suddenly feeling less confident about my abilities.

"You will have to figure that out yourself," my father answered. "I cannot help you with that."

"But how will I know what to do?"

"Just answer any questions they ask you." My father looked at the boys. "Please, eat them—now."

The boys did as my father instructed. Sammy's eyes lit up as he chewed. "Hey, it tastes good."

"Can I have another one?" Joshua asked.

My father smirked and put the rest of the leaves away.

I noticed the boys' skin changing color.

Cory looked down at himself and stood. "What the hell is going on? Why am I turning pink?"

"It will subside in a few seconds," my father assured him. "You have nothing to fear."

He was right. The color faded, leaving behind a soft, pearlescent shimmer—subtle, but enough to see that something was different. The boys smelled sweet, like caramel apples.

"How long will the effect last?" Cory asked.

"Just a few hours," my father replied. "You will not be staying long today. When you come back, you must go straight to bed. I will put a sleeping spell on each of you the moment you return. When you wake, you must keep yourselves busy. Do not give yourselves time to think of my world. I suggest you go out during the day, and only come home when it is time to leave again. Most importantly: do not speak of my world to anyone, not even to each other."

He turned and reached for his ring. "Now, gather," he instructed. "You must all be touching Thea when she puts on this ring. This allows the ring to take you there, but there is no need to be touching her when she brings you back. The ring will know where to find you and will bring you back when she takes it off."

My father's instructions surprised me. It sounded like we'd be going to his world more than once. "Father, how many times do we have to go?"

"As many times as it takes," he said. "They won't trust you at first. The white energy you are looking for is well protected. They are not just going to hand it over to you. It could take several trips."

"Okay," Cory said. "Where do we find this white energy?"

"I will give you that information when you come

back. First I need to know that you can all make it there and back safely."

"What about James, Father?" I asked. "You said you would break the spell."

He walked to me and placed his hands on my shoulders. "Clear your mind, Thea," he said. "Just answer the questions they ask of you. Perhaps they will give you what I need to break the spell."

I nodded.

My father relayed a spell to me and told me that I would know when and how to use it. When he was done, he gently placed the ring in my hand.

I looked up at him. "How will I know where we're going?" I asked. "I don't even know what to look for."

"My friend Attor will greet you," he explained. "He will tell you everything you need to know. Simply relay the spell I just gave to you." My father retrieved a small crystal from his work table. He walked to me and placed it in my hand. "Break this, and give what lies inside to Attor. It is the capsule I have prepared."

"How will I know who he is? How will I find him?"

"He will find you, Thea."

I looked into his eyes. "When do I get my answers, Father?"

He smiled. "I left something there that belongs to you. Attor will see to it that you get it back. Then you will have your answers, my daughter. Then you will understand."

I hugged him tightly. "Watch over James," I said, pulling away. "Don't let Simon near him."

"I give you my word."

I closed my eyes and squeezed him again. "Is it

time for the truth?"

"It is time for you to understand why I cannot tell you things."

"Is it bad?" I asked, not sure I wanted to know the answer.

"Nothing about this is good, Thea."

It was another mysterious reply from my father, but enough to know that the truth would not be easy to hear. I kissed his cheek and looked at Cory, Sammy, Joshua, and Javier, who swiftly gathered around me.

"Are you all holding on to me?" I asked.

The boys nodded and closed their eyes.

I placed the ring on my finger and we were gone.

Chapter 7
The World of Magia

I felt streams of energy leaving my body. It slowly wrapped itself around the boys as we drifted toward my father's world. It looked like strands of ropes holding us together. With the end of the rope coming out of me. The boys gazed in amazement at the thousands of tiny speckles floating around us. Cory reached out to touch them.

"Don't," I said, blocking his hand. "They made me fall faster last time."

He pulled back his hand. "Is this some kind of vortex?"

Before I could answer, Javier said, "Holy crap, this is crazy!"

"I know," Sammy replied. "Like we're flying to the moon."

"What are these shiny things around us?" Joshua asked.

"I don't know," I said. "But I think they're carrying us." I smelled the flowers as a gust of wind hit my face. Soon we would feel the ground beneath our feet. "We're almost there."

"Stay close to me, Thea," Cory said, reaching for my hand.

When we landed, the boys gasped and looked around. I immediately recognized this as the same spot I had arrived at when I had last worn the ring.

"You've got to be kidding me," Cory said.

A warm, familiar feeling rose inside me, as though I was finally home. The place was exactly as I remembered it: an enormous, vibrant, magical garden. The wind whistled through the ivy-draped trees, and a carpet of purple flowers covered the surrounding mountains. Lush green grass bordered the trees and flowers.

The cherry trees, with their fluffy pink and white blossoms, looked as though God himself had pruned and trimmed them. Small creeks flowed with crystal clear water, and the rocks in their embankments gleamed like precious jewels. We were taking it all in when flowers suddenly opened up all around us.

Sammy reached out and touched one. "Hey, the flowers are full of glitter," he said, showing me his hand.

"Look at that lake!" Javier exclaimed. "I can see the fish jumping from here."

The lake looked too beautiful to be real. I wanted to get a closer look.

"Is it made of glass?" Sammy asked.

"Thea, this place is unbelievable," Cory said.

I looked up and beheld the thing that had amazed me most when I first came here. "Look at the sun," I said. "It's like we're on the other side of it."

The boys lifted their heads and gasped.

"Is that a backwards sun?" Cory asked. "Look at the rays! I can actually see them beaming down on the other side."

"Hey," Sammy exclaimed. "It doesn't hurt my eyes."

Javier pointed. "Look at that waterfall."

"What kind of waterfall is *that*?" Joshua asked.

"I don't know," Javier said. "But it's wicked cool."

The mist spraying from the falling water wasn't water at all, but sparkles of light that changed color as they flew. The water was so clear, the rocks were visible behind it.

"What are those things coming out of the water?" Joshua asked.

Before I could answer, Cory tapped me on the shoulder. "Thea, look at those clouds," he said. "Why are they moving like that?"

A giant white cloud sped toward us. "I don't know," I said. "I don't remember seeing any clouds when I came here the first time."

"Well, it's coming straight at us," he said. "Get ready to run." He flicked his arms but his blades didn't appear. Again he tried, but nothing happened. "My weapons aren't working." He looked at me questioningly.

I shrugged. "Stand behind me," I ordered the boys.

I stepped in front of them and tracked the mysterious cloud. As I watched it speeding toward us, a black image appeared from inside it—something I had seen before. Back then, I'd panicked and removed the ring before it reached me. I remembered my father being relieved that this thing was still here. Whatever it was, it knew I was back. I raised my hands and chanted the spell my father taught me before we left. I hoped this was the right time to use it.

"What is that thing?" Cory asked.

"I can't get my sword out of its sheath!" Joshua shouted.

I ignored them and continued chanting: "Here's my blood, here's my skin, find your answers from within. See her eyes, see her face, see I've sent her in my place. Break the spell from when we spoke, and let the skies be filled with smoke."

The creature from the cloud spread a pair of massive wings and halted abruptly. I watched in amazement as it hovered above us, darkening us with its shadow.

Cory stumbled back. "Is that what I think it is?"

"It's a freakin' dragon," Sammy gasped, "a real freakin' dragon!"

I pulled out the crystal my father had given me and cracked it open with a wave of my hand. I wasn't sure why the boys' weapons didn't work here, but I was glad my magic did. I held up the small black mushroom that was inside the crystal, hoping I was doing the right thing.

The ground shook as the dragon blew fire into the air. The sky filled with black smoke when the fire touched the cloud. The smoke spun up into a cone and moved toward us. Cory maneuvered to block it, but I pushed him away and faced the smoke.

"Thea, run," Cory whispered.

"No," I said. "I think this is supposed to happen."

I stood still as a statue as the smoke entered my nose and mouth. I could feel it move inside me, then gradually stream out of my body. I wasn't sure what to do, but the dragon seemed to be waiting for something. The smoke filled the sky around the dragon and turned into tiny crystals. They looked like shooting stars as they flew toward the strange sun. The dragon flew toward us.

"Stay behind me," I told the boys.

The dragon landed in front of me. He huffed, stooped over, and sniffed. I stood, frozen, as his nose touched my hair. The heat radiating from his mouth nearly burned my skin.

Cory leaned toward me. "What do we do?"

"Just stay still," I said. "I think he's checking me for my father's scent."

I could have sworn I saw the dragon nod, as if to agree with me. Could he understand us? He moved his head toward my hand and examined my father's ring carefully.

Sammy startled as the dragon lurched toward him. "Don't eat me!" Sammy cried. But the dragon only sniffed Sammy and huffed.

Our eyes widened in surprise when the dragon began to laugh. When he started talking, our jaws dropped.

"Witches are not welcome here," he said, eyeing the boys closely. "You would do well to leave—now."

I took two shaky steps forward. "Are you Attor?"

He nodded.

Again, I held up the mushroom. "My father instructed me to give this to you. He said to fill it with white energy."

Attor stepped closer and sniffed me again. He looked at the boys. "Wait here," he told them.

Before I had time to react, Attor picked me up with his talons and flew off.

~ 92 ~

"Thea!" Cory shouted.

I held on for dear life. Panic would have done no good here. I fought the impulse to use magic to free myself. I needed to know where he was taking me. It gave me a sense of security knowing that, if things got bad, I could always take off the ring. The ring would gather up the boys and bring them home with me.

Attor's talons were hard and smooth, like polished steel. His grip felt like it could cut me in two. I surveyed the surroundings as we flew. I could see the tips of what looked to be castle turrets a good distance away—some kind of village perhaps, or maybe that was where the wizards lived. The forest was too dense for me to get a clear view. Everything was so green and lush, and more beautiful than I remembered.

The boys were trying to keep pace, but I lost sight of them when Attor flew behind a mountain. There I saw another lake with several dragons sitting along the shore. They spread their wings and blew fire into the air at the sight of us. Attor, in turn, blasted fire back at them and flew toward the water.

The dragons on the ground screeched loudly as Attor hovered above the lake. I looked down and gasped at the beauty of the creatures that swam in its crystal clear water. There were schools of fish that looked almost like butterflies, each a different color. They swam with such grace, as though they were flying through the air.

Attor deposited me near the edge of a forest at the far end of the lake. He trudged over to the other dragons and spoke to them in a language I couldn't understand. The other dragons occasionally looked over at me as Attor spoke to them.

As Attor made his way back toward me, two of

the dragons immediately took to the sky. The others, nine of them, surrounded me and started sniffing. Their colors ran the spectrum of earth tones. Attor, on the other hand, was black as night. He had bright yellow eyes with red circles around the irises.

He flapped the other dragons out of his way. "Where is Xander?" he asked.

Before I could answer, one of the dragons spoke up. "Attor, this girl is half witch. She is not full-blooded wizard. We must kill her."

"Allow me my questions, Katu," Attor answered. "If she is who I think she is, then we have nothing to fear from her."

"Did she bring the witch Simon?" Katu asked. "Who are the others you sent Rasu and Paz to watch over?"

I looked at the one named Katu, surprised to hear Simon's name. The other dragons seemed to all be thinking the same thing. I shuddered under the scrutiny of their icy gazes.

"Silence!" Attor yelled. "I must ask my questions quickly, before the wizards find out she's here."

"Kill her, Attor," Katu cried. "Kill her quickly and get it over with."

"No," Attor replied. "She knew the spell. There is only one person who could have taught her that spell."

"But the wizards," Katu warned. "They will be furious."

Attor ignored Katu's appeals and looked deeply into my eyes.

"Then I will kill her," Katu said, lumbering toward me.

I stepped back as Attor took a swing at Katu, sending him stumbling back. "She will not be touched

~ 94 ~

until I have finished my questions!"

Katu glared at him, smoke puffing from his nose.

I started to feel dizzy and struggled to keep my mind on my mission. I stepped forward, again holding up the mushroom. "Kill me after you've helped my father," I said. "He's weak and needs this filled."

The two dragons looked at me and blasted fire into the air. I fell to the ground and slowly staggered back to my feet. "I'm not leaving until you fill this. I'll stay behind if you want. The others can take it to him." My limbs felt weak, but I pressed on. "You will not kill me until you have filled this."

"You dare give us orders," Attor hissed. "Why should we help you?"

I stepped closer and looked into his eyes. "Because my father said you were his friend."

They remained leery of trusting me. Attor looked into my eyes as though he was searching for something.

"Was my father lying?" I asked. "Are you not his friend?"

Katu took a step toward me.

Attor spread his wing and blocked him. "I have yet to ask my questions, Katu."

"Quickly, Attor," Katu said. "The wizards will never forgive us."

Attor nodded and looked at me. "Look at her eyes, Katu," he said. "It has to be her."

"It could be a spell, Attor," Katu said. "We must make sure."

Attor nodded again and leaned toward me. "What bonds do you and your father share?"

"We can read each other's thoughts."

"And why did he leave this place?" Attor asked.

"Because of my mother. He didn't want to bring

her here. He said it would change her, so he left to be with her."

"Is that what he told you?" Attor said, seemingly amused.

"Is that not the reason?"

Katu swung his wing toward me, but again Attor stopped him. "If you hurt her," Attor said, pushing him away. "I will kill you."

My questions seemed to fuel Katu's anger.

Attor studied me closely. "Who is your true love?" Attor asked.

"James," I said.

"So it has not yet happened," he whispered to himself.

"What?" I asked, stepping forward. "What has not yet happened?"

"You will answer questions," Attor said, "and nothing else." He looked down at my father's ring. "How weak is Xander?"

I sighed. "He has no powers at all. Simon cast a black spell on him."

"That's why he didn't use the ring himself," Attor said, looking at Katu.

"He was surprised it worked for me."

"The ring believes your father to be dead. He has no powers, so the ring moved on to its next owner—you."

"But he still has a little magic," I said. "He uses it sometimes."

"Then he is wasting what little energy he has left," Attor said, obviously annoyed. "He'll soon die if he continues."

"What do you mean?"

"Wizards are alive because of the white energy,"

Attor explained. "They need to drink from the secret river to replenish the energy they use. If they use it up without replacing it, they die." He paused. "Or turn human."

"Then you have to fill this," I said, holding up the mushroom again.

"You are here to answer questions, and nothing else," Katu yelled.

I glared at him. "I'm tired of answering questions. If my father dies because of you, I will return and kill you all."

Katu came at me. Quickly, I waved my hand and sent him hard into a pile of boulders. I spun to face the other dragons, who appeared to be stifling fits of laughter.

Attor smiled and looked at Katu. "Do you now see that she is who she says she is?"

Katu stood and brushed himself off. "Finish your questions," he said, glowering at the others.

Attor nodded. "Why has Simon not killed you?"

"I believe he'll try, but not before he gets what he wants from me, what I'm hiding from him."

"Yes, of course."

"You know about that?" I asked, surprised.

"Your father was a fool to bring that witch here. He was blind to the evil that lived inside the boy. The other wizards refuse to ever welcome your father back here because of the havoc Simon has wreaked at our expense. Your father put our world in danger when he brought the half-humans here."

"What happened, exactly?" I asked.

He didn't answer my question. He looked at the other dragons, who appeared furious at the very mention of Simon's name. I knew my father had spent many years here with Simon. Simon had, for the most part, grown up here. I wanted an answer to my question, but these dragons clearly weren't going to talk.

I wondered if the wizards could help me understand. "If you won't tell me anything, then take me to those castles I saw from the air. I'll ask the wizards."

"You foolish witch," Attor said. "Those are towers, not castles. The guards will kill you, and us along with you."

"Send her away, Attor," Katu said. "Give her nothing."

"But the white energy—my father said you would help me."

Attor gazed down into my eyes. "I don't know if we can trust you."

Anger began to rise inside me. Why were these dragons so frightened of Simon? Simon had no powers. He only knew the spells my father taught him. He possessed no real magic—not like me, not like the wizards of my father's world.

"I only came here to help my father replenish his powers," I said. "Please, my husband's life depends on it."

They remained silent and exchanged glances among each other.

"If you fear Simon that much," I said, "then just tell me where the energy is, and I'll get it myself."

The ground trembled as the dragons erupted in laughter.

"You think we fear the witch Simon?" Attor asked.

The dragons blasted shots of fire into the air. Their flames swirled together into a vortex and crashed to the ground, leaving a scorched crater in the soil. The ground beneath me singed my feet, and I quickly stepped onto a fresh patch of grass.

Attor trudged closer to me. "Why would we fear a simple witch like him?"

"If that's not it, then why won't you help me?"

"Because you have not yet said what I need to hear."

My frustration mounted. What was he talking about? I had answered all their questions. Suddenly, I remembered what my father had told me: that Attor had something of mine. He said Attor would give it back to me and that I would understand everything. In an instant, I realized there was only one thing that would answer my questions and help me reconcile my past with my present.

I locked eyes with Attor. "Give me back my memory."

Chapter 8
Only the Beginning

The dragons' laughter came to an abrupt halt as they turned to look at Attor. Attor nodded to one of the dragons, who quickly disappeared into a cave near the trees. The dragon came back holding a jewel in his mouth.

It looked similar to one of the jewels on Delia's memory box, the box my father had given to me as a gift when I was a little girl. He told me it was filled with magic from his world, that it could hold memories and keep them safe. I had used it to save my own precious memories, like those of when I first met James. Now I understood that it wasn't the box itself that was special, but rather, the jewels affixed to the box that held the magic.

My head was spinning when the dragon placed the jewel before me and rejoined the others. My knees were weak. I felt sleepy. I didn't understand what was happening to me, but I did my best to fight it.

"Place it in your hand," Attor ordered. "Then squeeze it."

I picked up the jewel and examined it carefully: a brilliant red ruby with a cluster of white diamonds embedded in the center.

"If you are not who you claim to be," Attor warned, "this memory will kill you."

I nodded, placed the ruby onto the palm of my hand, and wrapped my fingers around it. I closed my eyes and allowed the memory to flow back into my head. I was nine years old, and with my father along the shores of a lake—the lake I had seen when I first arrived in Magia . . .

~~~

My father walked behind me, laughing, as I chased the sparkles of light coming out of the water. He caught up to me, snatched up one of the sparkles, and placed it in my hand.

"Hold it up, Thea," he said. "It will change colors in your hand."

"I like these, Father," I replied. "What are they?"

"They are called Fairy Spirits, and they protect the animals and plant life here in Magia."

The light turned from bright red to yellow to green. "Why was it in the water?"

"They gather their energy from the water," he explained, "just as wizards replenish their energy from the secret river. It makes our powers very strong."

"Do I need the energy, Father?"

"I have often wondered that," he said. "There is only one like you, Thea. You are the first of your kind— half-witch, half-wizard. You may not need the things I do."

I released the sparkle and broke into a run. My father followed. I stopped at a flower and touched it. A glittery substance stuck to my hands. "Father, look!" I exclaimed, wiggling my fingers.

"That is called aging dust." He knelt beside me. "These are not like the flowers from back home. These have special powers."

"What kind of powers?"

He tore the flower in half and held it up to a strand of gray hair on his head. The hair turned brown when the flower touched it. He repaired the flower and placed it back on its stem.

"How did you do that?" I asked.

He smiled and gathered me into his arms. "Magia is filled with enchanted things, Thea. The flowers here keep wizards young, and one day they will help you, as well."

"Help me with what?"

He hugged me tighter. He tried to hide them, but I noticed tears forming in his eyes. He'd seemed so happy just moments before. He took my hand and we walked toward the waterfall.

Near the base of the falls he sat on a rock and pulled me onto his lap. "Thea, this place is your home. But there are those who do not want you here. I've kept you away from this place to protect you from them. They want to take what belongs to you, what belongs to me. But no one can take away what you are, what you were born to be."

He stroked my face as a single tear rolled down his cheek. "I want you to know that I love you with all of my heart. I would give my life to save yours. If there is a way to prevent you from suffering, I will find it. I will change what fate has written for you, my child. With my last dying breath, I will save you."

"Save me from what, Father?"

He sighed. "What I am about to say will make very little sense to you now, but one day you will return here and understand everything. You will see I keep no secrets from you. There is a reason I do not tell you things."

"I don't understand."

"I know," he replied. "But one day you will." He pulled me closer and breathed deeply. "When a wizard has a vision," he began, "he must never speak of what he sees because it would change the outcome. Only here can I warn you, and guide your way to the truth. I can't even allow you to read my thoughts because that, too, would change things that mustn't be changed."

He set me on my feet and reached for my hands. "Thea, do you remember when I went away after your mother died?"

"Yes, Father."

"I came back because I couldn't find the bad man I had been looking for. You see, I had a vision. It lasted for three whole days. I saw your future. And now I must do certain things to prepare you, to change how the vision ends. Do you understand?"

I shook my head.

He pulled me back into his arms, kissed my head,

and started to cry.

"Why are you crying?"

"Thea, one day a man will cause you great sorrow. He will kill someone you love very much, and turn many men against you. Even the man you love will leave your side. But before that happens, you will have your own vision, a vision I have passed on to you, so you can fight and protect someone you love—like I'm fighting to protect you. I will not be there to help you, so I have stored this vision in your mind. One day it will reveal itself to you and turn your life upside down. But these things need to happen. They must not be changed, not until I come back to you."

I stared at him, my eyes questioning.

My father was crying again and embraced me. "I'll come back to you, my child. I'll come back and fix everything."

"Don't leave me again, Father," I pleaded. "Please take me with you."

He held me tighter.

"Why are you thinking about needles?" I asked.

He pulled away. "Stop doing that, Thea," he said, shaking me. "You must never know what I am thinking. It will change things, do you understand?"

He stood, picked some flowers, and carefully placed them into a bag.

"Are we taking these home?" I asked.

"I'm going to dry them and plant them in the garden. They won't grow the same way they do here, but they will still work. I will use them to make you an anti-aging tea that will stop the years from passing you by. I will not be able to come here again, so I must take these now."

He raised his hand and threw a spell into the air.

Attor flew toward us. My father greeted him and took several jewels Attor held in his mouth. My father slipped them into the bag with the flowers.

"No wizards nearby yet, but you must hurry," Attor warned.

My father nodded.

Attor moved closer. "Does she know everything?" he asked.

"As much as she needs to," my father replied.

"You're sure about your vision, Xander?"

"I am, old friend. It took three days for the vision to unfold before me. There is no doubt."

"Change it, Xander," Attor said. "You have the power to change it if you want."

My father glanced at me and picked more flowers.

"Why will you not change it, Xander?"

My father shook the bag in frustration. "What the devil do you think I'm trying to do?"

"Kill him, Xander. Let us go and find Simon before he fathers the boy."

"I have been looking for him for many months. It is too late. The vision has already started to unfold."

"Stop her from meeting the boy." Attor leaned closer, lowering his voice. "So she never bonds with him."

"You cannot stop love, Attor," my father said. "It's more powerful than any spell I know. Even if I tried to change it, they would find each other. Fate would bring them together."

Attor nodded. "How can I help you, old friend?"

"There is something you can do for me, but we will discuss that later." My father picked up the bag and pulled out one of the jewels. "Hold out your hand,

~ 105 ~

Thea."

"Yes, Father."

Tears welled in his eyes as he handed me the glittering stone. He knelt down and gathered me in his arms. He kissed my head and whispered into my ear, "I love you, Thea. Be brave, my child. Search deep inside you to find the power you need to understand."

My father stood and waved his hand . . .

~~~

When the memory ended, I opened my eyes, dropped the mushroom, and collapsed to the ground. The tears came fast and furious. I thought the spell Simon had cast on James was the worst of my problems, but now I understood: it was only the beginning. There was more to come, more pain to endure. I was going to lose James, and someone I loved was going to die.

Why didn't my father tell me what to do?

I felt Attor's wing touch me. I pushed it away and scrambled to my feet. "Leave me alone," I said, wiping my tears.

"You must leave now," he ordered.

"You're not going to give me the energy, are you?"

"There is a wizard close by," he said. "You must not be seen here."

I was so tired I could barely stay upright. "I'm not leaving," I said, stumbling backward.

"Give us time to plan," Attor said. "The wizards guard the energy well."

"T-Take me to them," I stuttered, holding my head. "I can explain."

"They will kill you," Katu chimed in.

I dropped to my knees. "I'm not leaving."

Attor huffed and reached for me. Before I knew

what was happening, we were off and flying. I closed my eyes and let the wind hit my face. Within moments, I was with the boys again. I felt normal, no longer dizzy or weak.

"Thea," Cory called, dashing toward me.

"Are you guys okay?" I asked.

"Yeah," Cory replied. "Are you hurt?"

"I'm fine."

"Take the ring off, quickly," Attor ordered. "If they find you, they will kill you all."

"What is my father trying to change?" I asked. "Please tell me what he saw, tell me the truth."

Attor shot a glance at the dragons he'd sent to guard the boys and looked back to me. "When you come back, I will tell you everything. You have my word."

"How will I find you?" I asked.

"Give me the capsule," Attor said. "I will find you."

I held out my hand, and he took the mushroom in his mouth. He beckoned to the other dragons, and the group flew off.

I slipped the ring off my finger and we were gone.

Chapter 9
Do You Understand Now?

My father jumped to his feet when we reappeared in his room. I pulled away from Cory and ran into his arms. "I'm so sorry, Father. I failed you."

"You did not fail me." He held my face in his hands. "You will have another chance."

"Please forgive me," I said. "I didn't know, I didn't know."

"So you understand now?"

"I do, but you have to let me help you."

He smiled. "You are helping. You just don't know it."

"Tell me what to do to stop your vision, Father. Tell me how it ends."

"I can't do that yet. It's not time."

"What the hell is going on?" Cory asked.

I ignored Cory and buried my face in my father's chest. "Please stop using your magic. Attor told me everything."

"Did you give him the capsule?" my father asked.

I nodded. "Yes."

"That will be enough to keep me alive."

"But I didn't get the energy," I said, looking up at him.

"When you go back, Attor will give you what I need to stay alive."

Cory stepped forward, hands firmly planted on his hips. "Can someone tell me what the hell is going on?"

My father slowly broke away and faced the boys. "Forgive me, gentlemen. Please have a seat. We need to talk."

I handed the ring to my father and sat next to Cory. "Tomorrow when you go back," my father began, slipping the ring into his pocket, "I'm sure Attor will have a plan. Do whatever he tells you, no matter how strange it may sound. He will do his best to keep you all safe."

My father looked so tired. He had dark circles under his eyes.

"Why couldn't we use our weapons there?" Cory asked.

"I had to disable them," my father said. "I knew the impulse to attack Attor would be too great. I could not allow that to happen."

"Why didn't you tell us he was a dragon?" Cory asked.

"I'm sorry. I realize I could have better prepared you but time was running short."

Cory nodded. "Did you know Thea wouldn't be able to get the energy today?"

My father looked at me and smiled weakly. "I figured as much."

"Then what was the point?" Cory asked.

I kept looking into my father's eyes, desperately trying to read his mind. What Attor had said about the boy had not escaped me. He wanted my father to stop me from meeting James, but why?

"I can't answer that," my father replied, looking away. "At least, not yet."

"Why all the secrets?" Cory asked, his voice rising. "We're expected to make these potentially dangerous trips on your behalf, but you've barely told us anything."

"It is impossible to tell you, son."

Cory pressed on. "Why?"

My father regarded him for a moment and walked to his desk. He wrote something on a small slip of paper and handed it to Cory.

"What's this?" Cory asked.

My father nodded toward the piece of paper. "Read it."

After Cory read what my father had written, his head shot up. "Is this some kind of a joke?"

My father pointed at the note. "That was going to happen, exactly the way I wrote it. But because I have told you about it, it will now change."

Cory glanced at Sammy and looked back to my father. "But you could have stopped it."

"It will still happen," my father said wearily. "But now I have no control over it."

Cory was starting to come unglued. "Then why did you tell me?"

My father smiled. "Exactly."

Cory looked at me and again at Sammy. I wanted to know what was in that note. I had to stop myself from pulling it out of Cory's hand.

Cory looked at my father. "Now what?"

"Now we wait," my father replied. "Now we prepare. Because it will now change, the only thing to do is get ready for it."

I couldn't stand being left in the dark anymore. "Can I read the note?"

"I want to read it, too," Sammy added. He took two steps forward and tripped on Joshua's foot. When I noticed his head about to hit the corner of my father's desk, I promptly waved my hand. The desk shifted out of Sammy's way, and he hit the floor.

"Thanks, Thea," Sammy said, getting to his feet. "I think." Sammy's attention returned to the note. "What does that note say, Cory?"

Cory burst out laughing. He held up the note for Sammy to see. "It said you were going to fall down a flight of stairs and crack your head open real bad."

"What if I fell off a building instead?" Sammy asked. "I could have gotten killed!"

My father smiled. "Ah, but I didn't tell him you were going to fall here at home."

"You knew I was going to fall *here*?" Sammy asked.

"I would have never told Cory otherwise, young man." My father turned his attention back to Cory. "Do you understand now, son? It is impossible to tell you anything. You must trust me."

Cory nodded. "I understand."

"And you," my father said, turning to me. "Do you understand now why you must never read my thoughts? Or was sending you to my world a pointless exercise?"

I eyed the note in Cory's hand. "It wasn't pointless, Father," I said. "I understand now."

"Good," he said. "Maybe now you will leave

~ 111 ~

things alone."

I looked away, unworried. Attor had already promised to tell me everything. He'd given me his word, and for whatever reason, I knew his word was good. I didn't know what his vision had been, but I knew he was keeping something from me—something bad.

My father continued. "Now that we are on the same page, we have other matters to discuss."

"What is it, Father?"

"It seems Simon has convinced the warlocks that you have cast a death spell on them. They believe Simon will give them a reverse spell in exchange for their help."

"How did you find this out?" I asked.

"Jack is here," he replied. "We have been talking."

I was surprised to hear that Jack was in the house. After Delia removed his false memories, he'd disappeared and hadn't come back. He called James from time to time, but that was the only contact we'd had with him.

"Why is he here?" Cory asked.

"Jack is unwell, son," my father said. "I've set him up in one of the guest rooms."

"What's wrong with him, Father?"

"He is very weak. I have been giving him tea so he can rest. He has told me some interesting things, but we will discuss that later."

"Is there anything we can do?" Cory asked.

My father sighed. "Yes. Don't talk about where you've been, not even with each other. Don't give yourselves time to think of my world. Leave the house in the morning, spend the day doing whatever you wish, and return only before sundown. I will cast a sleeping spell on each of you. You have about two hours before it takes effect. There is food in the kitchen. I ask that you eat it quickly and retreat to the guest house."

Cory stood. "Okay, we'll leave right after breakfast. I'll take the guys to Newport. We have friends there."

"Thank you, young man."

"I'll put the sleeping spell on the boys, Father," I said, looking at him intently. "Stop using your magic."

My father smiled and nodded.

Suddenly feeling ravenous, I told the boys I would meet them in the kitchen in five minutes. I went to my room, changed, and hurried downstairs. When I walked in, Cory was already gone. Javier, Sammy, and Joshua were peeking into the pot on the stove.

"Where's Cory?" I asked.

Sammy ladled some stew into a bowl. "He said he was tired and headed to the guest house."

We each served ourselves some stew and sat at the table. Joshua kept talking about the dragons and the strange sun from my father's world.

"Shut up, Josh," Sammy ordered. "We're not supposed to talk about it."

"Talk about what?" Fish asked as he breezed into the kitchen.

"You'll find out tomorrow," Javier said.

I looked up at Fish and was surprised by what I saw. He wasn't wearing a shirt. Just like James, he was extremely fit. I could see why Delia was so attracted to him. With his blond hair and boyish face, he was very handsome.

"Hey, you going with us to Newport tomorrow?" Sammy asked Fish. "The girls will be happy to see you."

"Sorry guys," Fish said, reaching for a bowl.

"This stud is off the market."

He served himself some stew and sat next to me. I wanted to ask him to put a shirt on. I was having trouble keeping my eyes from drifting to his bare chest. I wanted to touch him, to feel every muscle on his body.

"So, I'll be going with you all tomorrow?" Fish asked.

I nodded and glanced at him from the corner of my eye. I had no romantic feelings for Fish but, for some reason, I couldn't seem to stop staring at him. As he ate, my gaze drifted toward him again. Before I knew it, I was undressing him with my eyes. I tried to force myself to look away, but I was helpless to the impulse.

At one point, he caught my eye and smirked. "You want me to put a shirt on, Thea?" he asked, grinning.

Male witches often lost focus when they saw a female witch's legs or some other alluring part of her body. They practically went into a trance, wanting her more than anything. I'd felt that trance-like state myself once when James removed his shirt in front of me. A stream of heat shot through my spine, just like I was experiencing now.

The boys erupted in laughter.

I shot them a look. "What's so funny?"

"You really don't know?" Javier asked.

Fish flexed his muscles and laughed again when I couldn't tear my eyes away from the display.

"I don't think she does," Fish said, returning to his stew.

"They'll never admit it," Sammy added, shaking his head.

Javier leaned across the table and tapped my nose. "You think the trance only happens to us?" he asked.

My face grew warm. "Well, no," I said, thoroughly embarrassed. "But I thought I could only feel like that with James."

Fish winked at the others. "Hey, take off your shirts, guys," he said. "Let's see how long Thea can take it."

The boys burst into laughter again, and I smacked Fish on the head.

James walked in. "I seem to have always just missed the joke when I walk into a room."

My face still flushed, I looked up at James and noticed how blue his eyes were. He was in a good mood, smiling even.

"So, what's so funny?" he asked.

"Fish," Javier answered.

"As always," James said, patting Fish on the back. He walked to the stove and peered into the pot. "Is this what you're eating, my love?" he asked.

The image of James kissing Helena appeared in my mind. I fought the urge to throw my stew in his face. I tried to get hold of myself. "Um, yes. It's beef stew," I replied, my appetite suddenly gone.

"May I join you?" he asked, grabbing a bowl. "I'm starving."

Fish stood. "You can sit here, man," he offered.

I closed my eyes as James approached the table. The rage in my heart was nearly uncontainable. I wanted to strike him when he kissed my head and sat down next to me.

"How was your day?" he asked. "Mine's been a bit slow, but it's better now that you're here." He winked and started eating the stew.

The boys stared at him, in awe of his unusually

good mood.

I looked at him from the corner of my eye. "Funny, I don't remember asking you about your day."

Sammy stood abruptly. "Come on, guys," he said. "We should get to bed."

Sammy, Javier, and Joshua said goodnight and walked out. Fish grabbed his bowl and followed them.

"Was it something I said?" James asked.

"Why don't you go ask Helena how her day was?" I said. "I'm sure she'll be more than willing to answer anything you ask."

"Thea, I don't understand. Did I say something to hurt you?"

"You can't hurt me anymore, James," I replied, pushing my bowl away. "You've pretty much killed any feelings I had for you."

He pushed his own bowl away, his eyes turning gray. "I don't know what I ever saw in you, witch. It baffles my mind how I could have ever loved you."

"I see we're on the same page then," I said. "I've been wondering the same thing about you." I stood up from the table and headed for the door.

James was immediately on my heels. He grabbed my arm and spun me to face him. "If that's the case, then get out of my house."

"Trust me," I said, "I'm planning to get as far away from you as possible."

"And run where?" he asked.

The impulse to lash out at him physically was nearly overwhelming. I shoved him aside and headed for the stairs.

James followed me. "Don't walk away from me!"

"Try and stop me," I said over my shoulder.

He caught up to me, grabbed a handful of my

hair, and wrapped his arm around my neck. "As you wish," he whispered into my ear.

I grabbed his arm and leaned forward. James flew over my head and landed on his back on the cold, stone floor of the foyer. "You'll have to do better than that, James."

"Is there a problem?"

James and I turned to see Jack standing at the bottom of the stairs. His appearance was shocking: dirty, disheveled, and rail-thin, as though he hadn't eaten in weeks.

Jack offered James his hand. "Rough day?"

I could see that James, too, was stunned by Jack's appearance. He grabbed Jack's hand and got to his feet. "You don't look too good, Jack."

"I'm fine, old friend," Jack said. "Just tired."

James' phone rang. He looked down at the number and glanced at me. "I'll talk to you tomorrow, Jack. Have a good night." James answered his phone and stepped across the foyer into his study. I heard him greet Helena before he closed the door.

"That spell is changing him fast," Jack said. "Did he hurt you?"

"No," I replied. "I can handle him. I mean, I'm getting used to it."

"Any closer to breaking the spell?" he asked. There were numerous scratch marks on his face, and bruises on his arms and neck. He held his stomach and coughed.

"Jack, are you okay?"

"I'll be fine," he said. "It's just the spell wearing off."

"Spell?" I asked. "What spell?"

He moaned and grabbed his stomach again. "I

needed to hide," he explained. "Simon was looking for me." A rueful smile tugged at his lips. "He wouldn't think to look for a cat, right?"

"You've been living as a cat?" I asked. "But that spell is so painful, Jack."

"I'm fine, Thea," he assured me. "It's not that bad." He was overwhelmed by another racking cough.

I reached for his arm and steadied him. "Why didn't you just stay here?"

He shook his head, unable to answer.

"Jack, you're in pain," I said. "Let's get you back in bed."

My father appeared at the top of the stairs and hurried down to help. "I told you to stay in bed, young man," he said, grabbing Jack's other arm.

"I was hungry," Jack replied, hunching over.

"I'll bring you up some food," I said. "Here, take him upstairs, Father."

As my father and Jack slowly climbed the steps, I went back to the kitchen. I couldn't understand why he'd chosen to turn himself into a cat; it was an excruciating spell. Few witches ever dared to chant it. It tore at your muscles and, when you changed yourself back, it took days to recover.

Jack was seriously ill. He looked and sounded awful. Animal spells were always hard to transition back from, but I had never known of one that made anyone as sick as Jack appeared now. Even Vera had fared better when Delia changed her into a mouse. She felt well enough to help Delia clean up the mess at the bakery the next day.

In the kitchen, I filled a bowl with stew and poured a glass of milk. I hurried back up the stairs and found the guest room where Jack was staying. My father had already helped him into bed.

"How is he, Father?"

"Not well. I will stay here with him tonight." He took a seat next to the bed.

I set the stew and the glass of milk on the nightstand. "I'll heal him right now," I offered. "Just tell me what the problem is."

My father smiled, a hint of pride in his eyes. "It will not help. Jack's spirit wishes to leave this world."

"What? But why?"

"His soul is tired. Sometimes death is the only peace one can find."

I tried to sit Jack up so he could eat, but my father gently pulled me away. "It's too late, Thea. Let him rest."

Jack grasped my hand. "Thea, let me die with the memories that haunt me."

I sat next to him on the bed and held his hand. "You were someone else back then, Jack. We all were."

"I killed innocent people," he continued, a tear rolling down his cheek. "I believed the words of a mad man. I burned poor souls alive. I don't deserve to live." He coughed and let go of my hand. He grabbed at his stomach and coughed up some blood.

In a panic, I stood and tried to wave my hand.

My father blocked the motion and shook his head. "Let him rest."

"Thea," Jack whispered.

I sat again on the bed and leaned toward Jack.

"I heard Simon say he needed you alive," Jack said. His voice was starting to fade. "He's instructed the warlocks not to kill you. There's something about a ball—a dance. He's ordered all the warlocks to attend."

"The Halloween Ball?" I asked.

Jack nodded. "But I wasn't able to learn of Simon's plan."

I reached for his hand. "Jack, please let me save you."

He shook his head. "Scout the woods near your old stomping grounds. Some of the warlocks have been taking humans there, to practice the wizard spells Simon has been teaching them. Many have already died."

Anger rose inside me. Simon knew no boundaries. He would stop at nothing to defeat me and return to my father's world. "I'll take care of it, Jack," I assured him. "I promise."

Jack's body began to tremble, and he looked toward the heavens. Tears welled in his eyes as he spoke his last words, his voice barely a whisper: "Forgive all that I have done." He gasped and slowly closed his eyes.

I felt my father's hands on my shoulders as I wept.

"There was nothing to be done, Thea," he said. "The warlocks practiced spells on him. They thought they were casting spells on a cat."

My blood began to boil. "Why did we let him die, Father?"

"Because he wanted to die, Thea. He was ready."

"Was this in your vision?" I asked.

"Yes."

Bitterness consumed me. I turned to face him. "And who's next?" I asked. "Who else has to die because of me, because I didn't change things?" I walked to the door and threw it open. "Stick!"

"Thea, no!"

But my father's words came too late. Perched on my stick, I descended the stairwell. I waved my hand to open the front doors and flew out into the night.

Chapter 10
Now You Squeal Like a Pig

I knew exactly where I was going, and who I was going to kill. I wanted nothing more than to see those warlocks die for hurting Jack, for killing things for their own amusement. Even as a little girl, I knew warlocks enjoyed torturing animals. They practiced spells on them. Now they'd moved onto humans.

Cory and the boys often lamented that they weren't considered warlocks. Why would they want to be warlocks? A warlock's heart was dead, unfeeling to love and emotion. My boys were nothing like that. Why couldn't they see that being a witch was nothing to be ashamed of?

I flew faster as rage coursed through my veins. All I could think about was killing the warlocks. My old stomping grounds were directly ahead—near the lake I loved so much, the place where I first met James. How dare they invade my world in such a way, to torture humans and animals, no less. They were going to die for this. I'd make sure of that.

As I flew over the forest, I spotted a fire. I flew in closer and saw a human dancing. He was jumping around like a monkey as the warlocks looked on and laughed. I landed a few feet away and snapped my stick in two. I moved slowly through the trees and tried to assess how many of them there were. I saw at least twenty, and two of them were nearby. They were throwing rocks at the human and shouting orders.

"Now bark like a dog!"

They exploded in laughter when the human complied.

I spun the sticks and turned them into swords. I stepped out from the trees and whistled at the warlocks. "Now you squeal like a pig!"

They had no time to throw spells. Two men came at me, and I ran at them, slamming the swords into the ground, using them to hold myself up as I drop-kicked them both. I pulled the swords from the earth and pierced their hearts.

Spells darted over my head as three warlocks ran toward me. I jumped backward off a tree and spun the swords. My feet hit the ground before the warlocks' heads did. I looked up and smiled as more warlocks came my way. One man swung a whip at me. It wrapped around my swords and pushed them together in my hands. I jumped on a twig and whispered, "Fly." I nearly went straight through the man as my swords sliced into him.

I kicked the dead warlock out of my way and spun to see another wave of warlocks coming at me. I twirled the swords and smiled; this was going to give me pleasure. Before I could strike, a spell hit my back, sending me flying forward ten feet. I caught my fall, but the swords flew from my hands. Before I knew it, a warlock towered above me, one of my swords in hand.

He stood, ready to strike. "Let me see you stop this," he said, swinging the sword over me.

I held out my hand for my other sword which came to me in an instant. Sparks flew as our swords clanged together. He swung again, but my sword was already through him before he could strike. I pulled my sword from his body and ran up a tree. The other warlocks had regrouped and were coming back. I heard spells spinning in their hands as they searched for me. There was a sound like that of a match striking each time one of the warlocks spat out a new one. I jumped off the tree as several men passed under me. They turned to face me.

"Use the spells," one of them shouted. "Don't kill her."

Before I could attack, one of the men was blasted with a spell. Over my shoulder, I spotted Ciro and his brothers running toward me. The warlocks tried to get to me before Ciro. I spun my sword, killing as many of them as I could.

Ciro came to fight by my side. We were back to back as Ciro swung his machete. A warlock charged at me and Ciro pulled me out of the way. I didn't have the heart to tell him I could fight these men by myself, that intervening wasn't necessary. But he had no way of knowing that I wanted to fight, and that I could kill them all with a wave of my hand. Fighting seemed the only way to conquer my anger, which was like a monster I could no longer control. I was changing, becoming something I didn't like.

We were surrounded by warlocks when I saw James' whip lash out and hit one of them.

"Thea!" Delia called out. She'd already put the human to sleep.

James stepped in front of her, swinging his whip. I saw the panic in his eyes as he fought his way to me. "Run this way," he shouted.

"I've got her, James," Ciro yelled back.

A warlock flew from a tree and nearly landed on top of me, but James swung his whip, slicing the man in two before he could reach me. Ciro turned and pushed me out of the way. He spun his machete around and held it in front of James.

"Ciro," I said, "what are you doing?"

"Making sure James wasn't aiming for you," Ciro replied.

James stopped and held up his hand. "It's still me, Ciro."

But Ciro kept his weapon at the ready. "Thea, what color are his eyes?"

"Blue," I said. "They're blue."

Ciro put his weapon away.

James ran to me. "What am I going to do with you?" he said, squeezing my arm. "Why did you run off like that?"

I yanked my arm away. I felt like punching him in the face. "What do you mean, it's still you?" I asked.

His eyes grew wide, as if I'd caught him in a lie. "I said: it's just me."

"No," Delia snapped. "You didn't."

James stared her down. "Leave it alone, Delia."

He knew about the spell, I was sure of that now.

"Why did you come here?" I asked. "I didn't need your help."

"Your father sent me," James said. "He was worried."

"Well, as you can see, I'm fine. No one needs your help. Why don't you go and help Helena?"

For a moment, James looked hurt. But soon rage grew on his face. He charged toward me.

Ciro stepped between us. "Now is not the time, James."

James ignored him. "You selfish witch," James said. "You don't care who you hurt, do you?"

"Not if I hurt you," I said, "if that's what you mean."

He tried to get closer, and again Ciro blocked his path.

"I wish I never married you," James shouted.

"James, please," Ciro said, holding him back.

"And I should have married Cory," I shot back. "He's the only one I ever really wanted!"

James stood, frozen, as all eyes turned to me. After a long, tension-filled moment, he started for his car. Ciro shot me a curious glance and followed James.

"Thea, what's gotten into you?" Delia asked.

The further away James got, the calmer I felt. I wondered why I felt like this every single time I was around him. "What the hell is going on?" I whispered.

"What are you talking about?" Delia asked.

"Something is wrong with me, Delia."

"What do you mean?"

"I don't know," I said, looking toward James. "But I'm changing."

"Funny you should say that," Delia said. "Your father told James if they caught you, it would change everything."

Alarm bells went off in my head. "Change what?" I asked.

"I don't know," she replied. "But James was very worried about it."

I looked at James again and my anger flared. I closed my eyes and breathed deep, trying to quell the urge to kill him.

"Are you okay?" Delia asked, rubbing my arm.

I turned to her. "Stop me if I go after James."

"Why would you go after James?" she asked, confused.

I swallowed my rising panic. "I need to get back to my father."

Ciro walked back to us and approached me. "You're making the spell work faster," he hissed. "Can't you see that?"

"How did you find me?" I asked.

"We couldn't get through the gates," Ciro explained. "You must have cast a spell around the house."

I sighed and closed my eyes.

"We saw you fly out of the house," he continued, "so we followed you."

I looked at James and back at Ciro. "I'm going to go check on the human."

Delia hurried behind me. "Why are you acting like this?" she asked.

I didn't have an answer to her question. I was terrified to even speculate why. Maybe Ciro was right. Maybe I was speeding up Simon's spell, playing right into that despicable man's hands.

"You're starting to scare me, Thea," Delia said. "Even your hair is changing."

I ignored her and started working on the human. I didn't want to tell her that I was scaring myself, too. "Jack is dead," I said. "Those warlocks were using him as a guinea pig for their spells."

"I know," she said, looking down. "Your father told us. We have to burn his body in the morning."

My heart raced as another wave of rage surged inside me. I looked up and spotted James walking back to us. I sighed in relief when he threw his keys to Delia and walked away, careful to avoid eye contact with me. I finished working on the human and took him home. I was able to find his house by following a trail of warlock scent.

We headed back to the mansion. I sat quietly looking out the window as Delia drove. I couldn't get rid of the disturbing thoughts swirling in my head. "What the hell is wrong with me?"

"Maybe you're just moody," she offered. "You are going through a lot."

"No, Delia, it's something else."

"Like what?"

I looked over at her. "Every time I'm near James, I want to kill him."

"I'm not surprised," she said. "He's cheating on you. The bond to him must be making you crazy."

"You think it's the bond?" I asked hopefully.

"I'm sure of it. I'm surprised you haven't killed James already."

That made me feel better. It did make sense. Now I understood why my father was so worried. He thought the bond would drive me to hurt James.

"Why don't we stop for some food," Delia suggested. "I think Cilantro might still be open."

"No," I said, gazing out the window. "Take me home."

I had calmed myself somewhat by the time we reached the house. When we walked in, James and the others were already there, gathered in the foyer. My father stood at the top of the stairs. I looked up at him, and he walked away.

"Father?" I called.

He ignored me and disappeared around the corner.

"Leave him alone," James snapped.

When I turned to look at him, I felt the monster inside me rise to the surface. "Don't tell me what to do, scum. This is between me and my father."

"Hate me all you want," he said. "But that man has done nothing but try to help you. I would have let you rot in hell."

"Why are you still talking to me?" I yelled. "Just leave me alone."

"Don't worry, witch. I have every intention of leaving you."

"Go to hell, James." I stormed into the kitchen. I needed to get away. It was getting harder not to wave my hand and strike him dead.

He stormed in after me. "If you have no respect for me," he shouted, "at least respect your father's wishes."

I reached a breaking point. "You're right, James," I said, facing him. "I have no respect for you."

I noticed his eyes grew dark as he stepped closer. "I should have let you rot in that grave, witch."

"And I should have let a real man take me."

His hands shook as he reached for my neck. "Ciro!" he shouted.

He was trying to stop himself, but the spell was winning. He clutched my neck and threw me against the wall, his eyes black as night as he leaned his face against mine. "A real man would have killed you long ago," he growled.

"That's why you're a coward!" I shot back.

He raised his hand and struck me across the face. He was reaching for his whip when Ciro dashed in and threw him to the floor.

"Do it, Ciro," James said. "Do it now!"

"No!" my father said, running into the kitchen. "Don't listen to him!"

James got up and tried to go after me again.

Ciro quickly grabbed him. "James, no!"

"You filthy witch! I've wasted my life on you."

"And I've wasted my time. Now we're even."

"Someone get her out of here!" my father shouted, helping Ciro hold James back.

James escaped their grasp and came at me. I waved my hand and sent him flying across the kitchen.

Ciro turned and grabbed me. "Delia!" he shouted toward the foyer. "Go get my brothers!"

I pounded my fist on Ciro's chest, knocking him across the kitchen and onto the stove. I turned to look at James again. He got up and smiled as he pulled out his whip.

"James, no!" my father cried.

I waved my hand and blasted everyone against the wall—everyone, that is, but James. I smiled at him and held out my hand. "Stick."

"Thea," my father called out. "You must stop yourself!"

I ignored him and caught my stick as it flew into my hand. "Ready to be a real man now?" I said to

James.

Ciro's brothers ran into the kitchen with Delia close behind.

"Thea, what are you doing?" Delia asked.

But I ignored her, too. "Any last wishes?" I asked James.

"Yes," he answered. "I wish I had never met you." He attempted to swing his whip at me, but Ciro's brothers caught his arm.

Delia ran out the back door.

"Thea, control your mind," my father commanded. "It's the spell. You can stop yourself. You must."

My father was too weak to break my spell. He remained glued to the wall as I stepped closer to James. "Let him go," I told Ciro's brothers. I waved my hand and they, too, were pinned against the wall.

James smiled, spinning his whip. "Now, where were we?"

I spun my stick. "I was about to kill you." I ran at him.

He tried to hit me with his whip.

I could hear everyone yelling for us to stop. I felt the whip cut deep into my arm, but it failed to sever my arm from my body.

"James, stop," my father shouted. "Run out of the room, James. Run!"

I smacked James across the face with my stick, spun, and kicked him in the chest. He sailed across the kitchen and smashed into the far wall, his whip flying from his hand and landing near my feet. I kicked it away as James regained his footing.

I waved my hand and threw a spell, hitting James in the chest. He grunted once and collapsed to the floor.

It gave me pleasure to see him in pain. I spotted Ciro's machete on the kitchen table. I snatched it and ran at James.

"Thea, no!" my father shouted.

Before I could reach James, Cory tackled me to the floor. We landed hard and slid through the kitchen door and into the foyer. I struggled to pull away.

Cory wrapped his arms tightly around me. "Snap out of it, Thea!"

I heard James cough and saw him spitting up blood. The sight of him shook me to the core. The fury that had been controlling me drained from my body. "James!" I screamed, trying to pull away from Cory.

Cory finally let me go, and I ran to my husband. I lifted his head and wiped the blood from his lips. "James," I cried. My heart was filled with panic as I waved my hand and healed him. I couldn't understand why I had hurt him. "What's happening to me?" I screamed into the air.

"Let us down!" my father shouted.

My hands trembled as I looked down at James. I had thrown a powerful spell at him, intending to kill him. I had never wanted anything so much in my life. But now the rage was gone, leaving behind only confusion and panic.

I screamed when James opened his eyes and they were still black. "Come back to me!" I sobbed.

"Thea," my father shouted. "Release us and get away from him!"

James reached up and touched my face. The anger returned the moment our skin made contact. I raised my hand, but Cory intervened and quickly dragged me away.

"Get her out of here!" my father ordered.

~ 132 ~

I tried to get to my feet again, but Cory was practically sitting on top of me. My father began chanting. He finally broke my spell and slid down off the wall. He ran to James and tapped his head, then reached over and tapped me.

I felt a great weight lifted from me, and darkness filled my head. I didn't fight it. I closed my eyes and allowed myself to drift away.

Chapter 11
It Works Both Ways

My slumber was filled with magical dreams. I felt soft hands touching my face, smooth lips kissing mine. Fingers slowly tangled themselves through my hair. The sensations were so real I didn't want to wake up.

The sound of pouring tea pulled me from my sleep. I opened my eyes. My father's back was to me, but he sensed I was awake. I sat up and tried to make sense of what had happened hours before.

"How are you feeling?" he asked, handing me a cup.

"James—how is he?"

My father hesitated, looking down at the floor. "He is . . . distraught."

I set my tea on the nightstand. "What the hell was all that, Father?" I asked. "And please don't lie to me." My insides churned. I ran my hands through my hair, noting how easily my fingers sliced through the smooth strands.

"Drink, Thea," he ordered. "I will tell you the truth."

"What's happening to me?" I looked up at him, my eyes filling.

"I wanted to spare you the pain of having to hear this, but after what happened last night, I have no choice." He sighed and sat next to me. "The spell Simon put on James, it works both ways. As his love dies for you, so shall yours die for him."

I leaned back against the headboard, tears spilling down my cheeks. "Why didn't you tell me? Why didn't you warn me about this?"

He handed me the cup again. "I tried to. But I realized, perhaps too late, that it was hastening the spell's effect."

"Simon put that spell on James. Why is it affecting my feelings?"

He regarded me with pity. "I told you, it works both ways. You are bonded to James. You share one love. When that love dies, it affects both of your hearts."

I sighed, finding a touch of comfort in his words. I didn't hate James. It was only the spell. "What am I going to do, Father? I would die if I hurt him again."

"And he feels the same way. It took a lot of convincing to stop him from leaving the house last night."

I bowed my head. "No. I'll leave. It's better for you to be close to him, to check on him." I looked up. "I'll stay in the guest house with the boys. I won't go near James again."

"That won't be necessary. I have thought of a way to keep you both strong."

A small smile found its way to my lips. "What do you mean?"

He pulled out Delia's memory box and handed it to me. "Here. I extracted one of your memories. I want you to visit it at least once a day. It will give you peace and keep your heart strong."

"And James?" I asked. "How will this help him?"

He removed a handkerchief from his pocket and dabbed at my tears. "Just do as I say, Thea. You will soon see." He stood. "It's a good thing you forgot to put that sleeping spell on the boys. Delia would have been trying for hours to wake Cory."

The sleeping spell! In all the commotion, I'd forgotten all about it. "I'm sorry, Father. It won't happen again."

His kind eyes lit up. "It seems your lapse in memory was fortuitous." He pointed to the tea. "Now drink. It will help your mood."

Obediently, I reached for the cup.

He headed for the door. "Oh, and Thea," he said, turning, "I have been thinking about what Jack said. If Simon is building an army, we will need reinforcements. I have asked Ciro to help you hunt the warlocks. He is taking you to meet some friends of his. But I do not want Cory and the boys going with you. The warlocks are too powerful. They could be killed."

"I don't need help. Why would I need Ciro's friends?"

He arched his brow. "I want you back before sundown. Attor will have good news today."

"Father, wait." I jumped out of bed and ran to him. "I'm sorry I always give you a hard time, that I always let you down."

"Don't say that again," he admonished. "You could never let me down. You have made me nothing but proud from the moment you were born." He kissed my head and started for the door.

"Wait," I said, grasping his hand. "James knows about the spell, doesn't he?"

He nodded. "Yes. He has known for oh, two hundred years or so."

"What? Why didn't you stop it?"

"That I cannot tell you."

Same old song and dance. "Where is he now?"

"With Helena. He left early this morning."

I lowered my head and blinked back the tears.

My father gathered me in his arms. "It is necessary, Thea. I swear I would not allow it if it were not."

"I know," I said, nodding. "No more questions, I promise."

"Visit your memories, child. They will comfort you. They will ease your pain." He pulled away. "Now go get dressed. Ciro is waiting."

I nodded again, and he opened the door.

Delia was waiting on the other side. "I was just about to knock."

"Come in, young Delia," my father said. "I was just leaving."

After he'd started down the hall, Delia closed the bedroom door behind her. "Are you okay?" she asked. She spied the box in my hand. "What are you doing with that—erasing James' memory?"

"Why would I want to do that?"

"Um, hello. Because of James' major breakdown last night?"

"What do you mean?"

"After your father put you to sleep, he woke James. When James saw your arm, he lost it."

"My father woke him?"

"Yeah. You didn't see James this morning? He was in here all night."

"James was here—with me?"

Delia nodded. "He refused to leave. He told your father the deal was off."

"The deal?" My stomach lurched. "What deal?"

Delia shrugged. "No clue. But they argued for a long time. James told your father that he was going to make Ciro do it.'"

"Do what?"

"How would I know? But your father was really upset about it."

"What the hell are they up to?" I muttered, mostly to myself.

"I assumed that's why you had the box. To find out."

Something clicked in my head. Why hadn't I thought of it before?

"Oh no," Delia said, eyeing me closely. "What did I just do?" She backed toward the door.

I grabbed her arm. "Where do you think you're going?"

"I'm out of here," she said. "I know that look." She peeled my fingers from around her arm. "I don't want any part of this."

"You have to help me, Delia."

She crossed her arms. "Give me one good reason why."

I told her about my father's vision, how he'd told me about Simon when I was a little girl. I told her the things he'd warned me about, and how he was trying to change them.

"All the more reason not to help you," she said.

"There's something my father doesn't want me to know. It's something bad. He said it would change things if we talked about it." I paused. "I think James knows what it is."

"Oh no you don't. I am not getting involved."

"Listen," I pleaded, "I just want to know what my father is hiding. I have to know why he would tell James and not me. My father already told me that James knows about the spell, and has for over two hundred years."

Her eyes widened. "He knows about the spell?"

"Yes, and I can't understand why my father would tell him. Why does James get to know everything, while I'm always left in the dark?"

I could see the gears of Delia's mind turning.

"You see what I'm talking about? They're hiding something from me, and you have to help me find out what it is."

"And how are you—we—going to do that?" she asked.

I held up the box and grinned.

Delia shook her head. "No way. I'm not messing with your father."

"He told me about a vision he had." I reached for her hands. "And in his vision, one of you dies."

She stood, her eyes darting around nervously. I knew she was worried for Fish.

Finally she squeezed my hands and exhaled. "When do we do it?"

I told her my plan. She was scared but agreed to help me.

"What are you going to do with the information once you have it?" she asked.

I sat on the bed. "I don't know."

"What if your father reads your mind? He'd know what we've been up to."

"I'll just have to be extra careful around him. Maybe I'll put a spell on myself or something."

We agreed to talk about it more when we got into Magia. I couldn't take the chance of my father overhearing us. I'd also have to find some way to block my thoughts from him.

"What time are we leaving today?" Delia asked.

"Sundown."

"Oh, I almost forgot—Gilly is here."

"He's here?" I asked, surprised.

"Yup, he heard Fish was staying here."

Gilly was Fish's good friend—another witch. He'd left Salem rather suddenly several hundred years ago. After my mother's death, many of the male witches fled Salem, but no one knew why. It certainly seemed that many of them were returning lately. I made a mental note to ask John-John about it next time I saw him.

"Well, I'll be in Steven's room if you need me," Delia said. "I got him a new video game."

I took a shower and dressed. When I walked into the guest house, my attention was drawn to a large map lying across the dining table, with certain areas circled in red. Before I could examine it closely, Ciro walked out of one of the bedrooms, followed by Sharron, who looked like a ghost. Her hair was a mess, more so than I'd ever seen it. Her petite frame looked tiny next to Ciro, who was the epitome of tall, dark, and handsome.

They seemed surprised to see me.

"Thea," Ciro said. "I didn't hear you come in."

"Hello, dear," Sharron said, smiling.

"Looking for something?" I asked, gesturing toward the map.

Ciro hastily folded the map and slipped it into the bookshelf in the living room. "I was thinking of doing some hunting."

He was lying. But why?

"Are you going with him?" I asked Sharron.

"No, dear. I was just asking Ciro if he was coming in for breakfast."

"Thank you, Sharron," Ciro said. "I'm not very hungry."

Sharron nodded and quickly excused herself. Ciro smiled nervously and fiddled with one of the placemats on the table. I considered pulling out Delia's memory box and using it on him, but thought better of it. I still didn't know why we were going to see these friends of his.

I decided to play along with their little game, play stupid and see where it took me. "Where are your brothers?"

"They had to leave," Ciro replied. "They said to say goodbye."

"Is everything okay?"

"Everything's fine." Again, the nervous smile. He offered me a seat. "How are you feeling?"

"I'm fine," I said as I sat at the table. "I'm sorry if I hurt you."

He sat across from me. "All is forgiven." He laced his fingers through the fringe of the placemat and looked out the window.

Ciro knew even more than I thought. "You knew about the spell," I said, "*before* I called and told you about it, didn't you?"

He peered at me from the corner of his eye. "Yes."

"How? And for how long?"

He faced me and sighed. "James told me about two hundred years ago."

My eyes narrowed. "Why are you really here?"

"Thea, please, don't make me do this."

I reached for his fidgety hand. "I deserve to know the truth."

"I wanted to tell you," he said. "I've never agreed with James and your father about keeping the truth from you."

"Then tell me. What exactly is the truth?"

He lowered his head. "It's not my place."

I pulled my hand away. "I thought you were a man of honor."

He stood. "You're putting me in a difficult position, Thea. I came to help, not to make decisions."

"And how are you helping exactly? What did James ask you to do last night?"

He exhaled and stared at me for a long, silent moment. "He wanted me to kill him."

"He what?"

"James asked me to kill him when the spell gets bad. He said he wouldn't be able to live with himself if he ever hurt you."

"So that's why he asked my father to kill him."

"Yes. James asked him first, but your father refused. So James came to me."

"You can't kill him, Ciro."

"I don't plan to. I'm trying to find a way to stop what's going on."

"What's going on?"

He sat down again at the table. "I can't tell you that. But if my friends can help us, I believe we can stop what your father fears most."

I looked into his eyes, searching for the truth.

"How bad is it?"

"Bad—if it happens."

I leaned back, my mind swarming with horrifying possibilities.

"Thea, come with me to see my friends," Ciro said, extending his arm across the table. "I promise if your father does not tell you the truth soon, I will."

I grasped his hand. "Give me your word."

"You have my word. I will tell you what I know."

He was telling the truth. I agreed to go with him, meet these friends of his, and not ask questions. I had no idea why we needed them, but I trusted Ciro.

We went to his car, which was parked in front of the house. "Have you ever been to Fall River?" he asked as he opened the door for me.

"Several times," I said, ducking into the passenger seat. "Maybe I know your friends."

He closed my door and walked around the front of the car. The car was filled with a pleasant scent that seemed to come from a cluster of dried leaves hanging from the rear view mirror. A feeling of peace and calm washed over me, and I drew a deep breath. I felt as though I could drift off in seconds.

Ciro jolted me from my tranquil state. "Don't think so," he said as he started the car.

"I'm sorry, what?"

"My friends—you said you might know them, but I don't see how that's possible." He pulled the car out of the driveway and onto the tree-lined street.

"So you trust these friends of yours?"

"I do, but I think we might have a problem with one of them. Justin is the youngest of the brothers and doesn't like anything about our world. He hates being a warlock."

"Then why are we going to see them?"

"I need them. I don't trust the warlocks in or around Salem. Most claim they don't follow Simon, but I still don't trust them. Your father wants us to hunt Simon's men. The Santos brothers are good fighters." He looked over at me. "They can help."

I was surprised. "So my father wasn't lying. We really do need them."

"Yes, they know how those warlocks fight. At one time, they followed Simon. They even know some of Simon's spells."

"And how do you know they aren't helping Simon now?"

"Because your father assured me we could trust them."

We talked all the way to Fall River. I told Ciro about the Halloween Ball, how Simon wanted all his men there. We agreed that it would be wise for all of us to attend and perhaps learn what Simon was up to.

"He must be preparing to cast a spell," Ciro said.

"On the warlocks?"

"No. On the humans. He must have some use for them."

"What use could he possibly have for humans?"

Before he could answer, he pulled up to a three-family tenement building. "This is it," he said, turning off the car.

I loved Fall River. The town had changed very little in a hundred years. The old fabric mills still stood, most of them housing shops and outlets now. The predominantly Portuguese-populated town was filled with beautiful old churches, and the Portuguese festivals brought crowds of tourists several times a year.

Ciro opened my door. "Shall we?"

Chapter 12
The Santos Brothers

Several cars occupied the driveway of the tenement building. Two empty chairs sat on the front porch.

Ciro started across the yard. "They usually use the side door. I'll go knock."

I waited by the front door, admiring the wind chimes that hung from the eaves of the porch.

He returned in less than a minute. "No answer. They must be next door. I'll check."

"Should I wait here?"

"Yeah. I'll be right back."

The chimes clinked in the breeze. They were unusual: various-sized crystal balls with little stars inside them. The stars seemed to come alive as I reached for them. The effect was mesmerizing. I leaned in to get a closer look, but was startled by a voice behind me.

"Tell your boss we already said no."

I glanced over my shoulder to find a young warlock, mildly overweight and surly.

"I'm sorry, were you talking to me?" I said.

"Is there another witch here?"

"You must have me confused with someone else. I came here with—"

He cut me off. "We already gave you our answer. Now get off my porch, before I forget you're a woman."

I stepped closer to him. "And I told you, you're confusing me with someone else."

"You can change what you look like, witch, but the answer is still no."

The front door opened, and another warlock appeared—older, thinner, and taller than the first. "Is there a problem, Justin?" he asked.

"Not at all, brother. This witch was just leaving."

I arched my eyebrow. "Actually, I'm not going anywhere. I'll tell you one last time: you're confusing me with someone else."

Justin pulled from his pocket what looked to be a silver straw. He twirled it through his fingers and grinned. The older warlock spat a spell into his hand. I watched as it spun and aimed itself at me.

I took two steps back. "My lords, I don't want to hurt you. If you could just wait for my friend, he can explain everything."

"Your friend?" Justin echoed. "He's here?" He raised the straw and blew into it, sending a spell directly at me. I waved my hand and blasted both of the spells away. The older warlock lunged for me, but I jumped back off the porch and onto the grass.

"Get her, Ryan!" Justin yelled.

A third, huskier warlock emerged from the house. He tossed what looked like marbles at my feet.

"Adam," Justin said, "get ready to grab her."

The one named Adam flew off the porch.

My feet were paralyzed. A surge of pain rushed up my leg. "Release," I commanded. The pain subsided, and I kicked several of the marbles toward Ryan and Adam. They jumped and spun to avoid them. Justin raised his straw and threw another spell at me.

I didn't want to hurt them, but it was getting harder to dodge their spells. I ran at the house and up the siding. I was shocked when Ryan and Adam ran up after me. As I stepped onto the roof, I spotted a tree in the backyard and called out, "Stick!" A sturdy branch from the tree broke off and flew into my open hand. I turned and hit the warlock named Adam across the face.

Without warning, two feet pounded into my back. I fell from the roof and onto the hard dirt of the backyard. I tried to get up, but I was hurt. I was about to heal myself when I felt a knife poking into my throat.

The one named Ryan towered above me. "Stay down, witch," he ordered. "You move, and I kill you." His eyes searched the yard. When he spotted Adam on the roof, he called out, "You okay?"

Adam gave a quick nod.

By the time Ryan looked back at me, I had healed myself. I hurled him across the yard with a wave of my hand. Adam tried to escape, but I jumped up and kicked him, sending him flying across the yard and smashing into the house.

I heard Justin's voice behind me. "That's it, witch. Now you die."

I turned to see him blowing into his straw. The spell slammed into my shoulder and knocked me to the ground. Before I could right myself, the other two came at me feet first, pounding my face into the ground. I heard a cracking sound as they stomped on my head repeatedly.

I wasn't going to let these warlocks finish me. I was done playing nice. I grabbed one of Adam's ankles. "Break," I said weakly.

Adam dropped to the ground.

I waved my hand at Ryan and heard his legs break. Blood ran down my face as I staggered to my feet. Things were getting fuzzy. Justin tried to blow another spell, but I managed to wave my hand and send it away from me. I raised my hand again, a death spell on my fingertips.

"Thea, stop!"

I glanced in the direction of Ciro's voice and collapsed to the ground. It took minutes for me to realize that my head was split open. I tried to heal myself, but I couldn't think straight. Ciro put his hands on my head, which was throbbing furiously. The pain was making me black out.

Ciro chanted a healing spell.

"Forgive us, Ciro," I heard the one named Ryan say. "We didn't know who she was."

"I already chanted a healing spell," Justin said, his voice tinged with panic. "It didn't work."

"Try again!" Ciro shouted.

The four chanted various healing spells, to no avail.

"Nothing is working," Justin said. "I think she's dying."

"If she dies," Ciro replied, "so will you."

Numb, I opened my eyes. I saw two of everything, and heard a strange buzzing in my head. I felt I was being held under water. My head was filled with a strange pressure.

Ciro grasped my hand. "Thea, are you able to

heal yourself?"

My eyes rolled back. I heard only chanting as my head filled with darkness.

~~~

"What happened? Why is she all covered in blood?" Delia's voice came to me through the enveloping darkness.

Ciro spoke: "It was a mistake. They thought Simon sent her."

"Who is they?" Delia asked.

I sensed the familiar surroundings of the mansion. I smelled my father's cooking. Hands wrapped under my back and legs, but I couldn't make out who was holding me. The sound of James' voice sent a surge of energy through my body.

"Thea!" James called. "Get away from her."

Through blurred vision I saw James running toward me and pushing someone out of the way.

"What did you do to her?" James shouted.

"James, it was a mistake," said Ciro. "They didn't know who she was."

"It's my fault," Justin said. "Don't blame Ciro."

"Then I will kill only you," James spat.

"James," Ciro continued, "they had no way of knowing."

I closed my eyes again as someone laid me down on the couch.

"James, put the whip away," Delia whispered.

"Please, James!" Ciro pleaded. "Thea's hurt. This is not the time. We have to take her to her father. The spells we've been chanting aren't working."

For a moment, there was silence. I felt James' arms lift me. I had the sensation of floating on air. I tried to talk, but couldn't get my mouth to work right. The sound of James' voice gave me comfort. I felt his kiss on my head.

"I'm here, my love," James whispered. "I've got you now."

I heard him kick open a door.

"James, what have you done?" my father said.

"It wasn't me, William," James explained. "It was the warlocks downstairs."

"The Santos brothers?" my father asked.

"We didn't know who she was." A voice from the door—Justin.

"Get out!" James shouted.

"It's her head," Justin continued, ignoring James. "I think her skull is cracked."

"How long has she been like this?" my father asked.

"An hour, maybe more," Justin answered.

"If she dies," James said, "your death will be slow and painful."

"We didn't know! We thought—"

"Thank you, young man," my father cut in. "Please wait outside now."

I felt something cold on my head, like ice melting on my face. Their voices started to fade away, leaving only the strange buzzing sound in my head.

I turned my head and vomited.

"Hurry, James!" my father shouted. "Get the boys. Her brain is swelling!"

"What?" James gasped. "No . . ."

"Hurry, James. We have no time to waste. I must put the ring on her finger as soon as possible."

"Heal her, William!"

"I'm too weak, son."

Soon after, I heard Cory's voice. "Should I pick her up?" he asked.

"Yes, quickly," my father answered. "Give her to Attor. He'll know what to do."

"Sam! Josh!" Cory yelled. "Get over here and hold onto her. Hurry!"

As Cory lifted me from my father's bed, someone slipped the ring onto my finger. In an instant, I felt myself drifting away. Cory's arms held me tight as he whispered into my ear. "You're going to be okay, Thea."

"What do we do when we get there?" Sammy asked.

"William said the dragon would help us," Cory said.

"What if he doesn't?" Sammy pressed. "What do we do then?"

"I won't take no for an answer, Sam. Keep an eye out, we're almost there."

I could smell the flowers and hear the rushing water of the falls as Cory set me down. I tried with all my will to open my eyes, but my body wouldn't respond to my brain's commands.

"Stand back," Cory said. "Give her some air."

Joshua pointed. "Here comes the dragon."

I heard Cory flick his arms and Joshua draw his sword.

"We're not leaving until she's healed guys," Cory told the others. "Get ready to fight."

I heard a thump, and then Attor's voice. "You're here early. It's not time yet."

"She's hurt," Cory answered. "Her father told us to bring her to you."

Moments later, I felt Attor's breath on me. "Anisa

Quisores," he whispered.

"What does that mean?" Cory asked.

"Silence!" Attor snapped.

Something wet dragged itself across my head. It took a few seconds for me to realize it was Attor's tongue. It felt like fire sealing my skull. Sensation started to return to my hands and feet. Cory's trembling hand held mine. I opened my eyes and smiled at him. He exhaled in relief.

"Can you speak?" Attor asked.

I breathed deeply. "Yes."

Attor looked at Cory. "How did this happen?"

"I'm not sure," Cory answered. "I was only told to bring her to you."

Attor turned his attention back to me. "Are you able to stand?"

"I don't think so," I said. "I can hardly move my legs."

"You will be better in a few minutes, but you must leave now. I was not prepared to receive you yet. You might be seen. You will continue to heal after you leave. Come back when it is time. I will be waiting for you."

I nodded and squeezed Cory's hand. I stumbled while trying to get to my feet. Cory caught me and looked at Sammy. "Take the ring off her."

"Wait," I said, reaching for Attor. "Thank you . . . for helping me."

"Tell your father he did the right thing," Attor replied. "Tell him we are almost prepared."

"Prepared for what?" I asked.

"He will know. Now, go."

"Okay," Cory said. "Let's get out of here."

A strange feeling came over me as I looked into

Cory's eyes, an urge to kiss him. I felt happy to be in his arms. I closed my eyes and leaned my head on his chest. He pulled me closer as Sammy reached for my hand and gently pulled the ring off.

"Thea," said James.

I opened my eyes.

He took two steps toward me, but my father held up his hand. "No, James," he said. "She is still very weak."

"Please, William," James pleaded. "Let me go to her."

"No, son."

James looked at me. His eyes were so dark. I felt my temper flare, but I closed my eyes and fought it. When I opened my eyes again, he was gone. The sour feeling drifted away.

"Do you think you can stand now?" Cory asked.

I nodded, and he set me down. I faltered as my feet touched the floor.

My father ran to my side and wrapped his arms around me. He sighed and gently kissed my head. "I am going to lose my mind over you one day, Thea."

"I'm okay now, Father. Attor healed me."

"Yes, I can see that." He smiled. "Please thank him for me when you go back tonight."

"He said you did the right thing, Father. He told me to tell you they were almost prepared."

He pulled away, his smile widening. "You see, he did have good news today."

"Why does the news please you so much?" I asked.

"Because it means that the other dragons have agreed to help you, and that will make things easier all around." He wrapped his arms around me again. "It's almost over, Thea. You can do this."

I started to cry. "But I don't know what to do."

"Follow your heart, child. In the end, I know you will make the right choice."

"But what if my heart is wrong?" I asked. "What then? Will I lose everything?"

"You will never lose me."

"And James?" I asked, looking into his eyes.

He handed me off to Cory. "There are some people downstairs who are anxious to know that you're okay."

The moment my father opened the door, Delia rushed in, breathless. "Thea, are you okay?"

My father disappeared down the hall as Delia ran to my side. "What the heck happened to you?"

"I got my butt kicked."

"What happened?" Cory asked.

I told them about the Santos brothers. Cory couldn't believe how vicious they'd been, how badly they'd hurt me.

"I tried not to hurt them," I said.

"And they were trying to kill you?" he asked. "But why?"

It hit me—the reason they had attacked.

Before I could explain, Justin walked into the room. "I am so sorry," he said. "We thought you were that witch."

"What witch?" Cory asked.

"A witch Simon sent," Justin explained. "She wanted us to help capture someone named Delia."

Delia spun around. "Me? He wanted you to capture me?"

My father walked back in, Fish on his heels.

Delia hurried to Fish. "Did you know Simon is

trying to capture me?"

"What?" Fish asked, confused.

"He sent someone to order these warlocks to take me to him," she said, gesturing to Justin.

Fish turned to Justin. "You'll have to get through me first."

"Calm down, Fish," I said. "They said no." On weak legs, I shuffled slowly to Justin. "What does this witch look like?"

"She's always changing what she looks like," he said, "so I can't really tell you."

"And why did you say no?"

"We're not Simon's puppets," he explained. "We do what we want, not what we're told."

"Perhaps you should all go downstairs and talk," my father suggested.

We all left my father's room. I told the others to go on, and that I would meet them in the living room. I was still covered in blood.

As I cleaned myself up, I heard the muffled voices of James and my father talking in my father's room. I put my ear up to the bedroom wall and closed my eyes. I heard something being shuffled from one place to another and the sound of a door open. The only door I knew of in my father's room was his closet door. Finally, I heard their voices.

"I'm sorry, William," James said. "I had to make sure it was still safe."

"I gave you my word," my father replied. "A thousand men could come into this house and not one of them would be able to find it."

"Is that where you were when Simon's men came here?" James asked. "I always wondered why they never found you."

"If you tried to find that door again," my father said, "you would grow old searching for it."

"Has she asked about it?" James asked.

"No. Not since I took it."

What were they talking about? What did my father take?

"How long before she forgets?" James asked.

"Do what I told you, James. It will help both of you."

"I can't go near her. What if I hurt her? I would never forgive myself."

"You must. You can't allow her heart to forget you, not now."

"Let me die with this spell. It would solve everything. She would learn to love another. She has a chance to be happy. Allow me to give her that gift."

I swung open my bedroom door and ran to my father's room. "Open up!" I shouted, pounding on the door.

When my father opened the door, I ran right past him, straight into James' arms. "I will never love another," I cried, throwing my arms around him. "If you die, I die with you."

He enfolded me in his arms. "Thea."

"Don't ever leave me."

His eyes turned dark as night. I could see he was trying hard to fight it. His hold on me tightened.

I, too, felt the change, but refused to let it control me. "I love you," I whispered.

He pushed me away and stormed from the room.

I tried to go after him, but my father stopped me. "Let him go, Thea. It's not safe."

I hung my head, the tears flowing freely. I knew

James had done the right thing. The desire to kill him grew inside me. If he had stayed one moment longer, we'd have ended up right back where we were the previous night.

My father put his arm around my shoulder. "I'll go tell the others you won't be coming down. You can speak to them when you come back tonight. I think you need some time to yourself."

Chapter 13
I Thought It Was a Dream

The fear of losing James was too much. I ran into my room, closed the door, and slid to the floor. I wanted to flee this world and be free from these destructive thoughts. How could he think I would ever learn to love another?

I decided to take my father's advice and escape into my memories. I pulled the box from my pocket and opened it. As the memory clouds drifted out and floated above me, I noticed one I hadn't seen before. The memory my father mentioned, no doubt. I rose to my feet, reached up, and pulled it toward me.

Seconds later, the warmth of the sun was on my face. I could see James swimming in the lake. I watched myself watching him from the shore. The look on my face was one of overwhelming happiness as he coaxed me to join him.

"Come, my lady!" he called out. *"I give you my word, I will be a gentleman."*

"That worries me not, my lord," I said. *"But I do worry about my dress. It is very thin and delicate. You*

might see things I do not wish you to."

James laughed and disappeared under the water. When he came up again he was near the shore. *"Then I shall come to you."*

He slowly rose out of the water. I couldn't help but giggle at my younger self, trying so hard to avert my gaze from James' beautiful body. Even now, his bare chest sent my heart racing. He sat next to me, stroked my face, and kissed me.

The memory didn't provide me the comfort I had hoped for. It only made me feel worse. I couldn't stand to see the happy us, the us that didn't have a care in the world. It only reminded me of how things would never be again, of just how much I was losing.

I finally looked away and started crying. There was no point in staying here and watching this. I looked down at the box; it was still open in my hand. I was about to pull myself out of the memory when I heard the sound of footsteps in the leaves. Someone was here. Someone was walking around.

I quickly closed the box and ducked behind a tree. There was some movement a few yards away, and James emerged from the trees. He looked towards the lake, watching the same scene I was. He sat near the water's edge and hung his head.

When he looked up again, I noticed how blue his eyes were. It was easy to see he was suffering as much as I was, searching for the same comfort I came here to find. I was terrified of making my presence known. There was no one here to stop us from killing each other.

But I felt no rage in this moment, only love. I stepped quietly out from behind the tree, hoping the anger wouldn't return. When a twig cracked under my foot, James shot to his feet. He spotted me and turned to leave, but then stopped himself.

Our eyes met, and we knew. There was no anger here, just me and him. Our hearts were free. This is what my father had been trying to tell us. Simon's spell had no power here.

When the realization hit, James ran toward me. I dropped the box and ran into his arms. My heart came alive with happiness. We came together like two lightning bolts, the surge from his touch nearly driving me mad. He held my face in his hands and crushed his lips to mine.

"James, James . . ."

He barely let me up for air, his kisses forcefully passionate. I thought my heart would explode. He kissed my head and I burst into tears. I wrapped my arms around his waist and sobbed. He took my face in his hands and looked into my eyes. "Don't cry, my love," he said, his sweet breath brushing over my face. "Please, don't cry."

"Say those words again," I said. "Call me your love."

"My love," he whispered, kissing me again.

I couldn't stop crying. As he held me in his arms, I couldn't believe that any of this was real. I kept touching his face to make sure I wasn't dreaming. He kissed my hand and pulled me to his lips again. His scent flooded through me.

I nestled closer to him. "I'm so sorry for everything I've said to you," I cried.

"No, my love," he replied. "Forgive me for all the pain I've caused you."

"Do you still love me?"

He smiled. "With all my soul."

"Then there is nothing to forgive."

"Helena—you know she means nothing to me, right?"

I placed my fingers to his lips. "Please, don't talk about her, not here."

He grabbed my hand, pulled me closer, and kissed me again.

"Please don't wake me from this dream," I said, resting my head on his chest.

"If anyone tries, I'll kill them."

I laughed and looked up at him. "Let's stay here and never go back."

"If only that were possible."

We turned to look at our younger selves.

"Look at them," he said. "What I wouldn't give to feel that free again."

"Don't give up on us, James," I pleaded. "Don't give your heart away."

He held my face in his hands. "How can you say that to me? My heart belongs to you—only you. It will never belong to anyone else, ever."

I looked away, but he turned me to face him again.

"Thea, I only see you when I'm with her. It's your lips I'm kissing when she's in my arms."

I turned my back on him. "I asked you not to talk about her. Can you not stop thinking of her, even here?"

He spun me around. "When this is all over, I want you to erase my memory of every evidence of her."

I was trying not to be childish, but jealousy consumed me. I hated the fact that he was with her, kissing her and holding her in his arms. I lowered my head. "And who will erase the pain in my heart? Who will erase the image of you kissing her from my head? Who will make me forget how much it kills me to see you with her?"

He kissed my head and enfolded me in his arms. "I will never forgive myself for the pain I've caused you. And I promise, you will never have to worry about any of that ever again. I know what I have to do."

"What are you going to do?" I asked, pushing away from him.

"Don't worry, my love," he assured me. "Everything's going to be okay."

"No, don't listen to me, James. Please, do not listen to me."

He tried to gather me in his arms, but I pushed away.

"Forget about what I said. I can handle it. I'll be fine."

"No, Thea."

"Yes!" I shouted. "I will never speak to you again. I'll leave you if I have to."

"I can't keep hurting you like this."

"Please, James," I screamed, pounding on his chest. "I know what you're thinking of doing. Don't you know it would kill me? I would lose my mind without you."

"Thea, I—"

"Promise me, James. Give me your word you will not harm yourself. Promise me you'll continue your relationship with her."

"I can't do that."

"You have to. I will never forgive you otherwise."

He held my face again. "Okay, but only under one condition."

~ 163 ~

"Anything."

He wrapped his arms around me. "Meet me here, every day. We can decide on the best time, but I want to see you here. Can you promise me that?"

I smiled. "I promise. I will be here waiting for you, every day."

"As long as we see each other every day, you will have my word."

I held him tighter. "I'll be here, my love."

"Even if you hate me, Thea. Even if you feel you no longer love me, you must still come here and see me. Do you understand?"

"I promise. I only ask the same of you."

He smiled and pulled my lips to his. I closed my eyes and melted into him. We spent over an hour just holding each other. We didn't talk about Helena again, or even Simon. We only spoke of our love. There was no room for anything else. It was as if nothing bad could follow us here. We sat under a tree and held each other, smiling together at the happy couple near the lake.

I was still lost in his scent when he pulled away. "I think we should go back now."

Panic flooded through me. I wasn't ready to let him go. "Please, just a moment longer."

He kissed my head and leaned back on the tree. "As you wish, my love."

I closed my eyes and leaned my head on his shoulder, losing myself in his scent. "You don't smell like this to me anymore," I whispered.

"Smell like what?" he asked.

"Like the sweetest smell I've ever known."

"And do I smell like that here?"

"Yes," I said, pulling him closer.

He stroked my hair and kissed my head. "Have

~ 164 ~

you noticed your hair?"

I swallowed hard. I'd been trying not to notice.

"What do you mean?" I asked, playing dumb. "What's wrong with it?"

"Nothing, my love."

As he ran his fingers through the smooth strands, I sensed there was something he wanted to ask.

"Did you mean what you said about marrying Cory?" he finally asked.

I tried to pull away, but he wouldn't let me.

"Just answer the question."

"I don't know why I said it," I replied sheepishly. "I guess I wanted to hurt you."

"Why did you pick him to hurt me with?"

"I didn't mean to hurt you. I don't know what came over me."

"Do you have feelings for him?"

"Do you have feelings for Helena?"

He brushed the hair away from my face. "If you ever feel the need to hurt me again, please—anybody but Cory."

"I'm so sorry, James. Like I said, I don't know what came over me."

"Don't get upset, my love. I'm sorry I brought it up." He leaned forward and gently pulled away. "We'd better get back."

"Can't we stay just a moment longer?"

He kissed my head and stood. "Come, my love. We will see each other tomorrow." He held out his hand and pulled me up into his arms. "Thank you."

"For what?"

"For not tormenting me with questions," he replied. "You allowed me to simply have this moment with you."

I looked into his shining blue eyes and smiled.

"Maybe I didn't ask you any questions because I already know the answers."

"If that were true, you wouldn't be here right now."

My heart skipped a beat. "What do you mean?"

"I love you, Thea. May those words stay alive inside you, may my touch and my kisses remind you of who you are."

"Kiss me," I replied. "Kiss me and I will never forget."

"I'm counting on that." He pulled me to his lips.

We walked back to where I had dropped the memory box. I picked it up and threw my arms around him again. "I don't want to ever leave here."

"Tomorrow, my love. I'll be waiting by our tree."

"I love you, James."

"Don't ever forget that."

"One more thing," I said, looking down.

He lifted my chin. "What is it?"

"It's silly, I know, but . . . please don't kiss Helena on the head anymore."

He sighed. "I promise."

After one last kiss, he was gone. I opened the box and withdrew from the memory. I was back in my room, overflowing with happiness. I heard someone bounding up the stairs as I slipped the box into my pocket. I heard my father's door open.

"You brilliant man!" James called out.

My heart swelled with joy. I whispered a command when James closed the door. I wanted to hear every word he had to say.

"So it went well?" my father asked.

"Yes, old friend. It went well. Thank you."

"And how did you both feel?"

"It was as if the spell never existed," James gushed. "It has no power at all there."

"That is good news, James," my father exclaimed. "Now that we have a weapon, we can drag her there if needed."

"It worked," James continued. "It was her, my Thea."

"Thank the heavens. This is such good news."

"I have faith again, William. She's given me hope."

"Fight for her, James. Remind her, as often as you can, of her love for you. She will need it."

What did he mean, they could drag me there if needed? Why would they have to drag me? Wouldn't it be James who would need dragging? More cryptic exchanges between my father and my husband. It seemed that each time I'd found my footing, someone was pulling the rug out from under me again.

"I plan on doing just that," said James. "She agreed to meet me there every day."

"Excellent. You did well, my son."

"Do you think I could tell her the truth while we're there?"

"No," my father said, his tone becoming serious. "It is not safe. It could change everything, and we would have to start all over again."

What truth? Why would I need to be reminded of loving James?

"Of course," James conceded. "You're right. Simon already believes that things are going well for him."

"And he must continue to think that. Do not

allow these moments with Thea to distract you from your mission with Helena. Simon will notice even the smallest of changes."

"Don't worry," James replied. "I'll go there now. Helena is surely waiting."

"Drink the tea before you leave. I left you a full pot on the stove."

"Thank you again, old friend. You've made me a very happy man."

I heard the door creak open and James heading for the stairs. I sat on my bed, trying to make sense of what I'd heard. What truth did James wish to share with me? When I'd heard them talking earlier, James asked my father how long before I'd forget. I know I told my father that I would trust him, but I hated being left in the dark. It felt so unfair.

A thought occurred to me: the tea pot. What was in the tea my father made especially for James? I opened my door quietly and crept toward the stairs. My father walked out of his room just as I passed his door.

"Oh, there you are," he called.

Startled, I jumped and turned to face him.

"The Santos brothers are waiting."

"I was just heading down to meet them," I lied. I started to walk away.

"Do you not have good news for me, child?"

"Good news?"

"Yes, from where you were just now . . ." He arched an eyebrow, a playful smile tugging at the corner of his mouth.

I was so distracted by the tea that I'd nearly forgotten about my reunion with James. Normally I would have jumped into my father's arms and thanked him. I swallowed hard and grinned. "Oh, of course! I'm just so happy right now, I feel sort of numb." More lies.

He looked deeply into my eyes for a long, silent moment. Panic rose inside me. *Is he reading my thoughts?*

Finally he smiled and nodded toward the stairs. "Go. The others are waiting."

I nodded and went down into the kitchen. James was there, drinking his tea. My mood changed instantly as James' eyes changed from blue to black. He set down his cup and walked out of the kitchen. I looked the other way as he passed me, balling my fist to stop from waving my hand at him.

I walked over to the counter and peered into James' cup, which was still half full. I picked it up and drank what was left. At first, I was seemingly unaffected. After a few minutes, my skin began to feel strange—thick and tight. The feeling passed quickly, and a moment later, my eyes began to itch.

"Where have you been?" Delia asked, suddenly appearing at the kitchen door.

When I turned to look at her, she leaned in closer, her eyes narrowing. "Thea, why are your eyes blue?"

Cory walked in—at least, I was pretty sure it was Cory. Several of the others filed in behind him. I couldn't be sure how many.

"Thea, your eyes," I heard someone say.

I stood still as a statue. Were my eyes deceiving me?

Delia stepped closer. "What did you do to your eyes?"

"Are you okay, Thea?" One of the others asked, though I wasn't sure who.

"I . . . I'm fine."

I turned my back to them and closed my eyes tightly, trying to clear my head. I felt a set of hands on my shoulders.

"Thea, is everything okay?"

I opened my eyes and turned around, but the horror was still there in front of me: everyone in the room looked like Helena.

"Really, I'm fine," I lied. "I'm just tired. I was practicing a spell."

"Do you want us to leave so you can rest?"

My head was so clouded that, save for Delia, I couldn't distinguish between their voices. I took a shot in the dark. "No, Sammy, I'm fine."

"Thea, I'm Justin."

"Are you okay?" Delia asked again.

"I'm fine," I said, shaking my head. I decided to change the subject. "So, what did you all find out?"

"It looks like the witch changes what she looks like every time she talks to them," Delia said. "It could be anyone."

"Did she tell you why Simon wanted Delia captured?" I asked. I looked around at the others and tried to act normal. I was hoping Justin would somehow know I was talking to him because I couldn't tell which one he was.

I concentrated on their voices.

"Um, you don't look so hot, Thea." It was Cory's voice. "Maybe you should go and get some rest. We have to leave in a couple of hours."

My father walked in, looking like himself. I tried to snap myself out of the spell.

He walked over to the stove and started brewing more tea. "Perhaps you should stay here in town tonight, gentlemen," my father said over his shoulder. "You can speak to Thea in the morning."

"Who, us?" Justin asked.

"Yes, you can stay in Thea's apartment," my father suggested. "There is plenty of room for you and your brothers there."

He added several different kinds of leaves to the tea. I wondered if it was James' tea.

"Our apartment is available, too," Cory added. "Ciro is welcome to stay there if he likes."

I couldn't bring myself to look at any of them. The sight of Helena, much less multiple Helenas, was making me physically ill.

"That sounds perfect," my father replied. "Perhaps you should all be on your way. Cory will give you the keys. We'll see you all here for breakfast in the morning."

"Come on," Cory said, leading them out of the kitchen. "I'll tell you where to find the blankets and stuff like that."

"I'll be upstairs with Steven," Delia called on her way out. "I have another game for him."

I desperately wanted to ask my father about the tea. Why was he giving James a potion that made everyone look like Helena?

"I know what you're going to ask," my father said. He handed me a cup of the freshly prepared tea. "Here, drink this."

I shook my head.

"Drink it, Thea," he ordered. "It will take the effect away."

"You know?"

"When will you learn, child?" he chuckled. "You can hide nothing from me."

I took the cup and sipped.

~ 171 ~

My father shook his head, chuckled again, and sat down. "Don't waste your time trying to sort through James' head. I've already made sure Delia's memory box will not work on him—or me." He raised his brow, the look of amusement still in his eyes.

My shoulders slumped. "How did you know?" I asked.

"I'm a wizard, and your father, Thea. Try as you might, you cannot keep secrets from me."

"Oh, but I can," I said, taking another sip.

"Oh, really? How so?"

"I heard you talking to James. You didn't know how things had gone with him and me today—not until he told you."

"I would have known the moment I looked into your eyes."

I took another sip of tea. "So what's the tea for?" I asked, pointing to James' cup.

"I use it to remind James who he's with, to remind his heart."

"What do you mean?" I asked, confused. "I thought he could see only me."

He searched his mind for a way to explain. He was thinking about lying to me again.

"If I don't allow James to see that he's with Helena, he would truly fall in love with her. The tea reminds him it's her, and also allows *her* to see his eyes as blue."

"So she can believe he loves her?"

"No, so Simon can think James no longer loves you. But you should know, the spell is getting harder to control. His heart is starting to feel love for her. This is why visiting your memories is so important."

I set the cup down. "He loves her?"

"Not yet. It's up to you to stop that from happening."

"How can I do that, Father? He's always with her."

"Visit your memories," he said. "Don't miss a single day. Fight for him, Thea. Do not allow him to forget he loves you."

I looked into my father's eyes. How stupid did he think I was? It was obvious he was making sure I would meet James in my memories. I heard him say the same thing to James. And I knew he was lying about the tea, too.

"Can I ask you a question, Father?"

"I will answer just one," he replied.

"Am I supposed to forget who James is?"

"Yes."

"Why?"

He took the cup from me and walked to the stove.

"I said I would answer just one question," he said, filling the cup.

"Tell me what to do, Father."

"I already have, Thea. Pay attention." He walked back and set the cup in front of me. "Drink this and get some rest. You have to leave in a few hours."

"Why won't you tell me everything? What are you hiding?"

He looked deep into my eyes. For a split second, he seemed to contemplate telling me the truth.

"I lost your mother, and it almost killed me," he said. "I will not lose my only child to the man who killed my wife. Please understand if I don't share certain details with you, Thea. I only ask that you bring me back that energy, and I promise all this will end."

~ 173 ~

"Will we get the energy today?"

"Perhaps enough to keep me alive. I am truly counting on that."

I sighed. "Are you okay?"

"I'll be fine. Attor will give you what I need for now."

"Will it be enough to replenish your powers?" I asked, hopeful.

"No," he replied, shaking his head. "He won't be giving you the white energy. He'll be giving you something to help me stay alive."

"Stop using your magic, Father. I'll bring back what you need to get better."

"I will, if you promise me one thing."

"Anything."

"Stop trying to figure everything out. You're making things very difficult for me."

I didn't understand what he meant, but I promised him anyway.

I was finishing my tea when Fish walked in through the back door—again, not wearing a shirt. "Do we have any fruit?" he asked.

I averted my eyes. "Fish, what are you doing here?"

"I'm hungry, and we're all out of fruit back there." He opened the refrigerator.

I was actually happy the tea had worked. I could see every muscle on Fish's body. In fact, I couldn't look away. I ogled him as he leaned over and searched the refrigerator, momentarily forgetting that my father was sitting across from me.

"Is that my girl?" Gilly asked, striding in through the back door.

I looked over my shoulder and smiled. He leaned over my chair and planted a kiss on my cheek. I stood, taken aback when I saw his shirt hanging over his shoulder.

He threw his arms around me and lifted me off my feet. "I missed you, girl."

The touch of his bare skin was nearly too much. Gilly set me down and planted another kiss on my cheek. "It's good to see you."

"Aren't you cold?" I asked, pulling away from him.

Fish shrugged. "We were working out."

"Damn, you look good," Gilly exclaimed.

I looked into his brown eyes. His dark, silky skin called to me. "W-What brings you here?" I asked.

"I moved back, couldn't stay away from my girl forever," he said, pulling me back into his arms.

I tried to pull away when Fish started laughing. "Gilly, give Thea a big, sloppy kiss."

"Oh yeah, I forgot how witches get," Gilly said, pulling me closer. "Kiss me, Thea."

My father shook his head, but said nothing.

I pushed Gilly away. "You two are horrible."

Fish laughed and threw Gilly an orange. "Here, it's all we've got."

I was glad when Gilly turned away from me to catch the fruit. I couldn't help wondering again why all the male witches were suddenly returning to Salem.

"That's okay," Gilly said. "I have to get back to mom's anyway."

"You coming over tomorrow?" Fish asked.

"Yeah, see you then." Gilly pulled his shirt over his head, gave me a kiss on the cheek, and strode out the back door.

I felt normal for a moment, until I spied Fish from the corner of my eye. His bare chest was more than I could stand. I looked away and returned to my tea.

"Are you ready for tonight?" my father asked Fish.

Fish grabbed an orange for himself and closed the refrigerator door. "I'm ready. I'm dying to see what the guys can't talk about."

"And you will not be able to either," my father reminded him.

"Yeah, I know," he said, peeling the orange." I still can't wait to see what Oz looks like."

"Oz?" my father asked, eyebrow arched.

Fish smiled and shook his head. "Anyone know if Delia's still awake?"

"Yes," my father replied. "I believe she is playing a game with Steven."

Fish pulled off a section of orange and stuffed it into his mouth. He winked when he noticed me staring at him. He flexed his arms and laughed when I couldn't tear my eyes away.

I felt my face flush. "Fish. Shirt."

"Okay, okay." He took another bite of the orange. "I'm out of here."

"I'll see you in a few hours," my father said.

My eyes were still glued to him as he walked out. When he was gone, I looked at my father, who was grinning from ear to ear.

"What?" I asked, taking another sip of tea.

"Interesting," he muttered.

Chapter 14
The Fighting Game

I finished my tea and went to my room to lie down, hoping to get some rest before leaving for Magia. As I approached the door of Steven's room, I heard laughter. I peeked my head in and smiled. Fish, Delia, and Steven were plunked down in front of the television set, atop a mound of pillows. Snacks of all kinds were scattered about the room. Model cars—gifts from the boys—littered the floor.

"What's going on in here?" I asked.

"Sister, look!" Steven said. "I already opened a new guy!"

"A new guy?"

"I told you," Delia cut in, "I got him a new video game."

I stepped into the room and closed the door. On the TV screen was some kind of martial-arts game.

"Yeah," Fish said over his shoulder. "When he beats the main guy, a new character opens up for him."

I was relieved to see that Fish had put on a shirt.

"Want to see my finishing move?" Steven asked.

"Sure, sweetie," I replied. "Show me."

"Show her how your guy dives into the ground," Delia suggested.

I squatted down behind them as the game played on, fascinated with the moves Steven was pulling off. I watched as his "guy" dropped down into the ground as if he were phasing through it. The ground swallowed him up and spit him out behind his enemy. He made his kill and quickly disappeared into the ground again.

I moved in closer as Steven whipped his guy around the enemy. He dove into the ground, dragging his enemy with him.

"Do that again," I said, plunking down next to Steven. I couldn't pull my eyes away from the screen. This was too good to be true.

"What," Steven asked. "Dive into the ground?"

"Yeah. Show me that again."

As Steven obliged my request, an idea brewed in my head. It couldn't be this easy.

"Show her the move you just learned," Delia said.

"Hold on," Steven replied. "Let me change guys."

"You mean each one performs different moves?" I asked.

Steven nodded. "Yeah, they have lots of moves."

I couldn't believe what I was seeing, how intricate the action was—on a video game, no less. How did I let this get by me for so long? "Show them all to me," I said, my excitement building. I stared intently at the screen, impressed by the skillfulness of the fighters.

Fish warned me not to touch the controller. "You'll break it."

I shot him an indignant look and sat quietly, watching Steven play. "Are those warlocks?"

Fish burst out laughing.

Delia rolled her eyes. "Thea, even warlocks can't pull off moves like these."

"No," Fish chimed in. "But someone like Thea could."

The room went silent; the same light had just gone on in their heads that had already turned on in mine. Fish reached for the controller and went through a list of moves which he asked Steven to show me. I was careful not to get too close, but I desperately wished I could just jump into the game and try them out.

When Steven was done, I wanted more. "Do you have any more games like this?"

Steven got up and pulled another game from the shelf beside the TV. "This is my favorite," he said.

I sat next to him, my eyes glued to the screen. He chose a fighter—this time a woman. Her weapon was a sword that opened up and transformed into a whip whenever she swung toward a far-away enemy. The whip was edged with razor-sharp blades. When she fought someone close up, the whip reformed back into the sword.

"Isn't her sword cool?" Steven asked.

I nodded silently, mouth agape, as she brought down her enemy from twenty feet away. She pushed the sword into the ground and it reappeared in front of her enemy, piercing his heart. She swung the weapon into the air when her enemy moved to jump her. The sword wrapped itself around the enemy and slammed him into the ground. I tried to memorize every detail.

By the fourth disk, Steven was spent. Fish took over the controller and showed me more moves. "Look," he said. "This guy moves fast as a whip. He dizzies his enemies by flying past them before he kills them."

I inched closer to the screen. "Show me."

"Do you really think you can pull off these moves?" Delia asked.

I didn't think, I knew. "Only one way to find out."

"Thea," Fish said, "you should try playing the games with us. You should see what Javier can do."

"You have these games, too?" I asked, surprised.

Delia shot me a look of disbelief. "Thea, is this the first time you've seen these games?"

I frowned. "Why would you ask that? You know I've never played."

"But you've seen them before, right?"

I shook my head.

She exchanged a worried glance with Fish. "Thea, I'm telling you, you've seen these games before."

"What, when?"

"When I used to take you to the boys' apartment. You got a kick out of watching them play. I had to erase the memories at one time, but I've since restored them." She looked thoughtful for a moment. "Why do I feel like a broken record?"

"The cell phones," Fish replied.

"That's right," Delia exclaimed. "You didn't remember about the cell phones blowing up either."

My stomach lurched. "I'm just tired," I offered lamely. "There's been a lot going on." I looked at Fish. "Keep playing."

I felt Delia's eyes on me as Fish showed me more moves. My friends were starting to notice what I'd been fearing for weeks. But I couldn't let my father find out. I didn't want to give him another excuse for keeping secrets.

"I'm fine, Delia," I insisted. "Like I said, I'm just tired."

"Tired," she echoed. "Being tired affects your long-term memory?"

I was starting to get annoyed. "You know, I think you're wrong, Delia. Maybe I have seen these games before, but you obviously never restored the memories."

Fish flashed Delia a look. "Hey, maybe you should go and get some rest, Thea," he said, turning off the game.

"You're both crazy," I snapped, getting to my feet. "I'm fine."

"You've been acting weird," Delia said, rubbing my arm. "I think we should tell your father."

My anger rose to the surface. "Leave it alone."

Delia stepped back, her hands on her hips. "Hey, I'm not scared of you, witch," she shot back. "And I'm telling you, something's wrong."

My father appeared in the doorway. "Is there a problem?" he asked.

"I don't know," Delia said, staring me down. "Is there?"

"Leave it alone, Delia," I repeated.

Steven jumped up off the pillows. "Please don't fight."

I had forgotten he was even in the room. I looked down at him and smiled. "We're not fighting, sweetie."

"Steven, I left some food in the kitchen for you," said my father. "Why don't you go join Joshua."

Steven flashed Delia and me a curious glance before walking out of the room. My father closed the door.

"Tell him, Thea," Delia demanded.

"There's nothing to tell," my father said. "She is just tired. Now let us move on." He sighed. "Why have the three of you kept me waiting?"

"Kept you waiting?" Fish asked.

My father raised his eyebrows. "Have you forgotten where you are going tonight?"

"Oh, Father, I'm so sorry," I replied. "We lost track of time."

"In my room—now," he ordered.

Delia and Fish followed my father. I stopped by my room to change clothes, throwing on a pair of jeans and a T-shirt. On my way to my father's room, I spied Delia and my father talking outside his door. They stepped inside the room as soon as they saw me.

The look on Delia's face when I walked into the room made me uneasy. My father cleared his throat and asked everyone to take a seat. Delia seemed nervous. She kept looking at me, concern in her eyes. Cory nudged her and told her to pay attention.

My father pulled out the gold leaves and handed them out. "You will feel normal again in a few minutes," he told Delia and Fish.

"What are these?" Fish asked.

"Just eat them," Cory said, taking one from my father.

My father gave them the same speech he had given Cory and the boys, but Delia was distracted. She kept glancing over at me and biting her lip.

"Delia, please pay attention," he admonished.

She nodded and placed the leaf in her mouth, but her worried glances continued through the corner of her eye. How stupid did they think I was? It was obvious my father had just told her something about me. He seemed to have no problem telling everyone what was going on—everyone except me, that is.

I stood beside him, stewing. He wouldn't even look me in the eye when he handed me the ring. I snatched it from him and sniffed.

He leaned toward me. "It is not what you think," he whispered.

I ignored his words and shot Delia a dirty look. I couldn't help feeling betrayed. In fact, I was starting to feel angry with all of them. I no longer trusted them. They were all lying to me. For all I knew, the whole thing was a ruse and they were all in Simon's back pocket.

"Stop it!" my father said, seizing my shoulders. "You cannot allow those kinds of thoughts to enter your head."

"What do you care?" I snapped. "All you ever do is lie and keep things from me."

He looked into my eyes for a long, tense moment. Finally he spoke. "I think you had better put the ring on now." His hands shook as he pulled them away.

My mood changed in an instant. "Father, why are you shaking?" The dark circles under his eyes made him look like he'd aged twenty years overnight. "Have you been using your magic?"

"I told you, I'm very weak."

I was angry, this time at myself. How could I not notice how weak and ill he was? He'd been telling me how he needed Attor's help to stay alive. I was too busy trying to find out what he was hiding, even turning on my friends. What was happening to me?

"I'll get back as fast as I can," I said, ashamed.

"I know you will. And I will be here waiting."

I threw my arms around him. "I'm so sorry, Father. I've been a fool."

"It's not your fault. After today, you will understand why."

"Will I finally learn the truth?"

"Yes, Thea. It's time."

"I'm scared."

"No, you're brave. You always have been."

"Brave enough to hear the truth?"

He smiled. "Brave enough to change the truth." He stroked my face with his trembling hand.

"Please don't die on me, Father."

"Do not worry. Attor will give you something that will help me. Now go, or Attor will grow anxious."

The others gathered around and held onto me.

I slipped the ring on my finger and we were gone.

Chapter 15
The Spell Within

Delia gasped as we spiraled toward my father's world. She held tight to my hand as her feet searched frantically for some kind of foundation. "What the hell is this?" she screamed.

Cory threw his head back and laughed. "Shut up and enjoy the ride!"

Fish gazed at the swirling sparkles. "Did I just see Tinker Bell?"

We all laughed—everyone but Delia.

"Are we falling?" she shouted frantically.

Fish pulled her into his arms. "Don't be scared, baby," he soothed. "We're going to get Cory a heart, and Joshua a new brain." The boys laughed again when Fish told Delia he wouldn't allow anyone to throw a bucket of water on her when we got there. She glared at him, panic in her eyes. I began to wonder whether bringing Delia along was a good idea.

I smelled the flowers and knew we were close.

Delia's eyes were squeezed shut when our feet hit the ground. After a moment, she opened them and gazed around in awe. "Am I dreaming?"

Fish, too, was mesmerized by our surroundings. "Thea, run!"

"What?" I said, alarmed. "What do you see?"

"I think a house is about to fall on you!"

My friends erupted into laughter, Delia included. I looked at them, confused.

Cory shook his head and pointed to the lake. "Check it out, you guys."

"It's the most beautiful thing I've ever seen," Delia muttered.

"Why would your father ever want to leave this place?" Fish asked.

"Don't talk like that," Cory said. "Don't even think it."

"Why?" Fish asked. "What's the big deal?"

Cory looked incredulous. "Fish, did you not pay attention to what William told us?"

Fish rolled his eyes and looked at Delia, who was still gazing, glassy eyed, toward the lake. She looked up at the sun. "Fish, look at that."

He looked up at the sky and stumbled backward. "What the hell is that?" he asked, grabbing Delia's arm.

I looked up. "It's okay. It's just Attor."

Delia screamed and tried to take off running, but Cory pulled her back to the group. "He's not going to hurt us."

Attor landed a few yards away, accompanied by three other dragons.

"What the—"

"Shut up, Fish." Cory snapped. "Just stay still."

Attor trudged closer and sniffed the area around my neck. The intense heat from his mouth made me wince. Why was he checking my neck?

"Look into my eyes," he ordered.

His demeanor was off-putting, but I did as I was told. When he was done examining me, he nodded toward the other dragons and huffed once. His cronies moved in and rounded up Delia and the boys. Attor grabbed me, and we all flew away.

Delia was still screaming as we flew behind the nearest mountain. By the time the dragons skimmed the lake, she had passed out.

"Delia!" Fish shouted.

Attor blasted fire toward the other dragons, which I now realized was a signal for them to land. They blew fire back, and we all descended together. After they set us down on the ground, Fish ran to Delia. She was trembling, her eyes glazed over.

"It's okay, baby," Fish said, stroking her hair. "It's over." He wrapped his arms around her and pulled her close.

"Why did you bring that witch with you?" Attor asked. "She puts your mission at risk."

"What do you mean?" I asked.

Delia dropped to her knees and vomited. Fish leaned down and rubbed her back.

"Look at her," Attor said. "If she follows you into the forest, she will surely lose her mind."

"Why?" Cory asked. "What's in the forest?"

"Something only witches such as you have any chance of killing."

"We're wasting time," Katu said.

"What should I do?" I asked.

Attor looked at the other dragons. They nodded and flew away.

"We don't have much time," Katu warned Attor.

"We will make time," Attor replied. "They won't be long."

"Where did they go?" I asked.

"To check for any wizards nearby," Attor replied. "To buy you some time."

My frustration mounted. Why would my father allow Delia to go along if her presence risked the very thing we came to accomplish? "Time to do what?"

"You must take her back," Attor said. "And bring the other two here."

Delia's head shot up. "Please don't take me back."

"Delia, are you okay?" Fish asked.

"Don't let them take me," she repeated, grabbing Fish's shirt. "I want to stay."

"Maybe you should go back," Fish said. "You don't look so hot."

She stood and pushed Fish away, staggering to keep her balance. "I'm staying."

"That's it," Cory said. "You're going back. Take off the ring, Thea."

Attor used his wing to block me from the others. "Thea stays here!"

We looked at him, confused.

"She leaves with us," Cory said. "We'll be back."

I stepped closer to Attor. "How is that even possible?" I asked. "I have the ring."

Cory's face was resolute. "You're not staying here."

Attor turned to me. "Pull out a strand of your hair," he ordered.

As I pulled out the hair, Attor presented to Cory the mushroom I'd left with him the day before.

"What am I supposed to do with this?" Cory asked.

"Hold out your hand," Attor ordered. He placed the mushroom on Cory's palm and recited some unfamiliar words. The mushroom was now encased in solid gold. He instructed me to give Cory the strand of my hair and ordered him to place it in his pocket. "Give the mushroom to Xander. It will help make him strong."

"And what do I do with Thea's hair?" Cory asked.

"After you pull the ring off of Thea's finger, it will take you back home. When you are ready to come back, wrap her hair around the ring. It will bring you back."

I extended my hand toward Cory. "Pull it off."

He hesitated. "Are you going to be okay here?"

"I'll be fine. Get that back to my father."

Cory hesitated. "We'll be back as soon as we can."

Delia tried to pull away from Fish. "I want to stay!"

I looked into Cory's eyes. "Pull off the ring."

Cory took a deep breath and pulled the ring from my finger. My friends disappeared.

I turned to Attor. "Thank you for helping my father."

"Xander must be very weak by now."

I nodded. "What did you send him?"

"Some of my magic. It will give him strength."

A dizzy feeling came over me, and I stumbled.

Attor seemed to understand what was happening.

"Come with me. You will feel better inside."

I steadied myself to follow him into the cave, and was immediately enchanted by its beauty. The sparkling gems encrusted in the walls took my breath away. It was as though I were inside a giant crystal ball. I had expected the cave to be dark, and smell of dragon droppings. I couldn't have been more surprised. The walls were like huge sheets of ice, with colored crystals embedded in every inch of them. A giant oak tree was rooted in the middle of the cave and grew up through a hole in the ceiling.

Attor was right. Once inside, I started to feel normal again. He pushed forward a large rock and motioned for me to sit.

"Is this your home?" I asked.

He eyed me curiously. "Do you not remember this place?"

I gazed around again. "Should I?"

"The longer you stay here, the stronger your wizard-self will become. You will remember things you have lost in the human world."

"What do you mean? What have I lost?"

"Human air makes one forget this place. It's something the wizards discovered many years ago. The longer one stays in the human world, the less one remembers about Magia."

I thought about my recent memory problems. I'd been in the human world my entire life—or so I thought. "But my father remembers this world. And he's been in the human world for hundreds of years."

Attor nodded knowingly. "Your father has found a way to keep his mind strong. I do not doubt that somewhere in his home is a place like this cave, filled with crystals that remind him who he is."

My mind went back to the conversation I'd overheard between James and my father the day before. "I think he does. And I think he took my husband there." I wondered if it was safe to share the rest of what I'd learned with Attor. I decided to take a chance. "He's hiding something he took from me in that room." As I said the words, I realized what it was. "The crystal."

Attor regarded me carefully, quietly.

"Why would my father take it from me?" I asked. "What possible reason could he have?"

"Xander needs to stop using his magic on you. It will kill him, or make him human."

"He hasn't used his magic on me," I countered. "You healed me last, remember?"

Attor shook his head. "Then how do you explain your wizard shield?"

"Wizard shield? What are you talking about?"

Attor chuckled. "You haven't noticed how spells bounce off of you? How they knock you down but never out? Even healing spells fail to work on you."

I eyed him questioningly.

"That is your father's shield, Thea. He's protecting you from Simon, keeping him from casting another spell on you."

"What do you mean, *another* spell?"

"Everything your father has told you up to now is a lie. I think you know that. But you must understand, he is only trying to protect you."

I stood abruptly. "Protect me from what?"

Attor looked toward the entrance of the cave. "Xander is my friend. I will break my promise to him so that I may save him."

I dropped to my knees in front of him. "I beg you, I only want the truth."

"Xander saved our lives once, and now I will save his."

"What do you know, Attor? Please tell me."

He looked into my eyes. "The spell. You are the carrier of Simon's spell, not your husband."

I struggled for breath. Had I heard him correctly? I leaned back, speechless for several long moments. Finally I found the words. "Simon's spell . . . was cast on me?"

"Yes."

I scrambled to my feet. "What are you talking about? I heard Simon cast that spell on James. I saw the memory of it with my own eyes. I even saw it in Vera's head."

"Your father changed the memory," Attor explained, "so you wouldn't find out the truth. And so did the witch Vera; your father had prepared her."

I clung to my denial. "You're lying!"

"Dragons do not lie. We have no reason to."

"This can't be true." I ran my hands through my hair; the smooth, tangle-free locks did little to quell my panic.

Attor looked into my eyes. "Your father has always known Simon would cast that spell on you. He has always known he would have to save you and your husband."

"Save my husband?" I asked. "From what?"

"From the spell. It's going to kill him—if you don't kill him first."

My heart raced. "What are you talking about? The spell only kills our love. Why would it kill James?"

"And what is a heart without love?" Attor asked. "When his heart stops loving, it will stop beating."

"No!" I screamed. "You're lying!"

"I warned him. I told your father to prevent you from meeting that boy. If your father had listened to me, none of this would be happening."

"Exactly how does my father plan to save James?" I demanded.

Attor exhaled loudly. "The spell is a wizard spell. It brings death. Both you and your husband will die when your love dies. Your father plans to switch the spell, to turn it on himself, before that can happen. He will do this when you bring him the white energy. It will be his last act of love for you."

I buried my face in my hands. "No. He can break the spell. He told me he could break it."

"He can't break the spell without killing you both. But he can break it once he's turned it on himself. That's why he needs the energy."

I paced in front of Attor. "This can't be happening."

"It's true, Thea," he replied grimly. "With your father's last dying breath, he will save you."

I stood frozen. I knew those words. My father had said them to me when I was a little girl. I didn't know what he meant back then, but now they made perfect sense. "No, I won't let it happen," I cried. "I won't let him give his life for mine."

"And how then will you save your husband? If he dies before you kill him, the spell breaks. Your husband knows this. He's always known."

"What are you saying?"

"He cannot kill himself. But if he's killed, the spell breaks. The bond you share will be broken, thus the spell will no longer have control over you. Your father promised James he could break it, but your

~ 193 ~

husband has his own plan in mind."

"Oh my god . . . Ciro." Now I knew why James and my father had argued the night we fought. My father knew James was going to ask Ciro to kill him. I continued to pace, panic threatening to overcome me. "How can that spell be on me?" I muttered. "I love him. I still love him."

"Not for long. Soon the urge to kill him will overpower your efforts to continue loving him. The desire to destroy James will be more than you can bear. And, shortly after James is dead, you also will die."

"I don't understand. Why would Simon cast a spell on me, if he knew my mother's heart would be drained of any useful information as soon as I killed James?"

"Because Simon is not a wizard, he has no idea what he has done. He believes the spell is only killing your love so that you may bring him the heart. Simon doesn't realize that your husband no longer has the heart."

I gasped. "What?"

"Your father removed the heart and placed it into the crystal."

"What are you saying?"

Attor rustled his wings and sighed. "Thea, the only reason your husband encased the heart inside his own was because there was no other safe place to put it at the time. Once your father had the crystal back, there was no further need for James to carry the heart. Your father extracted it the night your memory returned, and deposited it into the crystal. There, it is incapable of stealing your thoughts."

I slapped my hands over my ears. I didn't want to hear anymore. "How could I have been so blind?" I cried, "Why would my father keep this from me?"

"Because it would change. He didn't lie about that. Your father is trying to prepare you, so that Simon can never bond with you."

I stared at him, shocked.. "Why on earth would my father need to prepare me for any such thing? I detest Simon, he knows that."

"By the time the spell takes you over completely, you will hate the one you love, feel betrayed by him *and* your friends. Your heart will then be tricked into thinking that Simon is your only friend. Simon is the keeper of the spell; so it goes that you will feel close to him as the spell takes full effect and kills your love for James. The desire to go to Simon will be all-consuming. There is nothing you can do to stop this. You will give Simon anything and everything he wants, do anything to please him."

I turned my back, drew a ragged breath, and tried to comprehend what Attor was telling me.

"Simon has heard of the box that can show him your memories," Attor continued. "He plans to steal it and use it to acquire the spell he needs to open the crystal. He knows that once his spell has taken you over, you will be more than willing to give him your powers. He knows the crystal is the only way."

"But he doesn't have the crystal."

"Why do you think your father took it from you? He knew you would give it to Simon. Xander knew what the spell would do to you, and did what was necessary to protect your son."

My heart skipped a beat. "My son."

"You had forgotten about him, hadn't you?"

"Oh my god, my son," I whispered as tears

streamed down my face.

"What the spell has made you forget," Attor said, placing his wing gently on my back, "you will remember here."

The spell was the reason I was forgetting. "That's what my father was showing James." I dropped to my knees. The nightmarish puzzle was coming together: why I wanted to kill James; why my poor father kept lying to hide the truth from me; why I felt myself changing, becoming the monster that now lived inside me. I wept into my hands as the truth sank in. I wanted to thrust a knife through my heart and end it all now. What was I going to do? How was I possibly going to change this?

"I can fight the spell," I cried. "I won't let it take me over."

"Your husband will still die."

"Stop saying that!"

"You asked for the truth, Thea," Attor reminded me. "Even if you fight the spell, James will die. The moment the spell is broken, his heart will stop beating. You yourself will not live for long after that happens. This is the truth your father has been hiding from you."

I looked up at him. "So I will die, as well?"

"The chances of you surviving are close to none."

"And if my father succeeds in rechanneling the spell, he will die?"

"Yes."

I buried my face in my hands again and sobbed.

"Silence, witch," Attor commanded. "I am going to help you."

Chapter 16
Where No Wizards Dare To Enter

I jumped to my feet and tried to throw my arms around Attor's massive form. It was like trying to hug a mountain of jagged stones. His scales scratched at my arms, breaking the skin. "Tell me what to do, Attor," I begged. "I'll do whatever it takes."

"Will you chant a spell to save your husband's life?" he asked.

I pushed away and looked up into his eyes. "I can't let him die."

"He doesn't have to die," Attor said. "There is another way to save him."

I stepped back. "Tell me."

"It is not obvious to you?" he asked.

I shook my head.

"He dies when his heart stops loving. There is no rule that says he has to love *you*."

My breath caught. "What do you mean?"

"He doesn't have to love you, Thea. He only

needs to love. As long as his heart loves, he will be spared the grim outcome of the spell."

Helena. At last I understood what my father was trying to do. I searched Attor's dark, intelligent eyes. "Tell me what to do."

He met my gaze with alarming intensity. "You must give him up forever."

My head spun, my breaths coming in short rasps. "Why?"

"It's the only way to save him," Attor explained. "You must sever your connection to him. Your bond must be broken."

"But why forever? It seems so drastic."

"The spell I'm going to teach you cannot be broken. But it will save his life, and perhaps yours."

"Will it break Simon's spell?"

"No, it will only erase you from your husband's memory. He will then only love the woman you choose for him. He will remember nothing of you or the love you shared. He will be free of the spell, because his heart will still love."

His words cut deeply. I felt the physical pain of my heart breaking. I couldn't imagine my life without James. What kind of life would be left for me? "Will I still feel the need to kill him?"

"Perhaps, but the spell will be easier to control once his connection to you is broken."

I closed my eyes. "And there is no other way?"

Attor shook his head. "Not if you want him to live."

"Does my father know you're giving me this spell?"

"Yes. He needed to save your husband before he did anything foolish. He's been trying to get himself killed. Your father sent Ciro's brothers to keep an eye on the areas James has been visiting in search of warlocks."

The map, I thought. That's where Ciro's brothers had gone. They were trying to stay one step ahead of James. My father was covering all the bases. I sighed in relief for that small comfort. Of course my father wouldn't allow James to get himself killed—he'd promised.

"And this spell you're going to teach me, you say it can never be broken?"

"It's one of ours," Attor answered. "Dragon spells last forever."

A thought suddenly occurred to me. "What if I put a love spell on him? One that makes him love another woman? Then he wouldn't have to forget me, only leave me until I can find a way to break the spell."

"Your father has been trying that with Helena, but so far he can't find a way to make it work. He even tried using your memories, but as soon as you leave them, the anger returns. The only way to save your husband is to erase yourself from his life. The bond you share will be broken, but he will be safe from the spell."

"Why must our bond be broken?" I asked.

"I told you, it's the only way to keep the spell from affecting him."

Tears continued to roll down my cheeks. "I don't think I can do it."

"Then he will die."

Katu walked in and stood beside Attor. "Did you tell her?"

Attor nodded.

I threw myself in front of them both. "What if he never stops loving me? What if he fights off the spell like I've been doing?"

"The witch part of him may fight it, but the human part of him will hate you. The spell works both ways, that much is true. You may have already seen signs of this."

I balled my fists. He was right, the signs were there. James' hatred for me was growing. We'd almost killed each other the other day. I thought it was because the spell was cast on him, but now I knew: I was the carrier. I bowed my head, realizing there was no other way. "Teach me the spell."

"You will cast the spell when the time is right," Attor explained, "when you feel you are losing control of who you are, and not a moment sooner."

"Will the spell make him forget who he is?" I asked.

"No. He will only forget you. It will be as if you were never born."

I closed my eyes. His words left an unbearable emptiness in my heart.

"What about my father and my friends? Will James forget them, too?"

"No, he will forget only you. Your father will still be William to him, although he will lose certain memories that include you. For example, he won't remember that your father has a daughter. He will remember your friends as his friends."

"Like I was never born," I said, looking away.

"Yes, you will be erased from his life—forever."

I looked at Attor, resolute. "Let's get it over with. Teach me the spell."

He leaned down and whispered the spell into my ear. When he was done, I broke into a sob.

"We will delay giving your father the energy," Attor said, "to buy you time."

"Time for what?"

"You must capture the master of the spell and bring him here to us."

I stared at him, confused. "Simon? I thought that was the last thing you wanted."

"We must be the ones to kill him. It's the only way to break the spell."

"You can break the spell?" I asked, getting to my feet again.

"Yes."

"Then let me bring Simon here at once, then there will be no need to cast the spell on James."

"That's not possible. The spell must be in full effect. It cannot be broken otherwise. By then, your husband would die."

I walked over to him. "What if I fight off the spell, Attor? What if my love for James never dies? Could he survive when you broke the spell?"

"No. You could possibly survive, because the wizard part of you may be strong enough to withstand the spell. But even so, it's a small chance. James is half-human. The odds of him surviving are practically nil."

"Please, Attor. Is there no other way?"

"Not if you wish for him to live. If you wait until we break the spell, he will not survive."

There was no other way. I would have to cast the spell and lose James forever.

"Tell her about the witch Simon," Katu snapped.

"What about him?" I asked.

Attor returned his attention to me. "You must gain his trust. He must believe you are helping him. He has something that belongs to us. We need you to find it and destroy it."

"He'll never believe I want to help him."

Attor shook his head. "He already believes you are changing, Thea. He's expecting you to join him. That is the only part of the spell he got right."

"And how am I supposed to stop myself from doing what he's counting on? What if I really do want to help him, what then?"

Attor looked at Katu and gestured for him to leave the cave. Katu shuffled off slowly, muttering under his breath.

"Where is he going?" I asked.

"To bring you some leaves," Attor replied. "You will need them to make a special tea. It will slow down the spell and give you enough time to deliver Simon to us."

I couldn't help but wonder why, all of a sudden, they wanted Simon here. They seemed so nervous about it before yet now they were eager for him to return.

"What about my father?" I asked. "How will I keep all this from him?"

"Your father knows everything that I have been telling you. It was he who told me to reveal the truth."

"My eyes," I whispered. "The two of you have been communicating through my eyes."

"Yes, but I am not following your father's orders. He wants me to help you get the white energy so he can switch the spell. What he doesn't know is that we will delay giving him the energy so we can first kill Simon. He does not yet know that there will be no need for rechanneling the spell."

"What about Simon?" I asked. "What if he uses the memory box on me?"

"Open your mouth," Attor ordered.

"Wha—?"

As soon as I parted my lips to question, Attor blasted fire into my mouth. I clutched my head and crumpled to the floor of the cave, twisting and contorting in pain.

Attor towered above me. "It will soon pass."

I smelled my hair burning, though the fire had gone straight into my mouth. I convulsed from the heat for what seemed like an eternity before the pain finally started to diminish. I staggered to my feet. "What the hell did you just do to me?"

"I planted a fireball in your head," he replied. "Your thoughts are safe now."

I was still reeling from the burning sensation in my head when Katu walked back in.

He set a collection of leaves near my feet and backed away. "Make sure your father never sees you making this tea. He will know what these are the moment he sees them."

"Are these the same leaves my father uses for my husband's the tea?"

"No," Attor said. "Your husband has been drinking a tea that makes his skin as tough as leather, so Simon can't get through to your mother's heart."

"But you said my father took out the heart."

A hint of a smile appeared on Attor's face. "Yes, but Simon doesn't know that."

"But I drank the tea," I said. "I saw the effect it had."

"I'm telling you, Thea, that is what the tea is for." Katu laughed.

I looked at him. "What's so funny?"

"I'm laughing because you're blind, witch. Your father can see the future. He must have known you would drink your husband's tea." He shook his head.

"Xander is a man of few mistakes."

"And don't you think he saw you telling me all of this?" I asked.

"Wizards can't see our future," Katu replied.

I was nervous about my next question, but I had to know the truth. "What did my father do? Why is he no longer welcome here?"

Katu immediately stopped laughing and turned to Attor. Attor shook his head and looked at me. "Not now, but I will tell you soon. You will need that information before you bring Simon to us."

I looked into Attor's eyes. "How do you know all of this?"

"I know the vision," he replied. "Your father showed me."

"And how does it end, Attor? What did my father see?"

He waited a moment before answering. "Your father would never forgive me if I told you."

I looked at Attor and Katu. I nodded and started for the entrance of the cave.

"Wait," Attor said. "There is one more thing you should know: your father is preparing your friends for battle."

I turned. "I already know about that." Attor's penetrating stare sent a tremor through my body.

"To battle you."

My mouth went dry.

"Not to kill you," he explained. "Only to stop you. He knows what the spell is doing to you, and he knows only warlocks can stop you."

"Ciro and the Santos brothers," I said.

"Yes, let them watch you," Attor instructed. "Their job is to learn how you fight, so they can stop you when you try to kill your husband."

I nodded and walked out. I needed to clear my head. My thoughts kept coming back to my poor father, who was willing to die so James and I could live. I couldn't let that happen. I would have to find a way to stay strong and fight the spell. I closed my eyes as I thought of what I had to do. It would be the most difficult test my heart would ever have to endure. My heart ached for James already.

I found a large rock not far from the cave entrance and sat. I understood everything now, all the secrets, the whispering behind my back. I had been foolish, always thinking I had the answers. I was so blinded by feelings of betrayal that I never bothered to look deeply into the eyes of my loved ones, never saw what they were trying to tell me. I thought of James and his constant asking that I not forget I loved him. How could I not see it?

"James," I cried.

In my heart I already knew the woman I would choose for him. Even though I hated her, there was comfort in knowing that Helena loved James. I knew she would do whatever it took to make him happy, give him all the love she could. I also knew I would have to leave the house, and remove any and all evidence of ever having lived there.

What would I do about my father? Where would I take him? I would have to find a way to move him safely. I would have to find a house near James, so I could see him from time to time.

I tried with little success to swallow back another flood of tears. What about our son? If James couldn't remember me, he'd never know he even had a son. My son would grow up without his father's love. As soon as

Simon was dead, I would release my son's spirit from the crystal and put him back inside me. But what would I tell him about his father?

I wiped away my tears when I saw the other dragons returning to the cave.

After a few moments, Attor came to find me. "Your friends are late," he announced. "We are running out of time."

"Maybe they had problems with the r—"

Before I could finish the word, Cory and the boys appeared. I was surprised they arrived here rather than the usual place.

I wiped at my tears again. "How's Delia?"

"She's fine," Cory replied. "Your father said we did the right thing in bringing her back." He looked into my eyes. "Have you been crying?" He seized my shoulders. "What did they do to you?"

"I'm fine, Cory," I lied. "I was just worried about her."

"We must hurry," Attor said.

Cory nodded to Attor. "William said to thank you. He said it worked."

Attor nodded and looked at me. "Are you ready?"

"Ready for what?" I asked.

"To go where no wizards dare to enter."

"I don't like the sound of that," Fish said.

Before Attor could reply, the other dragons came out of the cave. They formed a line behind me and flapped their wings. The wind blew my hair as I looked back at them, confused. One began to stomp the ground near a stand of trees, clearing some kind of a path. Before I could question, an awful noise came from the woods, like that of an injured animal.

"What the hell is that?" Samuel asked.

The dragons stopped abruptly, moving to one side as the awful sound filled the air.

"The wizards call them 'power eaters,'" Attor explained.

"What are they?" I asked.

"Something only half-humans like your friends can kill."

"We have to kill them?" Cory asked.

"No," Attor replied. "You have to make sure they don't kill Thea."

Cory flashed me a look and turned to Attor. "Are you crazy?" he asked. "She's not going in there."

"She must!" Katu snapped.

I looked back toward the woods, the sound of misery filling my head. My body tensed. I was nervous, not for me, but for the boys. Javier and Joshua stared toward the trees with fear in their eyes.

"Attor," I said quietly, "maybe I should go in there alone. The boys can wait here."

Cory stepped forward. "You're not going in there."

"There must be a reason, Cory. I have to do it."

"No," he insisted.

Attor blew fire between us. "She must go. It's the only way to know if her powers will work. That forest is the only way to get to the white energy without being seen by the wizards."

"Why wouldn't my powers work?" I asked.

"What lives through those trees renders a wizard's powers useless."

"Then why send her in there at all?" Cory asked.

I reached for Cory's arm. "It's okay, I want to do this."

"I won't let you," Cory said. "Not if you're in danger."

"That is why you are here," Attor said. "To pull her out."

"Attor, the wizards," Katu warned. "We have to hurry."

Cory approached Katu and Attor. "Why are you so afraid of the wizards?"

Chapter 17
The Power Eaters

Attor looked toward the forest. "We used to be hunted," he began. "The wizards feared our kind of magic, didn't understand our way of life. Our spells couldn't be broken by them." He looked back to us. "When they discovered they couldn't read our minds, they started hunting us. They hated not knowing what we were thinking, or what we were planning. So they killed us out of fear. This continued," he looked at me, his dark eyes softening, "until one became my friend."

"Your father realized how wrong the other wizards had been about us. He tried to make them understand, make them see we meant them no harm. But they wouldn't listen. One day, when he was trying to hide me from the other wizards, we flew into this forest. The others refused to hear him out, wanting only my death. But your father, he never saw what they saw. He called us 'majestic animals' and respected our magic.

"Xander wanted us to live in harmony, learn from each other. But the other wizards feared the unknown, the magic they couldn't understand. Your father saved me." He looked at Katu. "He saved us all. He released us from their spells and set us free.

"He also discovered what lives in these trees, and how it drains a wizard's power. It was I who pulled him out, when the forest had almost killed him. That is when an idea came to him."

"To bring you here," I said.

Attor nodded. "Yes. He found this place, a safe haven from those who hunted us. The wizards fear this forest more than anything else; the very scent of it renders their powers useless. That's why we stay close and live here in this cave. The wizards fear this forest so much that they have agreed to give us this part of the land. As long as we stay here, they leave us alone."

I looked back toward the forest. I now understood why I felt dizzy the first time Attor flew me here. Something in those trees was sapping my powers, killing me slowly.

"So tell us, then," Cory said. "Why does Thea need to go in there?"

"Because it's the only way she won't be seen by the wizards. The secret river of life is on the other side of those woods."

"Why don't you just fly us there?" I asked.

"We are not allowed to go near the energy. If they see us flying over this forest, they will know we have violated our agreement. We would be at war."

Something clicked in my head. "I know what my father did," I said, turning to Attor. "Simon took something from this forest, didn't he?"

Attor stared at me silently.

"My father told Simon about this forest," I continued. "That's why the wizards are angry with him, isn't it?"

The dragons blasted fire into the sky.

Their reaction was all the answer I needed.

"Is that what you need me to retrieve for you?" I asked. "What Simon took from this forest?"

Attor nodded.

"Do the wizards fear that Simon will return and steal their powers?" I asked.

"No," Attor replied. "They fear that Simon will use what he took from that forest to kill them. They know that without their powers, they will be at his mercy." Attor stooped over and looked deeply into my eyes. "Why do you think Simon is building an army?" he asked. "Did you think it is only to fight you?"

I gasped. "He's building an army to kill the wizards—the 'ones like me.'"

"What Simon took is the only thing the wizards fear. When someone told Simon about what he would find in those woods, they unwittingly gave him a very powerful weapon."

"Simon's building an army to kill the wizards?" Cory asked.

"Yes," Attor replied.

While reading Simon's mind, I learned that he planned to murder all the warlocks once the battle was done. I realized now I had the wrong battle. He wasn't referring to the battle against me, but rather the one against the wizards. Simon had called it the most important battle of their lives. "How will I know what to look for?" I asked.

"When you enter the forest," Attor said, "you will know."

"I'll find it."

"There is one thing your father never shared with Simon," Attor said.

"What?"

"Your father never told him about us. Simon does not know we exist."

"How is that possible?" I asked. "I thought Simon spent many years here."

"He did," Attor replied. "But we were the one secret your father kept from him."

"I told you," Katu snapped, looking down at me from his great height. "Xander is a man of few mistakes."

"Enough!" Attor yelled. "The wizards will soon be here. I must know if you lose your powers in there. If so, we will need to clear a path so you can get to the energy faster. You won't have much time once you reach the other side."

He told the dragons to move out of the way and looked at the boys. "Draw your weapons, gentlemen."

"What should I use?" I asked. "If my powers don't work, I'll need a weapon."

Katu stepped forward. "Give her Xander's weapon."

Attor nodded, and Katu quickly disappeared into the cave. When Katu returned, in his mouth he held a long crystal stick with a gold and silver handle. He placed it at my feet and stepped back.

"What is it?" I asked. "A knife?"

"It's your father's wand," Attor replied.

I picked it up and turned it in my hands. "Do I wave it?"

Laughter erupted among the dragons. Attor shot them a look and they quieted. "Just hold fast to it," he said. "The wand will know what you need. It works symbiotically with your mind. There is no need to wave it."

"How will I—"

"No more questions, witch," Attor said. "We don't have much time." He shuffled over to the boys. "Try not to kill them," he instructed. "Only stop them. But I will understand if violence becomes necessary."

"What do they look like?" Sammy asked.

"They are the only things in the forest that move."

Cory flicked his arms. "How long do we stay?"

"Just go to the end of the path we created," Attor replied. "We will join you if needed."

We drew our weapons and faced the forest. I took my place at the front, the wand secure in my hand. Attor nodded to the dragons, who again flapped their wings. The wind blew my hair toward the trees. That awful sound—the sound of misery—brought the image of a thousand tortured souls into my head. I tightened my grip on the wand and set off along the path.

A tingling sensation surged through my body as I passed the first tree, the unnerving sound growing louder. The boys followed close behind. My eyes nervously combed the forest for any sign of movement. I spotted a shining light beyond the edge of the trees, gold with tiny silver speckles. The wind increased, and with it the intensity of the blood-curdling sound. I had an impulse to touch something, because it all seemed so unreal. The ground looked strangely clean, with no leaf litter like you would expect to find on the floor of such a dense forest.

"Are those rake marks?" Sammy asked, looking down.

"It looks like someone has been doing yard work," Joshua added.

"Yeah," Cory said. "Everything looks so clean— unnaturally so."

"Not even a twig," I said, searching the ground.

"Hey," Fish whispered. "The sound—it stopped."

We halted and looked around. The forest was eerily quiet and still. Even the leaves were no longer blowing in the breeze.

"What's happening?" Javier asked, circling around me.

"Keep Thea in the middle," Cory ordered.

They surrounded me and we inched ahead. The wand quivered in my hand. I was stunned when it transformed into a sword. I raised it up, mesmerized by the beauty of its crystal-clear blade.

"That thing's going to shatter," Cory said.

I gripped the handle with both hands. "No, it's not."

Suddenly, an avalanche of leaves fell on me, which drained my powers the moment they made contact. Cory pulled me behind him as the boys started in on the leaves, hacking and swinging. "It's just leaves!" Cory shouted.

The ghastly noise erupted again, this time coming from behind us. Before I could turn, I was plagued by another round of leaves. I noticed that the first set was now swirling together in the air like a giant swarm of bees. Cory pulled me to him but the leaves followed. Every time I moved, more leaves fell from the trees and threatened to paralyze me. I couldn't escape them. My energy was draining fast.

"How in the hell are we supposed to fight

leaves?" Sammy shouted over the din.

I waved my hand, trying to blow the leaves away, but my powers were useless. Javier swung his mesh chain at them, to no avail. The chain merely passed through the cloud of leaves as they continued their relentless pursuit. Cory stepped in front of me and swung his blades, but what few leaves he managed to slice mended themselves and came after me again. "We have to get Thea out of here!" he shouted.

Coated in leaves, I struggled to breathe. I felt dizzy, weak. I could barely hold onto the sword. Another load fell, and I collapsed to the ground. Fish threw a hook, but his weapon missed the leaves and sank into a tree. As his hook hit the trunk, some of the leaves lost their grip on me and plummeted to the ground.

Fish threw his other hook at the tree, sending more leaves away from me. "Attack the trees!" he shouted.

Javier grabbed my father's sword, ran to a tree, and thrust the sword into it. The horrible sound increased, and a fresh crop of leaves blanketed me. Panic spread through me. A red liquid began to ooze from the tree Javier had just attacked. Blood.

More trees released their leaves and covered me. But I realized there was no pain, that they were only trying to block me. It hit me, why they were draining my energy: I was causing *them* pain. I was having the same effect on them as I had on the cell phones. My wizard energy was too much and they were doing the only they could to stop the pain.

As more leaves covered me, an idea come to me. I raised my hand and chanted, hoping the witch part of me would be allowed through.

"I take the air around me and turn it into glass.

Surround me like a bubble so my energy can't pass."

At once, a soft energy beaming out from all sides surrounded me. I could still feel the ground under my feet. I stretched out my hand and the bubble stretched with it. The shield looked like liquid glass, moving with every step I took.

The agitated leaves ceased their frantic motion. That horrible sound stopped. Some of the leaves flew back onto the trees. Some were gathered up by branches that reached from the trees, leaving behind marks like we had seen on the ground.

The boys abandoned their fight and stared in awe at the spectacle.

"What just happened?" Cory asked.

"Get me out of this forest," I said, leaning on the bubble. I pulled myself up. I could hardly stand, and barely had enough energy to breathe.

Cory hurried over to help and collided with the bubble. He stumbled back, shaking his head. "What the?"

I tried to stay on my feet. I had to get out of there. "Cory, I'm causing them pain. You have to get me out of here."

"Thea," Joshua called, "let me out!"

Over my shoulder, I saw that Joshua was trapped in the bubble with me. I carefully made my way to him and collapsed in his arms. I could barely keep my eyes open.

"Thea," Joshua gasped. "Your hair is gray."

"Get me out of here, Joshua."

He lifted me up and started walking back toward the entrance of the forest, with the boys right behind. "Are you in pain?" he asked.

"It's getting dark," I said, glancing around. "Why

is it getting dark?"

"Just hold on, Thea. I'll get you out of here."

I rested my head on his chest and closed my eyes. My body was tired; I felt like I was ready for death to take me. I only wanted to sleep, to drift off and never wake up.

"Is she okay?" I heard Cory ask.

"I don't think so," Joshua answered.

"Then walk faster!" Cory shouted.

The next thing I knew, Attor was reaching for me. He clashed with the bubble and stepped back. "What witchery is this?"

I tried to wave my hand and break the bubble, but I was too weak. I looked at Javier. "The sword."

Cory snatched the sword from Javier's hand and sliced at the shield. The noise resumed the moment I was free of the protective bubble. "Get me away from them."

"Put her down," Attor ordered. He turned to the dragons. "Grab the others!"

Chapter 18
That Funny Feeling

Attor's talons grasped me, and a moment later, wind rushed across my face. Attor flew fast, trying to blow off the scent from the leaves. I was weak, my skin wrinkled and old. Every bone in my body ached. Why wasn't I feeling better? I was away from the forest; my energy should be coming back by now. I looked down and spotted a leaf stuck to my sleeve. I carefully pulled at it and watched as it flew away on the wind.

Within seconds, my breathing improved. I grasped Attor's talon. I crumpled to the ground when Attor set me down. My head was still spinning. I lay, motionless, eyes closed.

Cory ran to my side. "Thea, is everything okay?" he asked, pulling me into his arms.

I opened my eyes. Cory looked so worried. I stroked his cheek. "You're a good man, Cory," I replied. "You really love me, don't you?"

He smiled. "And what good has it done me?"

I looked into his green eyes. I wanted to touch his lips, feel his tongue inside my mouth. "I love you, Cory," I said, pulling him closer.

Before our lips could meet, Fish pushed Cory away. "What are you doing, man?" he demanded. "Can't you see she's not herself?"

Sammy rushed over and helped me to my feet. Cory's eyes were still locked on mine. I had no idea what had gotten into me. The need to hold him arose suddenly. I felt I would die if I didn't kiss him. We continued staring at each other until Attor gave me a gentle push.

"What happened in there?" he asked, gesturing with his wing toward the forest.

I tore my eyes away from Cory. "Do you know why that forest drains the wizards' powers?"

"No one knows, witch," he replied. "It just happens."

"Well, I know. And I think I know a way to get past them without hurting them." I told him what I'd learned, and about my power over things like cell phones. He didn't understand the reference but, nonetheless, I was able to explain about how wizard energy caused the trees pain. "They only steal powers because they're trying to end the pain."

"But they hate wizards," Attor said. "They have gone as far as to kill them. I have seen it with my own eyes."

"They don't mean to, Attor," I explained. "They merely rob them of their powers until the pain stops. By then, it's too late. The wizards are too weak to survive."

"Are you sure about this?" he asked.

"You saw the bubble," I said. "They stopped screeching the moment I was inside it."

Attor looked at the other dragons. They seemed nervous. "You must not share this information with the wizards," he said, returning his attention to me.

I smiled. "I was going to say the same thing to you."

Attor gave me a quick nod. "We will talk about this when you return. But now, you must leave. A wizard will be here soon."

I wrapped my arms around his massive frame. "Thank you. Thank you for telling me the truth."

"Don't forget about the tea," he replied. "It will delay the spell and buy you precious time. I will see you in four days."

I pulled away. "Why four days?"

Attor didn't answer. He took to the sky, followed by the other dragons.

I drew the leaves Katu had given me from my pocket. I walked to Cory, purposely avoiding his eyes. "Here, hold these for me."

"What are they for?"

"I'll tell you later," I replied. "Just don't let my father see them."

He nodded and slipped them into his pocket.

"Thea, your hair is back to normal," Joshua exclaimed.

I ignored Joshua's comment and pulled off the ring. Within moments, we were back in my father's room. It was empty. Fish went off to find Delia. I set down the ring and hurried out of the room behind Fish, in an attempt to avoid Cory.

"Where are you going?" Cory asked when I'd reached the top of the stairs.

I stopped but didn't turn around. "To look for my

father."

"I'll come with you."

I peered down the flight of steps, annoyed. I still didn't understand what had gotten into me, and I didn't want Cory getting the wrong idea.

My father walked out of Delia's room.

"Father," I exclaimed.

He walked over and held out his hand. "The ring?"

"I left it in your room."

I couldn't stop staring. He looked forty years younger. His hair was free of gray and his eyes twinkled in a way I hadn't seen since I was a child.

He looked at Cory. "There is food ready in the kitchen. Don't forget to leave the house in the morning."

Cory nodded and headed down the stairs. My father flashed me another look, walked back down the hall and disappeared into his room. His demeanor took me aback. He was usually full of questions when we returned, but this time he was cool and distant.

I gave up trying to figure him out and went downstairs. Cory was waiting for me at the bottom of the steps. I started to ask him for the leaves when I felt a chill come over me. Rage bubbled under the surface, an ugly hate filling my heart.

"What's wrong?" Cory asked.

I ignored his question and slowly looked toward the study. I caught a glimpse of James and seized Cory's arm. "Stop me if I move." My heart raced intensely at the thought of hurting James. The idea of his death seemed sweeter to me than ever. I imagined his dead body lying at my feet.

"Thea," Cory whispered. "Your hair, it's . . ."

James turned on his heel and walked back into his

study.

"James," I called.

He looked over his shoulder.

"Today. Right now."

He nodded and slammed the door behind him. My mood instantly reverted.

"What's going on?" Cory asked. "Your hair."

I ran my fingers through the smooth, silky strands. Not a curl or knot to be found. The spell. I knew the truth now. I understood. But it didn't make curbing the desire to kill James any easier.

"Thea, what are these for?" Cory asked, pulling the tea leaves from his pocket.

I looked at him. The urge to kiss him was so strong, I could barely resist throwing my arms around him. I stepped back up a stair. "Meet me in the guest house later," I said. "I'll explain everything."

He nodded, and I followed him into the kitchen. The boys were rounding up the pots on the stove. "We're going to warm up the food in the guest house," Sammy said, heading out the back door.

I turned to Cory. "I'll be there shortly."

He nodded again and left with the boys. From the kitchen, I heard James walk out of his study. I peeked through the kitchen door and watched as he climbed the stairs. I knew he was going into my father's room. I closed my eyes and commanded to listen in. A moment later, I heard my father's door open and close.

"She wants to see me, William," James said.

Silence.

"William, is everything okay?"

"Then you should go," my father finally answered.

"What do you think she wants?" James asked. "I

wasn't supposed to see her until tomorrow."

"I don't know. But I need you to give me your word that you will relay to me everything she tells you."

"Of course. Why wouldn't I?"

"Just give me your word, James."

"You have my word."

"No matter what, you must tell me."

"I've given my word," James said. "What is going on?"

"I can no longer read her mind."

"The part of the vision you were worried about."

"Yes. Now go, see what she wants."

I backed away from the kitchen door as James came hurrying back down the stairs. My father couldn't read my mind—Attor's fireball. I heard James stomp across the foyer and slam the door to his study. I slipped out the back door and found a secluded spot in the garden. I pulled Delia's memory box from my pocket and slipped into the memory by the lake. I walked over to our tree and waited.

Though I'm sure it frustrated him, I was thankful my father couldn't read my thoughts. I didn't want him to discover what Attor and I were planning. A troubling thought occurred to me: how would I keep James from telling my father what transpired between us while in the memory? James had promised to tell my father everything and James was nothing if not a man of his word, especially when it came to my father.

I had to be careful. My father was clever. He would surely read between the lines of anything I said to James. I even wondered if it was my father who had asked Attor to give me that spell. Maybe that was my father's way of keeping his word to me that James would not die. He never promised I wouldn't lose him, though. In fact, he'd warned me about it.

But my other problems would have to wait. I wanted only to think about James now—couldn't wait to be with him. I would soon have to find a way to say goodbye to him, so I could cast the spell. I already felt Simon's spell working its evil. I could feel James before I even saw him. Just breathing the same air as him bothered me.

I grabbed a strand of my hair. Here at least, it reverted to its usual form—messy and knotted. If keeping James alive meant I had to set him free, then that's what I would do. Tears filled my eyes. I knew I would have to endure seeing him with Helena. I would have no choice but to stand by and watch as they walked the streets of Salem, hand in hand.

I leaned back on the tree and closed my eyes, allowing tears to roll down my face. Suddenly, I felt James' lips on mine.

"James," I said, throwing my arms around him. "I love you."

He pressed his body against mine, his hands firmly planted on the tree's trunk. He smiled. "I know." His lips were inches from mine. "And I love you."

He brushed his tongue across my lips. His sweet scent filled my mouth. I closed my eyes when his hand found my breast.

"And now I would like to show you how much," he said, sliding his tongue into my mouth.

He picked me up and carried me over to a patch of grass. He laid me down and climbed on top of me. I wrapped my legs around him and pulled his face to mine. "Tell me you love me," I begged.

He smiled. "Thea, the word 'love' is not enough for what I feel for you. Such a word doesn't even exist.

It lives only in my heart, only in my eyes, when I look at you. It lives in my soul when I'm with you, and it lives in my arms when I'm holding you."

I touched his face. "Kiss me now."

He smiled again. "Yes, ma'am."

He crushed his lips to mine. I delighted in his touch as he peeled off my clothes. The warmth of his body next to mine felt like home. I was safe here. Nothing could touch me. Nothing could hurt me.

I closed my eyes, allowing his hands to explore every inch of my body. He ran his fingers along my thigh and kissed my breasts. I couldn't tear my thoughts away from his beautiful, muscular body. It called to me, drew me in closer with each passing second of ecstasy.

Chapter 19
How Do I Keep This From My Father?

I didn't know how much time had passed, and I didn't care. I rested my head on James' chest as he fiddled with my matted locks.

He kissed my head and ran his hands along my naked body. "What are you thinking of?" he asked.

I looked up at him and smiled. "I'm thinking I never want to leave this place."

He smiled and kissed my head again. "And when I was coming out of my study, what were you thinking then?"

I rolled over, away from his gaze.

"Thea, don't you trust me?"

I closed my eyes. "I should ask you that question."

I felt his hand on my shoulder. He turned me over and made me look at hm.

"You think I don't trust you?"

"Am I wrong?"

"Thea, how can you say that?"

I got up and started to dress. I hated to ruin this

moment, but right now I didn't have a choice. I knew my father was waiting for a full report, and I had to find a way to stop James from relaying the details of our conversation. We dressed in silence, but I could feel James looking at me. I couldn't let his gaze weaken me.

"What did I do?" he asked.

I turned to leave.

He grabbed my arm. "Thea, please."

I pulled away. "How come you never told me that Simon put that spell on you?" I couldn't tell him I knew that the spell had been cast on me.

He looked down and didn't answer.

"I'll tell you why," I said. "It's because you have no faith in me."

"It's not like that, Thea," he replied. "You don't understand."

"No, you don't understand, James. You're the one person I thought I could count on. The one person I trusted not to lie to me. I thought you were on my side."

"I am on your side," he said, stepping toward me.

"Prove it!"

He grabbed my shoulders. "Tell me how."

"Have faith in me, James."

He sighed and pulled me closer. "I have faith in our love. I believe in it."

"But do you have faith in me? Not just in our love, but in me?"

"I do, but you don't understand."

"Then why must you plot with my father? Why didn't you come to me, why didn't you believe in me enough to help you?"

He looked into my eyes. "A desperate man will do anything to save the one he loves, even lie if it means saving her life."

I held his gaze. "I can take a few bumps and scratches."

"So can I." He grabbed my hand and placed it over his heart. "You feel that? Can you feel my heart beating? It would stop if I ever lost you. I would have nothing to live for. Without you, I would have no life."

"And do you think mine would be better without you?"

"I don't want to lose you, Thea. I would give my life to save yours."

"Would you have me give up mine, to save you?"

"If you ever did that, I would die with you."

"And what do you think I would do, James?"

He sighed and bowed his head.

"Have faith in me," I said, reaching for his hand. "Not in my father, but in me."

He looked at me for a long moment. "Tell me what to do."

"Stop giving my father information. He's out of this now. I'm going to fix this. But I can't tell you how."

"Will I lose you?"

"I will always be yours, my love."

He pulled me into his arms. "But will I lose you?"

My heart was breaking inside, but I held back my tears. "You will never lose me, James."

He slowly pulled away from me, a strange expression passing across his face. He stared deeply into my eyes, as if studying them. It almost seemed like he was reading my mind, something I knew wasn't possible. Suddenly, he grabbed my shoulders and drew me against him. "My heart would find you, Thea. Even if you were in the depths of hell, my heart would find you."

He didn't give me a chance to answer. He pulled my lips to his and kissed me passionately. I felt myself panic a little. I wasn't sure what to make of his cryptic words. It was as if he had figured it out, saw through me somehow. But that couldn't be; there was no way he could possibly know what I was planning.

"My heart would find you," he repeated, between kisses.

He tightened his embrace, almost more than I could stand. He smelled sweeter than ever. I breathed in his scent. "I love how you smell to me," I whispered.

James stiffened. He pulled away from me, a strange expression on his face. After a moment, a smile broke across his face.

Why was he suddenly so happy? I was about to question him when he pulled me into his arms again. "I give you my word," he said. "I won't share any more information with your father, even if it means breaking my word to him."

I sighed in relief and melted in his arms. "Thank you."

"Don't forget to drink the tea," he whispered into my ear.

My head shot up. "What?" I asked nervously.

"The tea, so you won't be with child."

"Oh," I said, exhaling. "I won't forget."

"I suppose that means you might not make it here tomorrow. I know the tea makes you sleepy."

"I'll be here. I'll be fine."

He kissed my head. "What time then—tomorrow, I mean?"

"Before the ball. I'll be here waiting."

His smile disappeared, and he pulled away.

"Please don't go to the ball. Please stay home."

"Why?" Then it occurred to me. "Oh, you're taking Helena."

He nodded.

I reached for his hand. "It's okay. I understand. I'll stay away from you."

His smile returned. "We should get back now. It's late."

"Look at me," I said, brushing my hand across his cheek.

He looked into my eyes, seeming nervous. I smiled and stroked his face. "I'm not going to hurt you. I will never hurt you."

"And I'll never hurt you, Thea."

"We can stop ourselves. Have faith in us."

"I do."

"Then I'll see you here," I said, smiling. "Before the ball."

"Tomorrow then," he whispered.

We kissed goodbye, and I watched as James disappeared into the woods. After opening the box and pulling myself out of the memory, I quietly slipped in through the back and peeked through the kitchen door. I caught James running up the stairs, presumably to my father's room. I prayed he would keep his word. I closed my eyes and commanded to listen.

"What did you find out?" my father asked.

My heart raced. "Please, James," I whispered to myself.

"I'm sorry, William," James said. "We got carried away in the moment."

"I see. I will make her a batch of the tea then."

"I'm sorry I wasn't able to help, but she seemed fine."

"Good, good. Thank you, James. That will be all."

I opened my eyes and sighed, deeply relieved. One less thing to worry about. I slipped the box into my pocket and headed to the guest house. When I walked in, the boys were still eating. I wondered how long James and I had been gone.

"Where's Cory?" I asked.

"He's out back with Delia," Fish replied, his mouth full of food.

I walked out the back door of the guest house and spotted Delia and Cory sitting on a garden bench.

"What do you mean you already knew?" Delia asked Cory.

They were talking about the spell. But how did Cory know about it?

I approached them. "What's going on?" I asked, pretending I hadn't heard Delia's question.

Delia stood and brushed at her skirt. She stepped away from Cory and smiled nervously. "Oh, I was telling Cory about the Halloween Ball."

"What about it?"

"I was telling him that I don't think we can make it this year."

"Why not? I don't see any reason why we can't go."

"Well, I just figured with everything that's going on . . ."

"Well, you figured wrong. We're going, all of us."

Delia avoided my eyes. She kept glancing at Cory.

I turned my attention to him. "I need to speak with you."

"I'll just go inside," Delia said, hurrying toward the back door. She couldn't get out of there fast enough, it seemed.

"What's going on?" Cory asked.

I waited until Delia was inside before speaking. "We need to go to your apartment. Do you have the leaves?"

"Yes, but did you forget about the sleeping spell?"

"I'll cast it now, and you can sleep there tonight."

He nodded, and we went inside. He told the boys to hurry up and eat because I was casting the spell.

"Where are you guys going?" Sammy asked.

"Don't worry about it," Cory replied. "I'll see you guys in the morning."

"Are we going to the Halloween Ball tomorrow night?" Javier asked.

Cory nodded. "Yeah, so get some rest."

Javier high-fived Sammy, calling out, "We're going to the ball, guys."

When Cory and I walked into the kitchen, there was a cup of tea waiting on the table. That's my father: dutiful as ever. I picked up the cup and started drinking.

"What's that for?" Cory asked.

"Nothing," I replied, downing the last of it. "Let's get out of here."

When we pulled up to Cory's apartment building, most of the lights were still on. I smiled at the old place. It felt like years since I'd been there. The boys lived on the first and second floors, and my apartment was on the third. It was small, but I loved it—quaint and cozy. The building had a giant front porch with two rocking chairs and numerous pots filled with flowers. I thought of the many hours I'd spent nestled on that porch, reading my books.

"Looks like they're still awake," I said, stepping out of the truck.

I saw Justin spying out the front window. He opened it. "Wait there!" he called.

He came storming out the front door, pointing behind us.

I looked over my shoulder and saw two men standing near the vacant lot across the street.

"Do you know them?" Justin asked.

The men disappeared behind some trees. I didn't get a good look at them, but I could tell they were warlocks.

"No, why?" Cory asked.

"They were looking for your friend Delia."

I turned and ran at them. The warlocks promptly took off running. I wanted to wave my hand, but there were far too many tourists milling about. I'd have to find another way. If only I could bound off the trees. That way, I'd be able to catch up to them.

I heard Cory and Justin behind me, and saw a spell flying past. Over my shoulder, I saw that Justin had his straw out. His spell hit one of the warlocks in the back of the head.

The warlock stumbled to the ground but quickly got to his feet and faced me. "Take your best shot, witch," he said, glaring at me.

I stopped just a few feet from him. "I'm not trying to kill you, you fool."

"No, you're just trying to cast your death spell on me."

"Trust me, if I wanted you dead, you would be."

He glanced over his shoulder; the other warlock was nowhere to be seen.

~ 233 ~

"You can stop looking for the witch Delia," I said. "She doesn't have what you're looking for."

Cory and Justin approached and stood on either side of the warlock.

"She's talking to you," Cory said, kicking him to the ground.

The man fell hard. "You're going to regret that, half-human scum."

Cory smiled and flicked his arms.

The warlock's eyes widened.

"We can settle it right now," Cory replied.

The warlock scrambled to his feet and spat a spell into his hand. I spun and kicked the spell away from him. A noise, like matches being lit, sounded behind us. I knew that sound—there were more warlocks here. I saw them, ten of Simon's men, coming out from behind the trees. I looked again at the numerous tourists walking about. This was going to get ugly.

"Thea, catch," Cory yelled.

My father's wand soared through the air and into my hand.

The warlock smiled at Cory. "Let's see you kick me down now," he said.

Cory spun around and kicked the man down again. The other warlocks ran at us. The wand vibrated in my hand. When it transformed into a memory box, I knew exactly what to do.

I held it up.

The warlocks halted abruptly. They couldn't take their eyes off of it.

"Is this what you're looking for?" I asked.

The warlocks surrounded us. Cory and Justin stepped in front of me.

I pushed through them and confronted the

warlocks. "Tell Simon the witch Delia no longer has it. It belongs to me now. And if Simon wants it, he'll have to come after me himself."

"That can be arranged, witch," one of the warlocks replied.

"Good, it will save me the trouble of looking for him."

The warlocks looked skyward and stepped back, expressions of shock on their faces. Ciro ran toward us, with Justin's brothers close behind. I wanted to look up and see what the warlocks were so scared of, but I kept my eyes fixed on the group. I couldn't risk one of them throwing a spell and catching us off guard. Ciro and the others surrounded them, but the warlocks stood frozen, their eyes transfixed on the sky.

Ciro prepared to swing his machete into the group.

I put up my hand. "There are too many tourists around," I shouted. The tourists were a good distance away, but I didn't want to spark a panic.

When Adam and Ryan looked up, they too stepped back in astonishment. My curiosity took over. I looked toward the sky and spotted several ninja stars floating above us. I stifled a laugh. Sammy was high up in a tree somewhere, probably upside-down, dangling his stars.

I leaned toward the band of warlocks. "Those are my death spells," I hissed. "If you move, I'll throw them at you."

A collective look of horror crossed their faces.

Sammy waved the stars again.

"No, please!" one of the warlocks shouted.

"Leave now!" I ordered. "Tell Simon what I said."

Two of the men grabbed the warlock Cory had kicked, and dragged him away. The rest of the pack took off running.

Justin and his brothers were still looking up toward the sky in awe. Cory and I exchanged an amused glanced and erupted in laughter.

"Sam," Cory called, "Get down here!"

Chapter 20
Cory's Blue Eyes

We heard the sound of feet hitting the ground. "Man, I thought they were going to pee their pants."

Ryan looked in the direction of the voice and, finding nothing, asked, "What kind of witchery is this?"

Sammy waved his stars in front of Ryan and Adam, sending Cory into another fit of giggles. Sammy chuckled as he circled mercilessly around the Santos brothers. Ciro nearly fell to the ground laughing.

When Justin raised his straw, I was forced to step in. "Okay, Sammy," I said, trying not to laugh. "That's enough."

Sammy pulled off his head piece, revealing only his head, which looked to be floating on air.

"Where the hell did you learn an invisibility spell?" Justin asked.

"It's not a spell," Sammy replied. "It's a special ninja suit."

Justin stepped closer to Sammy. "That is the coolest thing I have ever seen. Where did you get it?"

"It was a gift from Thea's husband."

~ 237 ~

"Sam!" Cory snapped. "Put the head piece back on, you're going to scare the tourists."

Sammy complied as the Santos brothers watched in amazement.

"Where did your husband learn an invisibility spell?" Justin asked.

I shrugged. "You'll have to ask him."

I knew the answer, of course; my father had put a spell on the suit. There was no such thing as an invisibility spell, not in this world. Although hundreds had tried to create one, it remained something witches only dreamed of.

The brothers were still expressing their admiration for Sammy's suit when Cory walked over to me. "Why do you think Simon wants the box?"

"He wants to use it on me," I replied.

"How the hell did he find out about it?"

"I don't know. But I have a feeling Helena has something to do with all of this." While waiting for the box to turn back into a wand, I spotted James' car coming down the road. Helena was in the passenger seat. Cory turned to see what I was looking at and swiftly threaded his arm through mine.

"Isn't that your husband?" Justin asked.

I prayed that James was just driving by, but no such luck. He pulled the car to the curb in front of the little grocery store across the street. He walked around and opened the door for Helena. She kissed his cheek as she stepped out of the car. He smiled and put his arm around her as they walked toward the store together.

I started for the happy couple.

Cory tightened his hold. "Let's get back to the house," he said.

Ciro held fast to my other arm, but my eyes were transfixed on James and Helena, standing together on the sidewalk. My blood began to boil.

"Thea," Cory said quietly into my ear. "There are tourists everywhere."

James leaned away from Helena as if he was listening to someone speaking into his ear. Sammy was telling James I was here. James glanced over his shoulder. Helena nestled in closer to him as they walked into the store. They came out moments later, James holding a bag of groceries.

I tried to look away as he opened the car door for her. Helena flashed me a smug smile before kissing him. I shoved Ciro and Cory away and into the trees. I ran at James, the Santos brothers close on my heels. One of them grabbed my shirt. I kicked whoever it was in the stomach and sent him flying across the street.

James shoved Helena into the car, ran to the driver's side and attempted to get in. I waved my hand. James slammed into the car and fell to the ground. Helena got out and ran to him.

"Get back in the car!" James shouted.

When I got to within a few feet of James, Ciro tackled me to the ground. The others soon piled on. They tried holding me down with spells, but I waved my hand and sent them flying. I scrambled to my feet and glared at Helena. A wave of my hand sent her crashing into the store window.

James pulled himself up, his expression forbidding, and brandished his whip. Before he could reach me with it, he crumpled to the ground. Sammy was trying to subdue him.

Cory grabbed me from behind. "Snap out of it!" he shouted.

Justin seized my feet as his brothers fastened ropes around my arms and legs.

"Get in the car and get out of here!" Cory shouted at James.

I kicked Justin away and pulled off the ropes. I waved my hand, sending Cory into a tree. Someone kicked me, and I stumbled to the ground. I jumped to my feet, spun around, and jumped over Ciro.

"We have to snap her out of it!" Cory shouted, running after me.

Somewhere deep inside, I knew I had to stop, but my rage was stronger than my will to do what was right. "Control yourself, witch!" I said to myself. I had to find a way to distract my mind, find something to take me away.

Cory caught me from behind. I spun around and grabbed his face. I pressed my lips to his.

Cory pulled back. "What are you doing?"

"Kiss me, Cory." I ordered. "Just kiss me."

He pressed himself against me and did as I asked. A sense of calm immediately washed over me. When I felt it working, I kissed him harder. Kissing Cory tamed the fire in my soul. I could think straight again, the anger no longer controlling me.

"Thea," Cory whispered, kissing me again.

I didn't want to stop until I felt every ounce of anger drain from my body. When it finally felt safe to pull away, I looked into Cory's eyes.

He smiled and pulled me back into his arms. "You still look pretty pissed," he said, kissing me again.

I ran my fingers through his hair and moaned. My heart was racing. I wanted—needed—Cory to kiss me.

"Uh, guys," Sammy cut in. "James is gone."

Cory kept kissing me.

I didn't pull away. "Kiss me again."

"As long as you want," he said, finding my lips again.

Sammy smacked Cory's head. "What the hell are you doing?" he asked.

"Get your hands off her!" Ciro added.

Cory ignored them both. He looked into my eyes, smiled, and kissed me again.

"Dude," Sammy said, trying his best to step in between us, "she's married."

Ciro seized my arm and pulled me away. "James is my friend."

Cory yanked me back toward him. "Don't touch her!" He glared at Ciro. "Don't ever put your hands on her again."

"What do you think you're doing?" Ciro asked.

"She's trying to calm herself down," Cory explained.

"Dude," Sammy said. "She looks plenty calm to me."

I looked around at my friends' faces, shame washing over me. I wanted to crawl under a rock. I touched my lips. What had I been thinking? How could I do that to James? I looked at Cory and stumbled back, fighting off the desperate urge to kiss him again. I turned and ran with no particular destination in mind. I just needed to get away.

"Thea!" Cory shouted. "I can explain."

I heard footsteps behind me and ran faster until I could no longer hear them. I didn't even care about the gawking tourists. I ran up the side of one of the buildings and jumped over it, landing on a tree. I broke off a branch, sat astride it, and flew away.

I couldn't explain what had come over me. It was

like I needed that kiss more than life itself. The moment my lips touched Cory's, I wanted more. He became the one thing I wanted most, even more than James.

"No!" I shouted into the wind.

My heart ached for James. I would beg his forgiveness, drop to my knees and tell him how sorry I was. I flew toward Helena's house. I knew it was a bad idea, but I had to see him.

When I arrived, James' car was just pulling into the drive. I flew to a tree and stepped onto a branch. I watched as Helena got out of the car, her face wearing a sour expression. She slammed the door shut and started toward the house, but James grabbed her and turned her to face him.

"All I've ever asked of you is not to provoke her," James said. "Why did you kiss me like that? This was your fault!"

"Why do you care?" she replied. "Or perhaps I should ask: why did it bother you so much to see Thea kissing Cory?" She struggled in his grasp. "You said you didn't love her. You said you loved me."

"I do love you."

"Then why were you shaking like that?" she asked. "Why did you say you were going to kill him?"

"It's the bond," James explained. "I can't help it."

"Then kill her!" She freed her arm from his grip. "Kill her and break that bond!"

He grabbed her shoulders and shook her. "Don't say that to me!"

"Kill her, James," Helena repeated. "If you really love me, then you'll kill her."

"I would kill you first!" he said, pushing her away.

I held tight to the tree, trying to keep my anger in

check. I wanted to fly down, cut off Helena's head, and drag James across a field of broken glass until only bones remained. I swallowed hard. I had to get out of there, but I had to fix things first. I couldn't let James lose her. I had to keep his heart loving her. It was the only way to keep him alive.

Against everything in my heart, I waved my hand. I looked away as James took her in his arms and kissed her.

When I looked back again, Helena was smiling. "Let's not fight like that again," she said, her hand on his cheek.

"I'm sorry I raised my voice," James replied.

She kissed his cheek and threaded her arm through his as they walked happily into the house.

I flew off like a bullet over the trees, trying to wash the image of them out of my head. It was strange to think that this horrible feeling inside me was actually good news. I still loved James; I still belonged to him. For once, my broken heart made me happy.

I was flying back to the boys when a spell knocked me off my branch. I hit the ground hard, but managed to scramble to my feet. I scanned the area and spotted a warlock standing behind a car. He stepped out into the open and spat into his hand. As I raised my hand to wave it, a flashlight appeared in my face. I tried to keep my eyes on the warlock, but he had disappeared into the shadows.

"What are you doing here, miss?" the officer asked.

I dropped my hand to my side. "I'm sorry, Officer," I replied. "I was just headed home."

He flashed the light in my face again. "Let me see some ID," he ordered.

I recognized the officer. He was the same one that stopped Cory. My senses told me he wasn't human. "Who are you?" I asked.

"Have you been drinking tonight, miss?" he asked.

He didn't smell like Simon's men, but I knew he was a witch. I leaned toward him. "Who are you?" I repeated.

"How much have you had to drink, young lady?"

"You don't know, do you?" I asked, stepping closer.

"Ma'am, stop walking toward me."

I knew that voice. "Have we met before?" I asked.

He talked into his radio: "Forty-eight, code one, send me another unit." He flashed his light at me again, and put his other hand on his service revolver. "Ma'am, stay where you are."

There was something familiar about him but I couldn't put my finger on it. Our paths had crossed before—numerous times.

I stepped closer. "You don't have to be afraid of me."

"That's it," he said. "Get on the ground, now!"

I ignored his command and stepped closer. "I'm not going to hurt you."

Into his radio: "Forty-eight, code three." He drew his gun. "Don't move!" he ordered. "Show me your hands."

"You're a witch," I said. "A full-blooded witch."

"What are you talking about?" he asked, pointing the gun at me.

"Why, you're not human at all."

"What?"

I was almost within arm's length when I saw flashing blue lights. I held my hand out for my branch and was gone before he knew what had happened. I flew back to the apartment building and started looking for the others.

"Thea," Sammy called, "you're back."

I walked in the direction of his voice. "Where is everyone?"

"They went looking for you," he replied. "I'll call Cory and tell him you're back."

Sammy briefly spoke with Cory, and then the phone snapped shut.

"Why did you do that, Thea?" Sammy asked. "You're going to hurt him."

"I had to run, Sammy," I replied. "I had to get away."

"No, why did you kiss Cory?"

"I . . . what do you mean I'm going to hurt him?"

"Cory loves you, he's always loved you."

"Take off that suit," I ordered. "I look like a freak talking to the air."

He sighed. "Hold on."

"I'll wait for you on the porch," I called, walking across the street.

When Sammy arrived, I was sitting on the front steps. "What do you mean, I'm going to hurt him?" I asked.

"Here, you dropped this when you ran away," he said, handing me the wand.

"Thanks. Now answer my question."

"He still loves you, Thea."

I hated how happy Sammy's words made me feel. I almost wanted to jump for joy.

"But his eyes," I said. "They're not blue, they're

green."

"That's his spell," he explained. "He didn't want you worrying about him. He wanted you to think he was over you."

"What?" I gasped.

Sammy tucked his suit under his arm and sat next to me. "He's never gotten over you, Thea. He's loved you as long as I can remember."

"Why would he hide it from me?"

"You have to ask? Because of James. When Cory and James became friends, Cory stepped aside."

"Are you sure he put a spell on himself?"

"Yes, I'm sure," he replied. "And if you don't believe me, break it and see for yourself."

Ciro's car pulled up, and Cory jumped out of the passenger side. I waved my hand and broke his spell. As he drew near, his blue eyes shone under the lights of the porch. My heart skipped a beat. I stood to greet him.

"Why did you run away like that?" Cory asked, grabbing my shoulders.

As I fought the urge to lean into him, I was overcome by a troubling realization. "Not like this, Cory."

"What do you mean?" he said, stepping back.

Ciro walked up. "Is everything okay?"

"Everything's fine, Ciro," I replied. "Can you give us a minute?"

"Thea, James is my friend," Ciro said. "I don't—"

"Please, Ciro," I said, cutting him off. "Everything's fine now."

He shot Cory another glance and went inside. Sammy followed him in.

When they were gone, I looked at Cory. "Not like

this. Not with a spell."

He looked away. "How did you figure it out?"

"It doesn't matter how," I said. "Why? Why would you cast a love spell on me?"

"Well, you're only half-right," he replied. "I didn't put the spell on you. I put it on me. But it only works when you're close to me."

"Why?"

"Why wouldn't I?" he said through clenched teeth. "How can you expect me to do nothing when I know you're going to stop loving him? When you told me you loved me first, and you would have married me."

I reached out and touched his face. "Because you deserve a woman to fall in love with you—not because of some spell, but because she can't live without you."

He placed his hand over mine and closed his eyes. "My heart's already taken."

"You never needed a spell," I said. "And you won't again."

He brightened. "What do you mean?"

"Let my heart see you, Cory. Let me find you when my heart is lost."

He looked at me, confused.

I didn't want to spell it out for him. I knew Cory was my only chance at giving my son a father, but I didn't want to love him because of a spell. I had once loved Cory, and I knew I could love him again. Someday he'd get the chance he'd always wanted because there would be no James to stop him.

He pulled me closer. I wanted to kiss him. The heat from his body drove me crazy. I could feel his heart pounding, his sweet breath on my face.

"Thea, what are you saying?"

~ 247 ~

"You once asked if things would have been different between us if I never met James." I paused. "You may get the answer to that question."

He looked into my eyes, a smile tugging at his lips. He took my face in his hands. "I will always be here, Thea," he said, "waiting to give your heart a home."

I closed my eyes as he pulled me to his lips. I wanted to pull away, but his spell was so powerful. Cory's hands were reaching for places they shouldn't. I pushed away and waved my hand.

He reached for me again.

I put up my hand. "Not until my heart finds you, Cory."

His shoulders slumped. "You broke it, didn't you?"

I backed away. "I shouldn't have kissed you again. I'm sorry."

"I kissed you," he corrected. "You were only reacting to the spell."

"Can we be just friends again?"

He nodded. "And I promise, no more spells."

"Not even on your eyes."

"I'm going to kill Sam."

"Come on," I said, taking his arm. "I need to speak with you and Ciro." He rubbed his eyes as we walked inside. "You getting tired?" I asked.

"I think your sleeping spell just kicked in."

When we walked into the boys' apartment, Sammy was already dead asleep on the sofa.

Cory stretched out on the floor. "I'm just going to rest my eyes." Moments later, he was snoring.

I threw a blanket over him, turned out the lights, and went looking for Ciro.

Ciro flashed me a dirty look when I walked into the second floor apartment. "You guys working out?" I asked.

Ciro paused his workout but said nothing. The Santos brothers were there, too. The room was jammed with exercise equipment—weights and benches. It looked more like a training gym than an apartment. Ciro went back to punching the bag hanging from the ceiling. Ryan, Adam, and Justin kept their distance. Ciro was disappointed in me. I had to make things right.

"Where's your boyfriend?" Ciro asked, punching the bag.

"It's not what you think."

"No," he said, turning to face me. "It's what I saw."

"It was a spell," I said. "Just a love spell."

He returned his attention to the bag. "Is that what you're going to tell James?"

"Yes," I replied, annoyed. "Because it's the truth."

"I suppose it's an easy out," he said.

"Ciro," I said, stepping closer, "it was a spell."

"No," he said. "It's called cheating." He punched the bag harder.

I kicked the bag and sent it flying across the room. I slapped Ciro across the face. Justin and his brothers readied themselves into a stance, but Ciro held up his hand.

"Don't you ever talk to me like that again," I said.

"Don't ever cheat on my friend again," he shot back.

I opened the door to leave. "Go to hell, Ciro."

Chapter 21
The Blood Line

I stormed outside, slamming the main door behind me. I wanted to kill Ciro. How dare he tell me I was taking the easy way out? What part of my life seemed easy to him? I stomped across the lawn in a fury. I felt my father's wand quiver and quickly transform into a sword. I eyed it curiously; I didn't want to kill Ciro that badly.

I was trying to make it change back, when I saw the band of warlocks from earlier had returned with reinforcements. They were gathered in a vacant lot across the street. I spotted the warlock Cory had kicked; he was clearly back for revenge.

"Find him and cut off his head!" he shouted.

When our eyes met, a wicked grin spread across his face. The warlocks readied their weapons. Most held steel bats, the same bats that nearly killed me before.

They had chosen the wrong day to test my patience. I was still fuming about what Ciro had said to me. I looked around, the streets were empty. I smiled and walked across the street, straight into the center of their circle. I held the sword down as I scanned their faces.

They pounded the bats into their palms, ready to pounce. Wicked smiles spread across their faces.

"I was wondering when I'd get a chance to practice," I said.

"Practice what?" one of them snapped.

I slammed the sword into the ground. It came up in front of the man and pierced his heart. "Seeing if my sword could kill you from here," I replied.

I pulled the sword out of the ground and swung it like a whip. It snaked through the air and wrapped around another warlock. I pulled hard and cut the man in two. The sword sprang back to shape in my hand.

"Anyone else want to help me practice?" I asked, smiling.

They rushed me. I dove into the ground and came up behind them. A swing of the sword sent three heads flying. Dust filled the air as more warlocks fell. The monster inside me calmed. This was what I needed, a way to release my anger.

I refused to wave my hand. I could kill them in an instant if I had a mind to, but I wanted this, needed this. I had to feed the monster inside me. The sword looked beautiful as it came apart and glistened from the light of the moon. It sounded like a deck of cards made of metal when it would spring back together in my hand.

Another warlock ran at me, bat over his head. I swung the blade and removed his hands; his head soon followed. I searched for the one Cory had kicked. I knew I had to take him down. Some of the warlocks took off running, but I dragged them back into the melee with the sword. They ceased swinging their bats, and were only trying to stay alive now. Dust flew as I cut away heads and limbs.

When the dust finally settled, I saw him: Cory's warlock. He broke into a run, but I dove into the ground and emerged in front of him. "You forgot something." I thrust the sword straight through his heart.

As his dust swirled around me, I surveyed the area. Only their weapons remained, strewn about the ground. I saw Ciro and the others on the porch, their mouths hanging open. Ciro held his machete. He'd been ready to help, but now stood frozen. They all stood, like statues, fear in their eyes.

I walked back toward the building.

Justin was the first to speak. He looked at Ciro. "You want us to stop that?"

I tried not to smile as I climbed the porch steps. I wanted to tell Ciro how sorry I was for slapping him, but I was still angry about what he'd said. When I approached him, he took a step back.

"I'm sorry I slapped you," I said.

Ciro looked down.

Justin pushed Ryan and Adam forward. "Go ahead," he said. "Tell her how you've been bragging that you kicked her ass."

Ryan punched Justin's arm.

I stifled a giggle.

Justin rolled his eyes and looked at me again. "Where did you learn how to fight like that, witch?"

I approached him, tilting my head. "Why do you use a straw to throw your spells?"

He screwed up his face. "Because spitting into my hand is disgusting."

I chuckled. "I learned from watching video games."

We shared a laugh.

"Really?" he asked. "That's awesome."

I looked at Ciro, who was still avoiding my eyes.

"Are you heading home?" Justin asked.

"Yeah," I replied. "Cory and Sammy are staying here tonight."

"I'll walk you," Justin offered.

"Alone?" Ryan asked, his eyebrow arched.

"You really think she needs your help?" Justin asked.

I smiled and looked away. Justin waved over his head as we started walking toward the mansion. I wish I knew what was going through Ciro's head. I knew he and James were good friends, but I told him the truth. He should have believed me.

"I've decided I like you," Justin said out of nowhere.

"Excuse me?"

"At first I couldn't stand you," he confessed. "But I've decided I like you."

"Oh, really?" I asked, amused. "And what changed your mind?"

"You're not like the other witches, all stuck up and full of themselves. You're different."

His explanation puzzled me. Witches didn't get along with warlocks, but it wasn't because they were stuck up. "And you're not like the other power-hungry warlocks."

"Warlocks aren't power hungry, they're scared of you." He kicked a rock down the sidewalk. "I never knew why, until just now."

The night was clear and bright, the air brisk. The tourists were done for the day, and Salem was quiet. I loved this time, when the bright yellow and orange leaves called to me like a song in the night. I liked to walk Chestnut Street with its grand old nineteenth-century houses steeped in history. Corinthian porches, hand-tooled lintels, beaded molding. Sea captains built the houses, but I thought of them as built by angels.

As we cut through the park, I suggested we sit and talk. I wasn't quite ready to see James, or my father, for that matter. We found a bench and sat. I wanted to hear more about what this kid thought of me. I wasn't sure why it mattered, but it did.

Despite our violent introduction, I liked Justin. I felt comfortable with him. With all the lies swirling about my world right now, I appreciated his honest, up-front manner. He didn't look like the other warlocks, didn't act like them either. He wasn't muscular like the boys, and even carried a little extra weight like me.

I could tell he was an old soul. His honesty surely got him into trouble from time to time, but he didn't seem to care. He was wise beyond his years and, even though he was the youngest of the Santos brothers, he was clearly the leader among them.

"So, what exactly did I do to win your favor?"

He smiled and looked down. "I thought you hated warlocks, but I'm starting to see that I was wrong. You could have killed us that day. We hurt you bad, but you held back. I can see that now."

"Why did you assume I hated warlocks? Ciro's a full-blooded witch, but I don't hate him."

"Simon told us you hated warlocks," he replied. "He said you wanted nothing more than to see us all dead."

"You believe Simon?" I asked, chuckling. "Well, I don't hate warlocks—not entirely. I do, however, hate how they treat my friends."

"What, the half humans?"

"Yes. What do warlocks have against them, anyway?"

He shrugged. "I don't mind half-humans, got nothing against 'em. But the others, well, they think male witches are weak for bonding with human girls. They think their blood line will be lost because of it."

What was this kid talking about? He had it all wrong. "So warlocks don't bond with human girls?" I asked.

"Never," he said. "They bond only with pure witches. They don't entertain any notions of human-witch attraction. They only care about the blood line."

"That is the dumbest thing I've ever heard," I said, shaking my head.

He looked at me, clearly annoyed. "They're dumb because they don't date humans?"

"No," I replied. "Because witches have nothing to do with the blood line."

"Yes, they do," he snapped. "Half-humans can't father warlocks."

I burst out laughing. I couldn't believe how clueless Justin was. "You warlocks are so arrogant. You think you know everything."

"And you witches are rude, especially that Delia."

We both laughed.

"Okay, I'll give you that one. But you have to understand, it's because of the way they've been treated."

"Is that why you defend them so much?"

A great sadness settled into my heart as I remembered things from my childhood: warlocks spitting on half-human witches, beating them and dragging them half to death. I never understood it. It was just something I got used to. They were always tormented, sometimes even by their own parents. Most of them were orphans, many left alone in the woods to die. But I changed all that and made the warlocks respect half-humans, even fear them.

Though I wasn't one of them, my father always told me they were an important part of my life, so I grew up defending them, protecting them from both warlocks and pure witches. They lived free, able to show their faces again. The shame of being half human disappeared, and it became accepted as a normal way of life.

"They were the only family I had after my father left." I looked at Justin. "They never turned their backs on me, and I will never turn mine on them. They live an almost-normal life now. No one cares that they're half human—except, of course, the warlocks."

"I told you," Justin snapped. "It's because half-human witches can't father a warlock. Only pure witches can do that. It has to be a pure blood line."

"So that's it?" I asked. "They're worried about the future?"

"Well, yeah," he replied. "Simon told us that you're power-hungry, that you want to be the most commanding one around here. And that's why you defend them so much."

I threw back my head and laughed.

Justin looked at me, confused. "What's so funny?"

"Oh, Justin," I said, shaking my head. "You know what I don't understand? Warlocks hate half-human witches with every fiber of their being, yet they follow Simon and do whatever he tells them to do. They allow themselves to be led by a half-human witch all the time."

Justin narrowed his eyes. "What are you talking about?"

"Simon," I said. "You know he's half human, right?"

"What?" Justin got to his feet.

I looked up at him. "You didn't know?"

"Simon's half human?"

"Um, yes," I replied. "I assumed you knew."

"No," he said, looking away. "I didn't know."

I leaned back against the bench. "You've got to be kidding me."

He didn't answer, just looked up into the sky.

I wondered what was going through his head. How many of Simon's lies had he believed? And why wasn't he helping Simon now? I knew they had told Simon no, but I still didn't know why. Justin seemed well informed about most things Simon was up to. I wondered how this could have gotten by him.

I stood and stepped beside him. "Well, here's something else you may not know then: you're not a warlock. You're a witch. Ciro and his men, your brothers, you're all witches."

He turned to face me. "What are you talking about?"

I sighed. "Warlocks are evil and greedy," I said. "They seek only power and fortune. Their hearts are dark and possess no capacity for compassion or love. The moment you decided to help me, you became a witch. You left the dark part of you behind, leaving only the good heart you have now. Warlocks don't feel,

Justin. Their hearts are empty, filled only with evil."

He looked at me like I was crazy. "But I'm not half human, that makes me a warlock."

"No, it doesn't. The witch is in our blood. We are born with it. Nothing can take that away from us, not even being born half human. Even now, there are humans walking around with witch blood, not knowing who they really are. But warlocks were born from greed and evil. They made the choice to be a warlock, to be the way they are."

"What about your friends?" he asked. "They think themselves to be warlocks."

I shook my head. "They're only trying to belong, to find their place in the world. But I've spent my life trying to show them that it's okay to be just a witch. That they have nothing to be ashamed of."

"What about powers?" he asked. "They can only chant spells."

"So what?" I replied. "That doesn't make them any less of a witch than you."

He looked away again. "Simon is half human," he muttered.

"Do the others think Simon is a full-blooded warlock?"

"No, they think he's half wizard."

I burst out laughing. How did Simon manage to convince a bunch of warlocks that he was half wizard? Was he that good of a liar? Justin looked annoyed. I drew a deep breath and tried to tame my laughter.

"He knows some weird spells, Thea," Justin said. "He said you took his powers. He promised us that when he got them back, he would share them with us."

Again, laughter overtook me. I sat back down on the bench, shaking my head.

"It's not funny," Justin said. "He's very convincing."

I composed myself and stood. "Then why are you not helping him?"

"Because I refuse to be one of his puppets!"

"You're all his puppets," I replied. "You believe everything he says."

"Don't say that!" he said, shoving me.

I flew back over the bench and toppled to the ground. I fought the impulse to wave my hand. I had provoked him, after all.

"I hate that man," Justin said. "He took everything from me." He kicked the bench and turned his back.

I got to my feet and approached him cautiously. "I'm sorry, Justin. I didn't mean to hurt you."

"How dare you call me his puppet? You have no idea who I am, no idea what I've been through." He kept his back turned.

"I'm sorry," I repeated, placing my hand on his shoulder.

He shrugged me off. "Just drop it."

"What did Simon do to you?"

Justin looked toward the night sky and closed his eyes. He sighed and bowed his head. "I once loved a human," he began. "I wanted to marry her. She was everything to me. I never loved anyone like I loved her."

"What happened to her?"

He sighed and turned to face me. "I left her."

"What, but why?"

"To save her," he replied. "To keep Simon away from her."

"Simon wanted to kill her?"

"No, but he would have. He said she was
distracting me, that he was disappointed in me for loving
a disgusting human."

"So you left her."

He nodded. "If I hadn't, sooner or later Simon
would have sent someone to kill her."

I knew it was true. Jack had once tried to kill me
when he thought I was human. He said I was distracting
James from his duties.

"Where is she now?" I asked.

His face fell. "She got married about six years
ago."

My heart broke for him. I could see how much he
still loved her.

"I've seen her a couple of times, with her little
girl. She seems happy."

"And you, are you happy?"

He shook his head. "That ship has sailed for me,
Thea," he said. "She was the one, and I let her go."

"Have you ever tried talking to her?"

"No," he said. "I just watch her sometimes, that's
enough."

"Is that why you refused to help Simon?"

"Yeah, but it's not the only reason."

"No?"

"I have my other reasons."

"Then you'd better share them with me," I said.
"You know too much about Simon as it is. How do I
know I can trust you?"

He looked thoughtful for a long moment,
seemingly struggling with whether or not to share any
more information with me.

I reached for his hand. "It's okay, Justin. You can

tell me."

His hands were trembling. He was having a hard time finding the words. I looked into his eyes. I knew that pain, that suffering. My heart put the puzzle together. His sadness told me everything.

"You left her to save the child she was carrying, didn't you?"

He pulled his hand away and turned his back on me again. I felt his pain in my heart, his sadness running through my veins. It was like I was inside him, suffering with him. I moved closer and put my hand on his back. "Believe me when I say I know what you're going through."

He laughed a little. "Yeah, I guess you sort of do," he replied. "You have a cheating husband."

I pushed him away. "Don't talk about James like that."

He turned around, a confused look on his face. "You're defending him?"

I shook my head. "It's not what it looks like."

"What then?" he asked. "All I know is that we're supposed to stop you from killing him."

"It's complicated."

"What, and my truth isn't?"

Justin was right. He'd shared the most painful thing in his heart. Who was I to hold back? We sat back down, and I told him my story, from the very beginning. He gasped when I told him about the needles, and again when I told him I'd been buried alive. I told him everything Simon had done, and was doing.

When I finished, Justin looked horrified. "So that's why you hate James sometimes?"

"Yes," I replied. "Because of Simon's spell."

"So you're just going to give him up, erase

yourself from James' life?"

"I have no choice. He'll die if I don't."

"I can understand that," he said, grabbing my hand.

"So, are we friends now?" I asked.

"Oh, I think we're more than friends," he replied, smiling.

"Am I interrupting?"

I turned to see Ciro walking up behind us. "What do you want?" I snapped.

He approached me. "I came to offer you a sincere apology."

I arched an eyebrow. "Because you believe me or because you're scared?"

"I guess I deserve that."

"You're lucky I didn't kill you."

"Forgive me," he said. "I did not mean to offend you."

I got to my feet. "I can understand how things may have looked, but it really was just a spell."

"Please, you don't have to explain yourself to me."

"Yes, I do. You're not only James' friend, you're my friend, too."

He looked me in the eye. "And I always will be."

"I need you to give me your word on something, Ciro."

"Anything," he replied. "You only have but to ask."

"I don't want you to keep your word to James. No matter what happens, don't ever lay a hand on him."

He smiled. "Done."

"Thank you."

Chapter 22
It's Only Getting Worse

We said goodbye to Ciro and walked to the mansion. The lights were still on. I spied James' car through the bars of the wrought iron fence. "He's home, Justin," I said. "Maybe I shouldn't go in."

Justin nodded. "Yeah, we should just go back. I don't know if I can stop you from hurting him."

I saw that the light was on in James' study, and decided Justin was right. The spell seemed to have reached a tipping point; I no longer had control over my anger when I was around James. "Come on," I said, offering him my arm. "Let's get out of here."

"Thea!"

I turned toward the sound of James' angry sounding voice. I looked toward the house but didn't see him.

Justin pulled on my arm. "Come on, let's go."

I pulled away and kept searching for James. I finally spotted him standing just left of the front door, in the shadows of the porch. My heart exploded with anger.

What was I thinking, coming back here? Why did I think anything would be different?

"The tea," I whispered to myself. In all the excitement back at the apartment, I'd forgotten about the tea leaves Katu had given me.

"Thea," Justin exclaimed, his eyes wide with shock.

He was pointing toward my hands on the iron fence. I was bending the bars without realizing what I was doing. I opened my hands and drew them toward me. The image of kicking Ciro's punching bag across the room flashed in my mind. I hadn't used a spell. My mind just knew what to do and my body followed suit.

Panic rose inside me. What if my mind wished James dead? What if I couldn't control what I was thinking? I felt my father's wand vibrate in my pocket. I pulled it out and it immediately transformed into my stick. I reached for Justin. "Hold on!"

As we flew out into the night sky, I heard James calling for me. I closed my eyes and chanted: "Fill my head with music; don't let me hear a sound. Keep the music playing until my feet have hit the ground."

James' voice faded away. I heard only a waltz in my head. Justin pounded my knee, but I didn't slow down. It was obvious he was terrified, his feet brushing the tops of the trees as we flew. I let him off in front of the apartment building and continued on up the front steps where I dismounted. The stick reverted to wand form as I hurried inside.

Once inside the boys' apartment, I knelt beside Cory and checked his pockets.

Justin followed me in. "Didn't you hear me screaming? I was falling."

"And did you fall?" I asked, pushing Cory onto his side.

"Well, no."

"Then shut up."

I searched all of Cory's pockets and came up with nothing. I stood, running my hand through my hair. "Damn! Where are they?" I waved my hand and woke him. He was startled at first but he jumped to his feet when he saw me. "What's wrong?"

"Where are the leaves I gave you?"

"In my sock, why?"

I rolled my eyes and held out my hand. Cory stumbled back as the leaves dislodged from his sock and flew into my open palm.

"What are those?" Justin asked.

I ignored his question, hurried to the kitchen, and filled a small pot with water. I didn't even bother to set it on the stove. A wave of my hand boiled the water in an instant. I dropped the leaves into the pot and waited for them to steep.

I felt Cory's hand on my shoulder. "Thea, what is it?"

I turned to face him. "Don't let me leave this house," I ordered.

"Are you okay?" Justin asked.

"Justin," Cory said. "Go get Ciro."

Justin nodded and rushed out.

I lifted the pot to my lips, drinking right out of it. I didn't care that it was burning my lips or hands; I only wanted this feeling to go away. The force pulling me back to James was like a hunger I couldn't satisfy.

I drank the tea so fast I nearly choked on the leaves. My hands trembled as I downed the last of it and threw the pot across the room. I held on to the counter as

I waited for the tea to take effect. The desire to feel James' blood on my hands was so great all I could think of was flying back to the house and tearing him apart. I looked toward the apartment door. I lacked the strength to fight off the urge to run for it.

"Stop me!" I shouted.

Cory reached for me, but I kicked him away and ran for the door. I was inches away when Ciro appeared and kicked me back. I fell to the floor and Ciro quickly threw himself over me. He grabbed my hands and held them to the floor. I was like a wild animal, screeching and wrestling to break free. My mind focused on one thing: killing James. Nothing else mattered, not even my own life.

"Kiss her!" Cory shouted.

"I can't do that!" Ciro shot back.

"Just kiss her, damn it!"

Ciro looked down, his eyes apologetic, and crushed his lips to mine. I pulled him closer when I felt myself calming. I was afraid to stop kissing him. When I finally pulled away, I burst into tears. Ciro got to his feet as I rolled over and banged on the floor. I felt so helpless. The spell was stronger than I was. I couldn't control it anymore. "It's going to happen," I cried. "I'm going to kill James."

Cory dropped to his knees at my side and gathered me in his arms. "You're not going to kill James," he said. "You can stop yourself."

"Kill me, Cory," I begged, my tears soaking his shirt. "Thrust a knife through my heart right now."

"Stop."

"The spell is on *me*, Cory." I clutched his shirt. "Simon put that spell on *me*."

Cory pulled me into his arms again. "I know, sweetie, I know."

I cried harder. "I can't stop myself. James is going to die, and his blood will be on my hands."

Cory tightened his embrace. "Not if we can help it."

Cory's phone rang. He handed me off to Ciro, stepped into the kitchen, and answered it.

"It's going to be okay," Ciro repeated, patting my back.

"Don't kill him, Ciro," I begged. "Kill me. Kill me instead."

"I'm not going to kill anyone," he replied.

Cory called from the kitchen: "Thea, will you wake up Sam?"

I nodded and waved my hand.

Sammy woke with a start and jumped to his feet. "Why are you crying?"

Before I could answer, Cory cut in. "Sam, you need to go back to the house."

"Why?" Sammy asked.

"Because I said so."

"But why is Thea crying?"

"Just go!" Cory shouted.

Sammy slipped into his suit and promptly left the apartment. Cory peeled me off the floor and we headed upstairs to my apartment.

"Who called?" I asked.

"Your father," he replied. "He wants to talk to me."

"I'm going with you."

"Uh, no," Cory said. "James is home. You're staying here."

"Is everything okay?"

Cory didn't answer my question. We walked into my apartment and he called for Justin. "I'll be back as soon as I can."

"What's going on, Cory?"

"It's nothing, sweetie," he replied. "Your father just needs to speak with me."

When Justin strode in, Cory ordered him to stay with me, waved goodbye, and headed out the door.

"Is everything okay?" Justin asked.

I quickly stepped to the window and looked out. "I have no idea."

Cory and Ciro were leaving together in a hurry. I wanted to follow, but Cory's words were still fresh in my mind. James was home. It was too dangerous. I sat on the window seat and pulled my knees to my chest.

"Do you feel any better?" Justin asked.

"I'm never going to feel better." I buried my face in my knees and shook my head.

Several hours passed, and Cory wasn't back yet. I sat by the window chewing on my lower lip. My nerves were shot. It was killing me not to know what was going on. Whatever it was, I had a bad feeling about it.

Justin snored on the couch. His brothers had come looking for him, but he'd refused to leave me here alone. I was glad for that. He kept my mind busy for a few hours at least. Adam and Ryan stuck around for an hour or so. Justin told them the truth about Simon. They seemed as shocked by the news as Justin was. Still, I didn't understand how they couldn't have known.

I walked into the kitchen to make some more tea. I had to stay awake until Cory got home. My eyes were heavy, my body numb. I hadn't slept well in days, and I was starting to feel it. I was filling the kettle with water when I heard a soft tap on the door. I left the pot in the sink and hurried to answer it.

"Cory." I threw my arms around him.

"Wow, I should leave more often," he said, wrapping his arms around me.

"I was so worried."

"Everything's fine," he assured me. "It was no big deal."

I pushed away from him. "What did my father want?

"It was nothing." He smiled weakly. "He just wanted to make sure you were okay."

I eyed him suspiciously. "You're lying. Why were you gone so long?"

He shrugged. "I had things to do."

I stepped back and examined him. There was blood on his shirt, and his clothes were filthy, as though he'd been rolling around in the dirt. His lip was bleeding.

I narrowed my eyes. "Tell me what happened, Cory," I ordered, "and do not even think about lying to me."

He lowered his head. "I got into a fight with James."

"What? But how? Why?"

He looked up and sighed. "Because I kissed his wife."

"What did James say to you?"

"We didn't talk much," he said. "His punch greeted me at the door. Guy's got a hell of a right hook." He rubbed his jaw. "Sent me flying all the way back into the driveway."

"What?"

"I tried to explain," Cory continued, "but he punched me again when I told him about the spell."

I raised an eyebrow. "You told him?"

"I had to," Cory said. "I didn't want him thinking you loved me."

I sighed and squeezed his hand. "Thank you, Cory."

"Don't thank me," he said. "It was all my fault in the first place." Cory came inside and followed me into the kitchen.

"So it was James that called you, not my father." I lifted the kettle out of the sink and filled it.

"Yeah. He said if I didn't show, he'd come here looking for me. I took Sam and Ciro with me so they could keep us from killing each other."

I placed the kettle on the stove. "I'm sorry he hit you."

"Ah, I'll be fine." He rubbed his jaw again. "I had it coming."

Ciro walked in, also covered in dirt. I wondered how long it had taken him to break up the fight.

He glanced at Cory as he quietly closed the door behind him. "I don't know if he believed you, man."

"He's just mad," Cory replied. "He'll get over it."

"Why?" I asked. "What did he tell you exactly?"

Ciro shot Cory a nervous glance.

Cory cleared his throat. "Hey, we'd all better get some rest. We have a ball to go to tomorrow."

"You're still going?" Ciro asked.

"We have to," Cory replied. "Simon is up to something."

"But James will be there."

I smiled at Ciro. "I'll be fine."

But I knew it was a lie. I didn't trust myself anymore. I hoped the tea would make me stronger, but I didn't feel any different.

"Oh?" Ciro replied. "And just how do you plan on stopping yourself from hurting James?"

I bit my lip. "Well, I can't seem to come up with anything besides kissing someone else. It seems to be the only thing that calms me down." I glanced at Cory, my face feeling suddenly warm. "Cory's kisses seem to calm me the fastest." I shrugged. "Maybe because I've known him the longest."

"And what about James?" Ciro asked. "What do we do when he goes after Cory again?"

"I'll being seeing James tomorrow," I replied. "I'll explain what happened."

"How is that even possible, Thea?" Cory asked.

I dropped some tea leaves into the bubbling water. "We found a way to see each other," I explained. "I can't tell you how, but I'll talk to him and explain everything."

"I'll tell the others to be prepared," Ciro said, turning for the door. "Just in case."

"I'm right behind you, man," Cory said.

When Ciro left, Cory asked if I was okay.

"I'll be fine, Cory. I'll see you back at the house tomorrow."

"You should stay here from now on, Thea."

"That's not necessary. I'll just stay in the guest house with you guys."

He looked skeptical for a moment and exhaled. "Okay, I'll see you back at the house then."

After Cory left, I covered Justin with a blanket and returned to the kitchen. I poured some tea into a mug, knowing full well it would keep me from getting any sleep. But I didn't care. I had to do everything I could to avoid another violent confrontation with James. He was going to the ball with Helena, meaning my temper was going to be put to the test. I took a sip and prayed for the tea to work. It was my only hope.

By the third pot, my body was buzzing with energy. I sat at the window and watched the sun come up. I couldn't get James out of my head. Simon's spell was taking me over. Time was running out. I fought with my heart, knowing that soon I would have to cast the spell. I didn't know how to say goodbye to him. Would today be the last time I held him? The last time my lips tasted his?

Justin stirred on the couch. "Are you crying again?"

"I'm not crying," I said, trying to muster a smile.

He pushed away the blanket and sat up. "Have you even been to bed?"

I shook my head. "I'm not tired."

"I'm wicked groggy," he said, getting to his feet and stretching his arms above his head. "I'm going to go shower."

"Justin, wait." I stood up from the window seat. "Will you make a call for me?"

"Sure. Who am I calling?"

"James," I said. "Just tell him to go there now."

"Go where?"

"He'll know."

He nodded and pulled his phone from his pocket. I jumped in the shower.

"He said to hurry," Justin called into the bathroom.

"Okay, thank you."

I finished my shower, dressed, and pulled out Delia's memory box. When I got to our memory, James was there, sitting under our tree, waiting. He stared out at the lake, plainly averting his gaze from our younger selves. I walked up behind him, filled with trepidation.

He didn't bother to look back at me. "You're late."

"I was taking a shower."

He pitched a rock into the water. "Then why did you say to come now?"

I bristled; he was so cold and abrupt. As I approached him, he stood. I reached up to kiss him.

He tipped his head back and away. "What did you need me for?" he asked. "I have to get back."

"I wanted to explain what happened yesterday, to tell you why I kissed Cory."

He folded his arms and looked away. "I'm listening."

He was so agitated, he couldn't even look at me. His stone-cold expression sent a chill through my spine.

"James, please," I said, reaching for his arm.

He yanked it away. "Just get it over with."

Suddenly, I was at a loss for words. I didn't know how to explain without telling him I knew about the spell. "The spell Simon put on you," I began. "I know it kills the love in both of our hearts. Every time I see you, I become enraged." I bowed my head. "Kissing someone else seems to be the only thing that calms me down, keeps me from . . ."

He glanced at me bitterly from the corner of his eye. "Is that why you kissed him again when I left?"

"What?" I asked, stepping back.

"I saw you, Thea," he said. "You were kissing him in front of your apartment building. What reason did you have then?"

I closed my eyes and drew a ragged breath. "You saw that?"

"I saw what I needed to see," he said.

Now I understood why he was so angry, why he had punched Cory. "It's not like that, James. You have to let me explain."

"I watched you, Thea!" he shouted. "I saw my wife throwing herself at another man."

"James, no! It's not what you think!"

"I always knew I would lose you to him, but I thought you'd at least have the courtesy to wait until I was dead."

Pain stabbed at my heart. "I was only trying to calm myself down. I didn't know Cory had put a spell on me."

"Do you think me a fool?"

"James, please. I love you, not him."

"Liar!" he said, seizing my shoulders. "You've always wanted him. I was just the fool who believed you loved me. You've never treated me like you treat him."

I shook my head. "That's not true."

"Go to him," he said, pushing me away. "I give you back your freedom; it's over between us."

"Please don't do this, James."

"Don't ever look for me again," he said. "I'm leaving for England as soon as I get back to the house." He started walking away. "Go, now. Be happy with your Cory."

"You have to believe me," I pleaded, following him.

"Get away from me!" he shouted. "How could you do this to us?"

"It was a spell, James. I swear it was a spell."

He started to leave again.

I grabbed his arm and tried to pull him back.

"You have to believe me!"

"Let go of me!" he said, pushing me away.

I fell back and hit my head on a rock. James stormed off and disappeared into the woods.

I got up, steadying myself against a tree, and tried to run after him. My head was spinning. "James!"

I staggered, then stumbled, collapsing to the ground. This would be the end of me. The thought of James leaving me was the ultimate blow. This should have been our last tender moment before having to cast the spell. The thought of him hating me was too painful to live with. How could I cast the spell if our final minutes together were spent like this?

That's it, I thought. *It's time to end it.* No one would get hurt if I died here. I struggled to open my eyes and attempted to wave my hand—a death spell would end it all.

James' hand stopped me mid-wave. He pulled me into his arms. "What did I do?" he said. "I'm so sorry, my love."

He kissed every inch of my face. "I was stupid, my love. I was so stupid."

"You broke my heart," I said through tears.

"I know. I'm so sorry. I was overcome with jealousy."

I tried to look up at him but I was too dizzy. "I only love you, James."

He pulled me closer, kissed my head, and held me.

I leaned my head on his chest and closed my eyes. "I'm so tired, James."

"Rest, my love, rest." He leaned against a tree and held me in his arms.

I drifted toward sleep. "Please don't leave me,

James," I uttered. "Please don't leave me."

Chapter 23
Just Tell Me If You Love Him

I opened my eyes and looked up at my husband. I wasn't sure how long I'd been asleep, but I felt rested.

James' face lit up. "Welcome back," he whispered. "How's your head?"

"Okay, I think. How long have I been asleep?"

"A few hours, my love." He kissed my head. "I chanted a healing spell while you were resting."

I wondered how his healing spell could have worked when no one else's could ever get through to me. I supposed, like with Simon's spell, the rules were different when visiting the memories inside the box.

I gazed up into my husband's shining blue eyes. "James, I'm so—"

"Shh," he said. "Let me go first." He kissed my head again. "I'm so sorry I said those things to you. I don't know what came over me. I wanted you to feel as badly as I did. I've never felt so jealous in all my life. I didn't even realize I'd hurt you until I came back."

He held me tighter. After a few moments he said, "Now I know how you feel."

I looked at him questioningly. "What do you mean?"

"When you see me with Helena," he replied. "Now I understand the pain I cause you."

I didn't answer him. I didn't want to talk about Helena.

"I've never felt my heart ache like that before," he said, stroking my hair. "I wanted to kill him, cut him to pieces, for touching you like that."

I tried to sit up. "James, it meant noth—"

His kiss cut me off. I didn't say another word. I wrapped my arms around him as he slid on top of me. Every painful word was instantly forgotten as he tore away my clothes. He held my hands above my head as his tongue traveled over my breasts. It felt like I was inside him, touching his soul with my heart.

Tears streamed from my eyes. This would be the last time. Never again would I give myself so completely to him. We gave into our passion. My trembling hands touched every part of him. I gave myself to him like never before. I allowed myself to dream for just one moment, pretended that we didn't have a care in the world.

I listened to birds as I lay naked in James' arms, my head buried in his chest. He stroked my hair as I breathed in his scent. Without warning, James started to laugh.

"What's so funny?" I asked.

He kissed my head. "Nothing, I was just thinking of something."

I giggled. "Tell me."

"It's your hair. I've been noticing how smooth

and straight it's been lately, and I just realized that when you were kissing Cory, it didn't change."

"Why is that so funny?"

He wrapped his arms around me and squeezed me tight. "Because I should have noticed that. It would have saved me—and you—a lot of pain."

"I'm so sorry you had to see that." I said, looking into his eyes. "And you're not going to like what I have to say next."

His smiled disappeared. "What?"

I took a deep breath and exhaled. "I may have to kiss him again."

James looked at me, his jaw tensing. "I see," he said. "To calm yourself?"

"And only for that, I swear."

He was quiet for a moment, then kissed my head. "I can handle it now," he said, jutting his jaw forward. "Do what you must."

"I think you should know . . ." I bit my lip. "I kissed Ciro, too."

"Well, I'd rather you kiss him than Cory."

I smiled sheepishly. "Cory's kiss calms me faster."

He chuckled. "Somehow, I knew you were going to say that."

"It means nothing to me, James," I said, sitting up. "Only your kisses can touch my heart."

He smiled. "I'm fine, my love. I think I understand things now."

"I wish I could say the same."

"What do you mean?"

"I heard you telling Helena that you loved her," I confessed, "that the only reason you became upset was because of our bond."

"You were there?"

I nodded. "Is it true?"

"I do not love that woman, Thea," he assured me. "I only said that to calm her down, so she wouldn't grow suspicious." He pulled me to him. "My heart belongs only to you."

As I gazed into his eyes, a question came into my mind. "If you had never met me, would you have fallen for her?"

"That's impossible to answer, Thea," he replied. "I *did* meet you, and nothing else matters now."

"I think she really loves you, James."

"We'll erase that when this is done."

But I needed to know. "But would you have loved her?"

He looked toward the lake. "No."

We didn't say another word about Helena, and held each other until it was time to leave. When we finally got dressed, I felt an overwhelming sadness in my heart. I knew my next words to him were going to be goodbye—forever.

"Don't forget to drink the tea," James said.

I threw my arms around him. "I love you, James."

He folded me in his arms and kissed my head. "Nothing in this world gives me more pleasure than hearing those words come out of your mouth."

I smiled and stroked his face. "Will you be home when I get there?"

"I'll shower quickly and leave, so you can come home and do what you need to do."

"What time are you arriving at the ball?" I asked, secretly hoping he'd decided not to go.

"I'm not sure," he replied. "But I'll stay away

from you."

"Thank you." I rested my head on his chest.

"Same time tomorrow?" he asked.

My heart sank. "Yes," I lied.

"Until tomorrow then."

We kissed goodbye, for the last time. I wanted to run after him, tell him how much I was going to miss him. But I knew it would only bring us both more pain. This was the smart way to end things, allowing James to leave with the hope of seeing me again, allowing our love—and not our pain—to be the last thing we shared together.

"Goodbye, James," I whispered as he disappeared into the trees.

I opened the memory box, looked one last time toward the woods, and left.

With a deep breath, I swallowed back my tears. I had a stop to make before going on to the mansion. I had to be sure I was doing the right thing.

The sun was setting as I made my way across the park and through town. When I finally arrived at the little blue house, I was relieved to find it empty. Delia would never understand why I picked Helena. Aside from her late sister and her cousin, I knew few who could tolerate Helena's cold, hostile manner. Some even considered her to be truly evil. I had certainly wondered about it myself, at times. But I sensed her love for James was real. His love could change her, just like it changed me. If there was anyone who could make Helena a better person, it was James.

I hurried up the walk and slipped into the empty house, unnoticed. I found her room and waited in the shadows. She would need to start getting ready for the ball soon. It was only a matter of waiting.

Several minutes passed. I heard the front door open and shut. Helena stepped into her room, holding her costume for the ball—a fairy costume. She set the wings gently on the bed, removed the dress from its plastic cover, and held it up to herself in the mirror. "You think he's going to like this?" she called.

"What does it matter?" Pam answered from somewhere in the house.

"Why can't you just be happy for me?" Helena asked, throwing the dress on the bed. "He loves me. He's going to leave her."

"He's a bonded man, Helena," Pam replied. "He can never leave her."

"We'll see about that," Helena shouted, retrieving the dress. She kicked the bedroom door shut and turned, admiring herself in the mirror again.

I stepped out from behind the closet door.

When she spied me behind her in the mirror, the blood drained from her face, and she broke for the door.

"Don't."

She halted and turned, a look of terror in her eyes. I could see her trembling as I approached.

"I'm not here to hurt you, Helena."

She dropped the dress and backed toward the wall. "What do you want?"

"I need to ask you something," I said, drawing near.

"I don't call him anymore, I swear."

I stepped closer. "Do you love him?"

She looked confused, unsure of how to respond. She shook her head. "I . . . no, I don't love him."

"This is no time for lies, Helena. I need to know the truth. I need to know if you truly love James."

"Why?" she asked, her voice cracking. "So you

~ 282 ~

can kill me?"

"No, so I can leave him."

Her eyes met mine. "What?"

"I'm going to leave him, Helena. But I need to know if you love him."

"You're lying," she said. "You want me out of his life."

"Helena, if it were that simple, I could have done away with you long ago."

She considered my words for a moment. "What do you want from me?"

"I want you to marry him," I replied, though it tore at my heart to say the words out loud. "But only if you truly love him."

Her trembling subsided, her expression smug. "Why, because you know you're losing him to me?"

I fought the urge to wave my hand. "Just answer the question, Helena. Do you love him?"

"You're trying to trick me," she said. "Why would you give him up just like that?"

My anger flared. She was seriously trying my patience. I stepped closer, my face inches from hers. "I'm trying to help you, you stupid witch."

"Why?" she asked. "I know you can't stand me. So why would you help me?"

"Fine, Helena. I'll just have to find someone else to marry my husband." I turned and started for the door.

"Wait," she said, clutching my arm. "You're really going to leave him?"

I yanked away from her bony grip. "Yes."

"Why?"

I studied her closely. She really was beautiful—at least on the outside. Tall, thin, long blond hair, green eyes.

"It's none of your business," I replied.

She jutted out her chin. "Does he know?"

"No," I said. "And you'd better not tell him."

"So you're really going to do it?"

"Damn it, Helena! Just answer the question."

Her eyes looked suddenly glassy. "I do. I love him with all my heart." She was telling me the truth.

"Good. Then I'll expect you to do everything in your power to be a good wife, and make him happy."

"What about you?" she asked. "How do I know you're not going to change your mind? What if you come looking for him again?"

"Even if I did, he wouldn't remember me."

Her eyes widened. "You're not going to . . ."

I started for the door.

"Wait," she said. "What about the bond? What kind of a husband is James going to be if he's bonded to you?"

"If he can't remember who I am, the bond is broken. He'll be free to bond with you."

Her eyes narrowed. "And you won't come looking for him?"

"I told you, he won't remember me."

That seemed to make her happy. "Why me, witch?" she asked.

"Because despite the fact that I despise you, you truly love James, and his happiness is important to me."

A smile tugged at the corner of her mouth. "And he won't ever remember you—ever?"

She was feeding on my misery. I didn't know how much more I could take. "It will be like I was never born." I could tell she was already imagining herself in James' bed. Bile rose in my throat.

"When can I bond with him?"

"I'm only going to erase myself from his life, Helena. I'm not going to put him in bed with you. You'll have to do that yourself."

She smiled wickedly. "Oh, don't worry. I will."

"I'm sure you've already tried many times, witch."

"I would invite you to our wedding," she said, flipping her hair. "But I don't think I want you there."

I'd had enough. I crossed the room and held my hand to her throat. "If you don't make him happy, I'll cut your heart out." The smile fell from her face.

I shoved her against the wall. "If I ever find out that you've hurt him, you'll have to hide from me forever."

"I won't hurt him," she said, "as long as you keep your word."

"Don't worry, witch. After today, you'll never have to worry about me again." I slammed her hard against the wall and let go.

I couldn't get out of there fast enough. I was breathless by the time I reached the front door. I wanted to wipe that smug look off her face. If I hadn't been so sure she loved James, I would have chosen someone else.

I made my way down the walk and took off running. My heart pounded in my chest as an image of James and Helena in bed together appeared in my mind. She was probably already making arrangements for the wedding. She would surely insist on a human wedding. Helena was all about material things and money. She lived for power and luxury, and James was her ticket.

James never flaunted his money, but he had plenty of it. He could give Helena the life she always dreamed of; buy her the things the rest of us couldn't care less about. Even warlocks had no use for money; all they wanted was power. In our world, power was like gold: the more you had, the more feared you were. It was the one thing that could keep you alive, the one thing money could never buy.

I knew spells to make money, but I refused to use them or teach them to anyone—another reason Helena hated me. Helena didn't like work, always wanted everything handed to her. But that kind of life never appealed to me. Most witches were humble. We didn't need money to be happy.

I was walking back through town when I noticed Donna's shop still open. She and her sister Kym owned a small place where they told fortunes and sold trinkets. The sisters had a knack for guessing the future, which kept the little shop busy. Delia refused to believe they could actually see the future, but I knew that some witches were born with the gift.

I walked into the shop, still swarming with tourists despite the late hour of the day. I spied Donna in the back room with a customer, her crystal ball between them. Donna was tall and blond with striking green eyes. Although her healing spells were the best around, of course they didn't work on me. Many came to her for help. Her sister Kym was a good six inches shorter, with dark, curly hair. She had a quick temper and penetrating black eyes. Kym adored cats, and cats apparently adored her. I rarely saw her without one, and once spotted her walking away from the shop with no fewer than four of the little critters following close on her heels.

"Mistress," Kym greeted.

"Hello, Kym," I replied. "How are you?"

"Fine. And what can I help you with this evening?"

I glanced around the shop: baskets of dried leaves, small bottles filled with different types of oils. I realized I hadn't seen the sisters since the battle. They had jumped in to fight alongside Sharron and Helena.

"Actually, I'm here about a council meeting," I replied.

"I wasn't aware there was one scheduled."

"There isn't, wasn't . . . I need to speak to everyone."

Kym gave me a short nod. "I'll spread the word, mistress."

"Please," I said. "You have to stop calling me that."

She nodded again. "As you wish. Please excuse me for a moment while I let my sister know you're here."

Moments later, Donna emerged from the back room, grinning. "Thea, what brings you into our little shop?"

"A council meeting. I have something to tell everyone."

She looked concerned. "Is everything okay?"

"No," I said, trying to muster a smile. "But it will be."

She looked into my eyes. "Did you know my son John was back?" she asked.

"I did, I saw him at Amanda's burial."

"I heard Pam is in town, as well," she said.

"Whatever it is, just ask me," I snapped. I felt bad for being so abrupt, but she was clearly getting at something. After my confrontation with Helena, I was in no mood to play games.

Her face flushed. She looked down for a moment, then back at me. "Well, now that Amanda is no longer with us, there's an empty seat on the council.."

"And you want to know who will fill that seat, yes?" It was a valid question. I softened my tone. "I'll go over that when we meet."

"Of course. And when and where will that be?"

"Immediately following the ball, at my apartment."

Kym stepped up behind Donna. "Your apartment? But James' house is so much bigger. Why not there?"

I stared at her, saying nothing.

"Is everything okay?" she asked.

"We'll talk at the meeting."

"As you wish, Thea."

Chapter 24
The Halloween Ball

By the time I got back to the mansion, James was gone.

Delia and the boys were waiting for me in the foyer. "Where have you been?" Delia asked.

"We'll be late for the ball," Javier added.

"Wow," I said. "You guys look great."

Delia was dressed as a dead bride, her makeup dark around her eyes. Delia even made dead look beautiful. She wore a fitted black wedding dress that hugged every curve of her body. Javier's costume fit him to a tee: Rudolph Valentino, the actor whose name was synonymous with the romantic era of Hollywood. Joshua's Conan the Barbarian costume surprised me. I would have thought he'd have chosen to be a hunter, or something of that sort.

"Where's Sammy?"

Giggles broke out among the group.

"The invisible man, at your service," Sammy announced. His voice came from just outside of James' office.

I was laughing along with the others when Cory emerged from the kitchen. My jaw dropped. He was dressed in army fatigues. His muscles filling out every part of the uniform. I couldn't get over how handsome he looked. His ridiculously long eyelashes were practically the only things I could see under his cap.

"Well, look at you," I said, suddenly aware of my heart racing.

"Where's your costume?" Cory asked.

I looked down at myself, embarrassed. "I . . . I sort of forgot to buy one."

Delia smirked. "No you didn't. There's one on your bed."

I looked at her, eyebrow arched. "Oh? And what am I going as?"

She smiled mischievously. "A witch," she said, shrugging. "What else?"

"I should have known." I scanned the room. "Where's Fish?"

"I'm up here," he sang.

All eyes were drawn to the top of the stairs.

"Why did you change your costume?" Delia asked.

He descended the steps, a toothy grin spread across his face. He was wearing a black tuxedo, his eyes blood red, bruises and scars all over his face. His hair was combed back and neat.

"And here comes the dead groom," I proclaimed.

Delia couldn't pull her eyes away from him. He looked handsome despite the gruesome makeup. "Why did you change your costume?" she asked again.

At the bottom of the stairs, Fish reached for Delia's hand. "What kind of bride would you be without a groom?" He got down on one knee and reached into his pocket, pulling out a ring.

Delia slapped her hand to her mouth. "What are you doing?"

He looked up at her. "I know I joke a lot, but the one thing I've never joked about is the way I feel about you. My heart comes alive when I'm around you. I'm only complete when I'm with you. I dream of sharing a life with you, of waking up every single day for the rest of my life with you in my arms. I've waited four hundred years to ask you this, Delia. Will you marry me and make me the happiest man alive?"

Delia stood, frozen, her hand still clasped to her mouth. Tears spilled over and streamed down her cheeks. "Are you sure about this?"

"I've never been more sure of anything in my life."

She looked at the ring and into Fish's eyes. "Yes."

Fish jumped to his feet and pulled Delia into his arms. The rest of us looked on, applauding, as they kissed. Fish slipped the ring onto Delia's finger and lifted her off her feet.

"Congratulations to you both," My father said, walking down the stairs.

I was shocked at his appearance. His gray hair had returned. He looked tired and weak.

Fish set Delia down and shook my father's hand. "Thank you, sir," he said, beaming.

The boys crowded around Fish, shaking his hand and patting his back.

I hugged Delia. "I'm so happy for you, old friend."

"Thank you, Thea," she said, sniffling. "Can you believe he did that?"

I looked at Fish and smiled. "Yes, I can."

I hugged her again and walked over to Fish. "About time," I said, wrapping my arms around him.

"She said yes, Thea. She said yes!"

"Who could say no to that face?" I asked, touching his cheek.

"Thank God is wasn't her."

I smiled and gave him another hug. "You'll make her happy, Fish."

"I'll die trying, Thea."

I kissed his cheek.

I left everyone celebrating, walked into the kitchen, and sat.

My father was already pouring tea. "They will have a happy life," he said, setting the cup in front of me.

"Father, what's going on with you?"

He pointed to the cup. "Drink."

I picked it up and took a sip. "You've been using your magic again, haven't you?"

He didn't answer. "Thea, I want you to know that I tried," he said, his eyes cast to the floor. "I did everything I could to change things." He looked up at me. "I'm truly sorry."

I set down my cup. "Why are you saying this to me?"

He sighed. "Because some things cannot be changed."

"Father, you're scaring me."

He reached over and touched my face. "Don't you know by now, that nothing has the power to truly scare you?"

"Then why am I shaking?"

"Never forget who you are, Thea. Remember, no spell can control your heart. Only you have power over it." He pecked my cheek and walked out. I picked up the cup and finished my tea.

When I walked out of the kitchen, Delia was showing off her ring. "It's perfect," she gushed.

I reached for her hand. "Let me see."

"He really knows me, Thea."

It was a simple silver ring with hearts engraved around the band. "You're right, it is perfect."

"I can have a diamond put on it if you want," Fish said.

"Don't you dare," Delia snapped. "This ring stays as is."

I started up the stairs as they kissed, so I could check out the costume Delia had gotten for me. I walked into my room and lifted the dress off the bed. "Oh, Delia," I muttered, knowing instantly I could never wear it. It was way too revealing. There was barely anything to it. I tossed it back on the bed and hopped into the shower, feeling no motivation to dress up at all.

What kind of costume would a half wizard, half witch wear anyway? As I rinsed off, an idea hit me. I was still getting ready when Delia walked in. I snatched the hooded cape from the back of a chair as Delia closed the door behind her.

"You're not wearing the costume I got for you?" she asked.

"You mean the threads you got me?"

She rolled her eyes. "Okay then, what are you supposed to be?"

I spun in a circle, my arms stretched out. "Isn't it obvious?" I asked. "I'm a wizard."

She sniffed. "It's a black pantsuit and cape, Thea.

Not sure how you get wizard from that."

I smiled and waved my hand down the length of my body.

Delia's mouth dropped. "Now we're talking," she exclaimed.

"So, how do I look?"

Delia gestured toward the mirror. "Check it out for yourself."

I stepped in front of the mirror, pleased with my work. Twinkling stars encircled my eyes. Crescent moons adorned my neatly combed hair. Painted on my purple velvet cape was a sparkling black dragon with yellow eyes and gold talons.

"Those aren't, like, real stars and moons, right?" Delia asked.

"I'll put 'em back when I'm done," I teased.

We headed downstairs and met the boys in the foyer.

Sammy's voice came from next to the front door. "Very cool, Thea."

"Wish I could say the same for you."

"What?" Sammy said, pretending to be offended. "I'm going to be the coolest one there."

Cory opened the front door. "No one's even going to *know* you're there, pal."

We walked into town, the streets too crowded for us to bother taking the car. Hundreds of tourists in costume flooded the town square. I couldn't walk an inch without bumping into someone. Even Salem's mayor and his wife were in costume, making the rounds and greeting the people.

"Nice turnout," Fish said, nodding and looking around.

I spotted several warlocks walking into the hall. I

could smell them from thirty feet away. I leaned toward Cory. "Simon's men."

"Yeah, I see them."

"Simon's already inside," I added. "I can feel him."

Cory grasped my hand. "We'd better get in there."

Salem buzzed with the usual excitement of the holiday, the smell of kettle corn and caramel apples wafting through the air. The haunted house across the street from the hall had a line of people around the building. There were the usual booths of services and wares, even a man selling lighted witch hats. The music from the nearby carnival pulsated through the streets.

The line to get into the ball was typically long and slow going. It seemed like every human under the sun was there. There were limousines parked outside the adjacent hotel, filled with out-of-towners, all in full costume.

"We should have gotten a room at the hotel," Delia said. "It would have been fun."

"Tried to," Fish replied, placing his hand on the small of her back. "They were booked."

Delia shrugged and smiled up at him.

"This is going to take forever," Joshua whined.

We trudged along slowly until we made it into the lobby and, eventually, the main hall. The place looked magnificent. Chandeliers with real burning candles hung from the ceiling. Red velvet curtains framed the giant, floor-to-ceiling windows. Hand-crafted spiders and goblins were hung about. Colored lights flashed through the room, making it look like real ghosts walked among us.

While looking for a place at the bar, we passed a

group of women who couldn't take their eyes off the boys. They whispered to each other as Cory and Fish strode by, and giggled when Javier winked at them. Delia eyed the women cattily and drew Fish in for a kiss.

Javier smiled at us. "If you'll excuse me, friends," he said, "I've got some business to attend to." He strolled into their little group. "Hello, ladies. Might I say you all look beautiful tonight?" He leaned on the bar and flashed his famous Javier smile—wide and full of bright white teeth.

Delia rolled her eyes and turned to Fish. "Come on, future husband. Let's cut a rug."

Fish nodded. "Your wish is my command, dear lady."

I laughed. "Oh, you're going to make a perfect husband with that attitude, Fish."

Delia grinned at me as they sashayed toward the dance floor.

I stayed behind and watched Javier at work.

"So, which one of you stunning beauties will be dancing with me tonight?" he asked, flashing each of the women his winning smile.

I clapped my hand to my mouth and stifled a chuckle.

"I'll go find us a table," Cory said.

All female eyes were on Cory as he strode through the room in search of a table. Of course, Cory didn't seem to notice. It was surprising to me that, with the exception of Fish, the boys remained eternally single. It certainly wasn't for lack of options.

I thought of James, who certainly turned more than his share of heads. He had a commanding presence—tall, confident, and handsome. A girl couldn't help but be mesmerized by him.

"Thea, you're here."

Startled from my daydream, I turned my head to see Kym standing beside me. Her costume was particularly dynamic—and fitting. She was dressed as a black cat. It looked so real, I almost thought she'd turned herself into one. She was covered in fur from head to toe. I had an impulse to scratch her ears.

"You look amazing, Kym."

"Meow," she answered, winking.

"Can I get you a saucer of milk?" Sammy asked.

As Kym searched in vain for the source of the voice, Donna appeared with a glass of red wine in her hand. Her face was painted green, and she donned a tall black witch hat on her head. I couldn't help but smile at her costume choice.

She hugged me. "What a creative costume," she said, pulling away.

"Thanks," I said. "Do you happen to know if everyone from the council is here?"

She nodded. "I think so. Nobody misses the ball if they can help it, right? It's the only time of year we're free to be ourselves."

We scanned the ballroom together.

"Pam and Sharron are here somewhere," Donna said.

"Did they bring Meaghan?" I asked.

"Yep," she replied, pointing. "She's right there, sitting by the stage."

Joshua's face lit up at the mention of Meaghan's name. He excused himself and headed off in the direction of the stage.

I still felt badly about snapping at Donna back at the shop. I pulled the sisters aside and discreetly shared with them my plans. I knew they would give Helena a hard time otherwise. Donna wasn't thrilled by my choice, but understood my reasons. Although she didn't like it, she agreed to honor my decision and leave Helena and James alone.

"Who'll take Amanda's place?" she asked.

"I'll cover that at the council meeting."

"Sounds good. I'll see you then." Kym and Donna left to joined Pam and Meaghan.

I spotted Ciro and the Santos brothers on the opposite side of the ballroom and waved them over. Fish wasted no time in telling them the good news. Cheers erupted as Fish embraced his future wife and Delia showed off her ring.

"Have you set a date yet?" Ciro asked.

Fish looked at Delia. "How's tomorrow sound?"

She rolled her eyes and chuckled. "Maybe the next full moon," she said to Ciro.

"So you'll be having a witch wedding?" Ciro asked.

"Yes. Human weddings don't interest me," Delia replied.

"Good choice," Ciro said. "The old ways are the best."

Justin was shaking Fish's hand when Cory came back.

"I found a table," Cory announced, grabbing my hand, "but we have to hurry."

We circled the table and claimed our places. Cory sat next to me and put his arm around the back of my chair. I felt a little uneasy as I scanned the room for James. I prayed we could avoid a fight tonight.

"Would you get me something to drink?" I asked Cory.

"Sure," he replied, standing. "What can I get you?"

"Just some water."

"Well, I'm springing for a bottle of champagne," Fish announced, removing some bills from his tux pocket.

"Put your money away, buddy," Cory said. "It's on me."

Fish slipped the bills back into his jacket and smiled. "Thanks, Cory."

After Cory left, I continued my search for James. I spotted Helena's wings by the bar and quickly looked away after glimpsing James beside her. I noted that he wasn't wearing a costume.

"Want to dance?" Fish asked Delia.

"Again?"

"Come on," he said, holding out his hand. "It's a slow one."

She smiled and took his hand. They were making their way to the dance floor when James stopped them to say hello. Fish presented Delia's left hand. James grabbed Fish's shoulders and said something to him. Fish nodded and smiled. James embraced Fish, and then Delia, who whispered something in his ear. James glanced toward our table and promptly walked off in the direction of the lobby.

Helena caught up to him and tried to pull him back, but James walked out of the ballroom. "I wanted to dance!" she called to him. She turned and flashed me a spiteful look and followed James out.

I closed my eyes to cast the spell, but Cory returned and interrupted me. "Did you want to dance?" he asked, setting a cup of water in front of me.

"Not now," I replied. "Maybe later."

"Dance with me," Sammy said.

I laughed. "Yeah, right, so people can think I'm crazy?"

"Oh, come on," he said. "It'll look cool."

"Later, I promise."

"A slow dance," he said.

I looked in his direction and shook my head. "Fine."

Cory sat next to me and again rested his arm on the back of my chair. I thought of asking him to pull it away, but realized he did this all the time. Since we were kids, we had always been physically affectionate with each other—sitting close, holding hands. I'd never given it a second thought, until now.

I decided to let it go and watched as Fish and Delia danced into the next song, seemingly unaware of anyone else in the room. Javier danced with one of the women he'd met earlier. She was practically melting in his arms. I spotted Joshua dancing with Meaghan. He looked flushed as he smiled at me over her shoulder. I smiled back and gave him a thumbs-up.

There was lightness in my heart for the first time in days. Even seeing James didn't bother me. My heart still ached for what I had to do, but I decided to enjoy this moment, watching my friends be happy. Even with everything going on, I counted myself lucky to have such dear friends. I smiled at Cory and looked back toward the dance floor.

The song ended and several couples walked off. My stomach lurched when I spotted him through the gap in the crowd.

Simon.

I swallowed hard. When he knew he'd caught my eye, a sinister smile spread across his face.

Cory snapped his fingers in front of me. "Earth to Thea," he said playfully.

But I couldn't respond. I sat, frozen, transfixed on the man who had caused me nothing but misery.

Cory caught on. "Where is he?"

"Sitting right across from us," I replied, never taking my eyes off Simon.

Cory stood, nearly knocking his chair over backward. "I'll get the others."

I kept my gaze on Simon, his dark eyes penetrating my soul. He sat alone at a table, wearing a dark suit, his black hair combed back off his face. I couldn't get over how much he looked like James. He was handsome—at least on the outside—and seemingly too young to have a son James' age. Simon oozed confidence. I grew more and more annoyed at how relaxed he seemed, how decidedly unworried he was.

He crossed his legs and picked up his drink, tilting his glass toward me. How I longed to wipe that smug expression from his face.

Warlocks occupied the neighboring tables— Simon's army, men gullible enough to fall for his lies and protect him despite his empty promises. His minions leaned in toward their fearless leader any time I moved so much as an inch. But Simon sat, unmoving, clearly enjoying this moment.

When I looked into his eyes, a peculiar feeling washed over me. I felt the sudden need to touch him, feel him close to me. I looked away, disgusted with myself, but I couldn't quell the desire to be near him.

"The spell," I muttered.

At that moment, Simon's plan for the evening revealed itself to me. He wasn't there to cause mayhem; he'd come to see if his spell was working. It all made sense now. This was a test. He wanted to see how far his spell had gotten.

His dark eyes followed my every move.

When James returned from the lobby, Simon looked at him and back at me. He was clearly hoping to witness a confrontation, but he'd be sorely disappointed. James had promised to stay away from me tonight.

"I'm pretty sure it's a trap," Cory said, slipping back in beside me.

"No," I replied, staring into Simon's eyes. "It's a test."

Simon sat calmly watching me. He leaned back and took another sip of his drink.

"What's he expecting you to do?" Cory asked.

I stood and removed my cape. "Maybe I should go find out."

"I'll have Sam follow you," Cory said. "He'll let us know if you need backup."

"I'm all over it," Sammy answered.

I felt something inside me change every time our eyes met. My mind raced with thoughts I couldn't understand. My heart knew the man sitting across from me was evil, that poison ran through his veins. But I pushed my anger aside. Simon was expecting something else. I wasn't sure what, but I was going to find out.

I placed my hand on Cory's arm. "Whatever you do, don't jump the gun."

I kept my eyes on Simon as I crossed the room, slowly making my way between the couples on the dance floor. The warlocks stood when they saw me coming.

Simon remained seated. He raised his hand to his minions as I drew nearer. "At ease, my brothers. Let us watch and see what happens."

The closer I got, the faster my heart raced. An involuntary smile appeared on my face when I looked into his eyes. The desire to touch him was nearly overwhelming—almost a protective impulse, to see if he was okay. It bothered me that the warlocks stood so close to him. I wanted to rip their throats out to protect Simon.

I tried to make sense of my conflicting feelings. I knew what I knew about Simon, but I wanted to be with him all the same. It was as if he was taking my pain away. My heart knew better, but my mind was in control, and it felt nothing but love. In a matter of minutes, Simon became the most important thing in my life. I would gladly die for him. I tried to fight the feelings, but that only made me want him more.

I shot the warlocks a dirty look when I arrived at Simon's table. "Get away from him," I ordered.

"You heard the lady," he said, getting to his feet.

I kept my eyes on the warlocks as they backed away, but Simon wouldn't take his eyes off of me. He seemed pleased with himself, practically beaming with delight.

I felt happy to be pleasing him. I looked away from the warlocks and into Simon's eyes.

"Care to dance with me, my lord?"

He looked over my shoulder toward Cory and the others.

"Don't worry," I said. "They're not going to hurt you."

He looked into my eyes. "No, I don't believe they are." He extended his elbow. "Shall we?"

The warlocks stepped toward me as I threaded my arm through Simon's. Simon raised his hand. "Stay back, you fools!"

His brainwashed slaves backed away.

"You'll have to forgive them," he said. "You make them very nervous."

I feigned ignorance. "I can't imagine why."

He threw back his head and laughed, and led me to the dance floor. I felt like an erupting volcano. I hated that I wanted to throw myself into his arms, but couldn't seem to suppress the feeling. The argument between my head and my heart intensified. I reminded myself that it was only a spell, but it didn't help. All I could do was gaze into his dark eyes as he wrapped his arm around my waist and drew me close.

I spied the look of shock on Delia's face as we sidled up next to her and Fish on the dance floor. Simon nodded and smiled. Understandably horrified, Delia grabbed Fish's hand and dragged him back to the table. Her arms waved madly as she talked to Cory, glancing intermittently toward the dance floor.

"It seems I make your friends nervous, as well," Simon said.

I looked toward my friends. "Maybe it's time we both make new friends."

My words clearly pleased him. "Perhaps you and I could be friends."

"I thought we already were, my lord."

He smiled and pulled me closer, his lips inches from mine. My heart thumped wildly in my chest.

"I have always been very fond of you, witch."

"Fond is such a cold word, my lord," I replied coyly. "I thought we were closer than that."

He hung on my every word. He ran his fingers along the back of my hand and pulled me to him. I was beyond happy, nearly in ecstasy, as our bodies became closer. I only wanted to please him more.

"We do have a lot of history, you and I," he said. "I've seen you flower into a beautiful woman right before my eyes."

"And are you pleased with what you see now?"

"All other witches are beneath me," he replied. "But I have always felt that you and I were perfectly suited to one another."

"Let's not talk about the past," I said. "None of that matters anymore."

"So all is forgiven?" he asked.

I pressed myself against him. "All is forgiven, my lord."

He smiled and placed his cheek next to mine. We danced into the next song—another slow one. I felt his heart racing. I was mad with desire for him. I had all but given up trying to stop it. I wanted to be alone with him, give him anything he wanted from me.

"I must see you again, Thea."

Happiness filled my world when I heard him speak my name. He wanted to see me again, just as much as I wanted to see him. I would go to the ends of the earth for him, say and do anything he desired. I trembled when I felt his lips near my cheek.

"You should come to me," he whispered.

"I thought I just did," I replied, leaning my head back.

I felt his lips on my neck. I wanted him to take me here and now. For a moment, I thought about fighting the spell. But when he looked into my eyes again, I lost all control of who I was.

"Do you know what would please me right now?" he asked.

"What is it, my lord?"

"If you shared all of your secrets with me."

"I'll share anything you wish me to."

"Anything?"

"You only have but to ask, my lord."

He looked down at my lips, and slowly pressed his to mine. I heard Delia gasp as Simon slid his tongue into my mouth and kissed me passionately.

I grabbed his face when he pulled away. "No, kiss me again."

He couldn't kiss me fast enough. I crushed my lips to his. I wanted to feel him inside my mouth, taste him. I ran my fingers through his hair. "Take me," I pleaded. "Please take me."

"Will you tell me all your secrets?" he asked, kissing my neck.

"Yes."

"What are you hiding in the crystal?"

Before I could answer, Simon was ripped from my grasp.

James threw him across the dance floor. "Stay away from my wife!" he said, pulling out his whip.

Simon landed on his back and slid several more feet before stopping. "Kill him!" he shouted.

All at once, the warlocks charged James.

I spun to face James but Sammy, out of nowhere, tackled me to the floor. Ciro leaped over us and swung his machete at the warlocks. Cory flicked out his blades and joined the fight. Fish's hooks flew through the air as Javier and the Santos brothers engaged. Simon scrambled to his feet. James swung his whip and tried to cut him in two.

Panic rose inside me at the thought of Simon getting hurt. "No!" I pushed Sammy aside and waved my hand at James, sending him flying toward the stage.

I jumped to my feet and ran to shield Simon with my body, facing my friends with Simon safely behind me.

I could see the witches trying to help Cory and the others. The humans were screaming and running for the doors.

"Cut out James' heart!" Simon ordered.

I looked at Ciro, held out my hand, and his machete flew into it. I ran to James and swung. I missed Cory's head by inches when he tackled me to the floor.

"No, Thea!" Cory yelled, as the machete flew from my grasp and slid across the dance floor. I searched my pockets for my father's wand.

Cory seized my hands and slammed them onto the floor above my head. "I won't let you do this!" he shouted. He tried kissing me, but I wished him off of me and he crashed into the bar.

James ran at Simon again. I jumped in front of Simon and kicked James away. Three warlocks attacked James as I turned to fight off the Santos brothers.

"Kill them!" Simon shouted.

Ryan tried to jump over me, but a knife thrust through his heart and he turned to dust.

"No!" Adam shouted. He ran to kill the warlock that threw the knife, only to have a sword slice through his chest. As Adam's body disintegrated, I realized I'd never told Justin about the faulty aging potion. I wanted to warn him, but my instinct to save Simon was stronger.

The sound of weapons clanging and clashing filled the hall as I scanned the mayhem for James. I spotted him fighting two warlocks over by the stage. I smiled and charged him but quickly changed direction. Simon's heart was calling out to me. The warlocks cleared a path, fighting off anyone who got in my way. I heard the back door open and turned to see Simon running out.

"Take me with you!" I shouted, and took off running.

Joshua knocked me down and tackled me to the ground.

"Simon!" I screamed. "Take me with you!"

He glanced at me one last time before ducking out of the ballroom. How could he leave me? I thought he wanted me. I thought he loved me.

Powder blew into my face, and Donna chanted.

"Use the spell I taught you!" Sharron shouted.

I tried with all my strength to pull away from Joshua and the others. I finally got to my feet and struggled from their grip. "No! Let me go to him!" I screamed.

"No, Thea!" Joshua said, wrapping his arms around me.

I fought the urge to kill the boys. "Simon!"

When James dared to come near me, he grabbed my face and looked into my eyes. "It's the spell, Thea," he said, shaking me. "You don't really love him, it's the spell!"

"No, let me go to him!"

"Remember who you are!"

"Simon!" I screamed. I waved my hand at James.

He slammed into a wall. Cory and the others were busy fighting off the remaining warlocks. I waved my hand and sent them all into the wall. I opened my palm and Ciro's machete flew into it again. I was prepared to kill them all for chasing Simon away, but James would be the first. It was his fault Simon had left, and now he was going to pay.

Screams of panic filled the ballroom, but the only thing I could see was James. I would torture him, and cut out his heart. I wanted to hold his still-beating heart in my hand. Excitement flowed through me at the thought. I knew how much it would please Simon. Yes, I would cut out James' heart and take it to Simon.

I smiled and walked toward James as he slowly rose from the floor of the ballroom. The others shouted from the wall for me to stop. James didn't try to run. His eyes were dark as night as he glared into mine. He was still holding his whip, smiling, as the spell took him over.

I could hear Helena screaming from somewhere behind us, begging James to run. He ignored her and kept his eyes on me, motioning with his hand for me to come closer. I couldn't take my eyes off his chest—his heart. It was like a precious jewel I had to have. I waved my hand and glued James to the wall. I waved it again and tore his whip from his hand. I could hear the others screaming but it was too late, I was already standing in front of James.

I slid the machete under his shirt and cut it open. James was gasping, trying to fight off the spell. He closed his eyes and yelled at himself to snap out of it. I raised the machete and thrust it toward him as hard as I could. I was stunned when the blade bent to one side. I waved my hand, straightened it, and struck him again. The blade shattered in my hand.

"It's because I still love you, Thea," James said.

I looked into his eyes and stepped back. I'd never seen them so blue.

"Come back to me," he pleaded.

I took another step back. The room spun.

~ 309 ~

"I love you, Thea," James repeated. "Come back to me."

I dropped the machete handle and stared into his piercing blue eyes. They were calling out to me. He had fought the spell and won. But I was still fighting.

"I trust you, my love," he said. "I will always trust you."

I slowly gazed around the room.

"Snap out of it, Thea!" Delia screamed.

We were the only ones left in the ballroom. I heard sirens and commotion just outside the front doors. Several warlocks hung near Cory and Ciro. In my fury, I had slammed everyone to the wall in mid-fight. I started to remember why we were here. Simon's image flashed in my mind. I drew my hand to my mouth.

"Put everyone down," James said.

I looked back into his eyes—still blue. "What have I done?" I asked, stumbling back.

"It was the spell, Thea," James explained. "Don't blame yourself."

I looked down at my hands. How could I have been so close to killing James? I had actually tried to cut out his heart. "Please forgive me," I begged.

I could feel the spell making me want to hurt him again. I backed up, slipped on something wet, and fell to the floor. I raised my hands to my face and gasped. They were covered in blood. I couldn't see anyone but, all around me, blood flooded the floor.

I looked back at the others. Sammy wasn't among them. I looked back down and waved my hand. My body went cold. I saw him, Sammy lying face down in a pool of his blood, a dagger in his back.

"No!" Delia screamed.

"Samuel!" Cory shouted.

I reached for him, hastily placed my hands on his back, and tried to heal him. "Please, Sammy," I cried. "Wake up!" He didn't move. I couldn't feel him breathing.

"Put us down, witch!" Delia shouted.

"Thea," James shouted. "Release us!"

When I looked into James' eyes again, the spell resurfaced. I had to get out of there. I waved my hand and released everyone from the wall. The warlocks gathered and ran for the door. I jumped to my feet and tried to run out, but the spell was compelling me to turn around.

"This way!" Justin said, pulling on my arm.

We headed for the back door.

I glanced at Sammy one last time before rushing out. "Heal!" I shouted as Justin pushed me out into the night.

Chapter 25
And Then There Were Four

Sirens echoed in the streets. Red and blue lights flashed everywhere. The sound of screaming humans blazed through my head. Simon had vanished, leaving devastation and panic in his wake.

Justin searched the area frantically as he pulled me behind him. "We have to get out of here!" he shouted.

I tried to run back in. "Sammy, I have to make sure he's okay."

"James is in there," Justin said, yanking me back. "We have to get out of here."

A spell hit Justin in the back of the head, and he dropped to the ground.

Four warlocks appeared from around the corner of the building and approached me. "Come with us," one of them said. "We'll take you to Simon."

I looked at the warlock's hand, took a step back, and shook my head. A warlock came from behind me and threw a rope around my neck. I couldn't move, couldn't even wave my hand.

The leaves, from the forest in Magia—the warlocks had infused the rope with the leaves, on Simon's order, no doubt. But I didn't feel drained like I had in my father's world. Here, the leaves only froze me, weakened my powers. I pulled at the ropes, but two of the warlocks swiftly wrapped more rope around my feet.

"Call Simon," one of them said. "Tell him we've got her."

I heard a commotion in front of the building and prayed for Cory to find me.

"Let me see your hands!" came a voice, seemingly out of nowhere.

The warlocks stood back and put their hands in the air. They were not immune to bullets.

"Forty-eight, code three," the officer said into his radio. He pointed his gun at the warlocks. "All of you, on the ground. Now!"

It was the officer that stopped me the other day, the one who seemed so familiar. "Spit into your hand," I said. "Throw a spell at them!"

He tilted his head. "It's you."

The warlocks moved in on him.

I yanked at the ropes. "Locate your anger and spit into your hand!"

One of the warlocks smiled. "She means like this," he said. He threw a spell at the officer, knocking him down.

The officer stood and fired his gun. "Shots fired! Shots fired!" he said into his radio. He dodged spells as the warlocks continued their siege. His vest was protecting him. I tried with all my might to pull the ropes away. He fired several more shots from his gun.

Justin shook off the spell that had knocked him down, and staggered to his feet.

"Get these ropes off of me!" I shouted.

Once free of the restraints, I waved my hand and sent the warlocks flying. I waved it again and destroyed them in midair. Police cars rolled into the back lot of the hall. I located my father's wand and pulled it out. As it turned into my stick, I grabbed Justin and the officer and flew off.

Justin tried to snatch the gun away from the officer. "Stop pointing that thing at me!" he shouted.

"What the hell is going on?" the officer asked, terrified.

Justin finally kicked the gun out into the night and held on for dear life.

I clutched at the officer's shirt to keep him from falling. "Stop fighting," I snapped. "You're going to fall."

"Please don't kill me," the officer screamed. His eyes were wide with terror, as though he were looking at the devil.

I landed abruptly several blocks away from the

scene.

Justin let go and rolled several feet. "I hate when you do that," he said, brushing himself off.

"Justin," I said, "Call Cory. Tell him to get James out of there so I can go help Sammy."

He nodded and pulled out his phone. I turned to the officer. He was hugging the trunk of a tree, petrified. "Please," he said. "Don't kill me."

I moved in closer. "Do you believe me now?" I asked.

"What the hell are you?"

"I'm a witch," I replied, "and so are you."

He looked at me like I was crazy. "No," he said, shaking his head. "Witches aren't real."

"Oh, yes they are," Justin sang out before returning to his call.

The officer slapped himself across the face as I stepped closer. I think he truly believed he was dreaming.

"I don't have time to explain things," I said, "but you are, in fact, a witch. And I'm pretty sure we know each other."

He looked to be on the verge of fainting. "I must be sleepwalking."

"You're wide awake, I assure you. This is real."

"I'm going crazy," he said to himself, "that's it. I've been working too hard."

"Did you not just fly with me through the air just now?" I asked.

He didn't answer. I readied my hand to wave. Perhaps a touch more gravity-free living would help to convince him.

"Thea, don't!" Kym shouted. She was hurrying toward us, tears streaming down her face. "Why did you take him?"

"Kym, what are you doing here?"

"Bring him back, Thea," she ordered. "I beg you to give him his life back."

"What are you talking about?" I asked, looking toward the officer. "Do you know this man?"

She held her hands out to me. "Please, Thea," she begged. "You have to erase what just happened. I'll get on my knees and beg if necessary, just don't tell him what he is."

"Kym, what is going on? Who is he?"

She looked at him and back to me. "I couldn't send him away, Thea," she explained. "Donna sent John away and it almost killed her. I needed him close, to make sure he was safe. No one knows what he is. I've managed to keep him safe from Simon with spells. Your father told us that Simon would have killed all the male witches." Kym dropped to her knees at my feet. "He's my only son. Please give him back the only life he's ever known."

The officer stepped forward. "What the hell is going on? This is not my mother."

I examined him closely: blue eyes, crooked smile. He was a lot younger when we knew each other back then, but I could never forget those eyes. "Jason Corser?" I uttered, incredulous.

"How do you know my name?" he asked.

Before I could answer, Justin was off the phone, a strange expression on his face.

"What did Cory say?" I asked.

"They took Sam home already," he replied. "Your father told me to go help the witches erase the humans' memories."

"And Sammy, how is he?"

Justin wouldn't look at me. Bile rose in my throat. I didn't wait for an answer. I held out my hand for my stick and flew away, racing through town in route to the mansion. I could barely breathe as fear filled my heart. I waved my hand at the front doors. I heard Delia screaming as I flew inside.

They were gathered around him in the sitting room. Sammy lay on the floor as the others frantically chanted spells. The dagger sat on a nearby table, covered in blood. My father stood outside the circle, his head down.

"No," I uttered.

I knew my father would be trying to save Sammy if there was a chance, if he had any life at all left inside him. I crept closer.

"Sam!" Cory shouted. "Come on, kid, wake up!"

Joshua pulled me down toward Sammy. "Wake him up, please!"

Cory lifted Sam's head. "Don't you die on me, kid. Don't you dare die on me." He reached for my hand and placed it over Sammy's heart. "Come on, Thea, wake him up. Make him open his eyes."

I slowly pulled my hand away and lowered my head. "He's gone, Cory."

"Don't say that," he said, forcibly retaking my hand. "You can wake him up! Keep trying."

Delia dropped to her knees and wept over Sammy as Cory gathered his dead friend into his arms. He held Sammy to his chest, tears filling his eyes. Javier burst into a sob. Joshua knelt beside Cory and cried. Fish was like a statue—stone-faced and in shock. He stood, frozen, his hooks still in his hands.

"I'm sorry, kid," Cory cried. "I'm so sorry."

I stood and stepped back, denial taking over. I

couldn't move or breathe. I felt numb inside, dead. It was like a bad dream I couldn't wake up from. I wanted to cover my ears to keep from hearing Cory's wails.

Everyone was crying—everyone, that is, but Fish. He hadn't moved an inch. I reached for him, but he pulled away. He glared at me with menacing eyes. He was right to hate me. All of this was my fault. I did this, put their lives in danger, caused this horrifying death in our family. I had no words of comfort for them. Nothing I could say would change things.

I just stood there, staring down at Sammy. No tears, only numbness. I wanted to scream from the pain, but my heart felt dead.

The front door flew open and James stormed in, whip at his side. He saw me and walked off. I closed my eyes as the spell kicked in. I reached for Javier, but he too pulled away from me.

"I am truly sorry for your loss," my father said to the boys.

Cory wouldn't let go of Sammy. He just kept repeating how sorry he was.

After a few more moments, my father stepped forward. "If you wish, I can make the funeral arrangements," he told Cory.

Cory shook his head. "He's getting a witch burial." He threw a venomous glance in my direction. "With only us."

My father nodded. "As you wish."

"We can do it at sunrise," Delia said, stroking Sammy's face. "Before his spirit finds its way home."

"There's plenty of space in the backyard," my father suggested.

I wanted to run to Sammy and hold him, tell him how much I loved him. But I could only stand—frozen, silent.

Cory pulled Sammy closer. "I'll build the platform tonight," he said, tears streaming down his face.

Fish stepped forward. "I'll help you," he said, suddenly overcome by choking sobs.

Delia stood and embraced him. He wept like a child in her arms. I stepped closer, hoping there was some way I could be of comfort. But I knew better.

Delia caught my eye. She released Fish and shoved me back into the foyer. "Get away from him. This is your fault."

My father stepped into the fray. "Delia, please," he said.

"No!" she shouted. "She caused all of this. Sam is dead because of her. She should be the one on the floor, not him."

"You will all live because of her," my father replied. "Never forget that."

"We're damned because of her!" Delia shot back.

They were all thinking the same thing. I could see it in the boys' eyes. They blamed me for Sammy's death.

Delia got in my face. "Get out of here!" she screamed.

I bowed my head. "I'm so sorry."

"Just leave!" Cory shouted.

The hatred in Cory's voice shattered me. Before I could react, I sensed James behind me on the stairs. I turned and saw the anguish in his eyes.

"James, no," my father warned.

James was coming to comfort me, to shield me from the harsh words of my friends. But I felt the anger returning. I rushed through the kitchen and out the back door, hurrying to the farthest corner of the yard. I wanted to sit, in darkness, away from the others. I sat on the ground, wrapped my arms around my knees, and waited for the tears to come.

But they never came. I looked out into the dark sky, the pain of this night threatening to swallow me whole. Delia was right; it should have been me on that floor. I started the fight. I walked right into Simon's trap, unable to fight off the effects of his spell. I'd been willing to give him anything he wanted. Sammy never would have been injured if I hadn't danced with Simon. Sammy's blood was on my hands.

It started to rain. I closed my eyes and clawed the ground around me. The ache in my heart was unbearable. I wanted to scream and burst into tears but I sat, silent, turning my face to the rain. "I'm sorry, Sammy . . ." It was the pain of losing my mother all over again. I couldn't cry, couldn't react to what I was feeling. Sammy was dead, and I couldn't accept it.

The back door opened and closed. Moments later, I heard Cory and the boys making their way into the garden. They had materials for a platform and began to build. Once finished, they would place Sammy on top and set it alight, and say goodbye to their friend. It was a traditional witch send-off: burning the body to ashes and allowing it to return to the earth. It was our way of keeping the memory of that person alive. To think of Sammy at one with the earth, the trees, and the flowers gave me a sliver of peace. We would keep him close to our hearts, show him he would never be forgotten.

I wanted to help, but knew they didn't want me around. I sat like a stone, unable to comprehend my pain. Every time I thought of Sammy, I wanted to die. I felt something inside me brewing—pain, or anger, I didn't know which. I was at a loss for what to do.

James walked out of the house and joined in helping the boys. I was so numb the sight of him didn't even affect me. It was like there was no spell at all. My heart felt completely dead.

"There you are." Justin was walking toward me, his expression intense.

"Please," I said, bowing my head. "Just leave me alone."

He kicked at my feet. "Did you know my brothers were dead?"

I slowly looked up at him. "Yes."

"Where are their bodies?" he asked. "What did you do with them?"

I looked away. "They turned to dust."

"You watched them die and did nothing, witch!"

I couldn't answer him, didn't know what to say. There was nothing I could have done. How could I have known they were going to die?

"Why did my brothers turn to dust?" he asked. "Why not Samuel?"

I couldn't look at him.

"Answer me!"

"You're mixing the aging tea wrong."

"I hate you!" he said, kicking mud in my face.

He turned on his heels and started for the house. James reached for him and asked what was wrong, then glanced over his shoulder when Justin pointed my way. James looked relieved to see me. Justin pulled away from him and went inside. James went back to helping the boys. I closed my eyes, hoping to find the tears that wouldn't come. I listened to the hammering. There were few words exchanged as the boys worked.

By the time they had finished building the pyre,

the sun was coming up. I hadn't moved. I was shaking from the cold, but couldn't bring myself to go inside. I watched as Fish and Javier brought Sammy out, his body wrapped in a sheet. Sharron followed and Delia, crying, was at her side.

An unbearable ache settled into my heart. I wanted to die and be with Sammy. I forced myself to get up and walk toward my friends. It was time to say goodbye to my precious Sammy. James was helping Joshua pile wood under the platform. Delia, still sobbing, dropped to her knees and buried her face in her hands. James turned his back when he saw me approaching. The others didn't even bother to look my way.

I stood a good distance away, watching as Cory set some of Sammy's things on top of his body. He placed his hand over Sammy's heart and started to cry. One by one, the boys broke down. Fish pulled out Sammy's ninja stars and set them on the pyre. Javier set the ninja suit beside them.

Joshua walked over and placed his bow and a quiver of arrows next to Sammy. "I always meant to give these to you," he said.

James helped Delia to her feet and held her as they walked to Sammy. Delia leaned over and kissed Sammy's forehead. "You live in our hearts now," she said. "You will always be happy there. You will always find love there."

James placed an item wrapped in silk cloth on top of Sammy and told him to "use it well."

Cory held his hand over his heart, made a fist, and held it to Sammy's chest. "I give you my heart, brother," he said. "May you always feel it beat. May you always know how much I loved you."

~ 322 ~

I swallowed thickly. It was my turn. I stepped forward.

Delia blocked me from getting any closer. "Go back to the hole you were in, witch," she spat. "You have no business being here."

"I will have my turn," I replied.

"Over my dead body."

I tried to go around her, but Fish and Joshua joined with Delia to block my way. I looked at Cory, who avoided my eyes. Javier joined Fish and Joshua. I looked to James but he, too, avoided my gaze.

Rage bubbled up inside me—but not because of James, or Delia, or the boys. Because of me. I hated myself more than they did. I stepped back. I couldn't stand the way they were looking at me, their eyes filled with contempt. I called for my stick and promptly flew off into the morning sky.

I entered the clouds and begged for tears to come. But I felt only rage—ugly, all-consuming rage. The monster in me was out for blood, and I knew just where to find it.

I flew over the campground, the same one they had taken me to after I'd been captured. There they were, hundreds of them, still sleeping. There were many more now, more than could fit into the cabins. Tents were pitched on every square inch of open space. I landed a few yards from the edge of the grounds. Simon was about to lose his army, and would have to face me alone.

I strode up the middle of the camp, sword at my side, and waited.

Chapter 26
Attor's Spell

The sun disappeared behind the clouds, and a thick layer of fog rolled in. The dampness of the morning air dripped from the ends of my hair. I was covered in mud from where I had been sitting. I should have been shivering from the cold, but the numbness had returned. I barely felt the earth beneath my feet. My eyes scanned the grounds as distant screams echoed through the fog—memories of when they burned me alive. But here, now, there was only silence. No signs remained of the battle we'd once fought.

My heart raced with excitement. I was done waiting. I drummed the tip of my sword on a nearby rock.

I stood, poised, head down.

The warlocks awakened and stepped out of their tents, weapons drawn. They eyed me, mystified by my unannounced visit. They spit spells into their hands and readied themselves to strike.

I slowly looked up, and spotted a warlock holding

a dagger exactly like the one that killed Sammy.

"I'm going to kill you last," I said, looking into his eyes.

He jutted his chin forward. "I'd like to see you try, witch."

I tightened my grip on the sword. The warlocks threw their spells at my feet, and the ground around me cracked. The soil turned black as the cracks made their way to my feet.

I thrust the sword into the ground, and the sound of breaking glass echoed through the grounds, rendering their spells useless. They were quick to throw more, and one flew straight at my face. I swung the sword sideways and sent the spell away. From the corner of my eye, I saw a tree shatter like toothpicks.

I'd never seen spells like these before. Simon had taught these warlocks well. They were better fighters, throwing better spells. I thought of Simon's right-hand men. What kind of spells had he taught them? They were bigger and more fit than these warlocks, and would be harder to kill.

I heard the spitting of more spells and looked up in time to see one flying straight at me. I pounded my foot on the ground, creating a wave of energy that sent the spells flying back at the warlocks. I was shocked when the warlocks exploded the spells in midair by merely chanting. Now I was sure: Simon had taught them the wizard spells.

"What's wrong, witch?" one of them asked. "Didn't know we could do that?"

I tilted my head and smiled. I looked down at the knife in his hand. When his hand moved toward his throat, the other warlocks stepped away in shock. They watched, horrified, as the man tried in vain to pull his hand away. When the knife made contact with his neck, the man looked at me, terror in his eyes.

"What's wrong, scum?" I asked. "Didn't know I could do that?"

With a blink of my eye, the man slit his own throat.

The other warlocks took off running. I waved my hand and dragged them back. I was a madwoman, cutting the men's bodies into pieces. My heart turned black. All I could think of was Sammy. Every time I imagined his face, I struck another warlock even harder than the one before him. My mind no longer belonged to me; it belonged to the monster inside me.

I spotted the warlock with the matching dagger running into the woods. I waved my hand and brought him to his knees. I raced to him as the rest of the pack escaped into the trees. I held the tip of my sword to his heart. "Beg," I ordered.

"Go to hell, witch!"

His feet sank into the ground. "I said, beg." His legs were gradually disappearing into the earth. "I want to hear you beg."

"Go to hell!"

I looked to the trees and sent branches coiling around his arms. I smiled as the branches began to pull his arms from his torso. I drew the sword away and tapped it on the ground. He sank further, his legs all but gone. "I can't hear you," I said.

"Please stop!" he cried.

I looked into his eyes, still smiling, and tapped the ground again. The branches pulled his arms harder. The sound of his suffering was music to my ears. I swung the sword at him, swung until there was nothing left but dust. I kept swinging at the warlock's ashy remains, unable to satisfy my need for vengeance. I swung the sword until I exhausted myself, dropped to my knees, and finally found my tears. "Sammy!" I shouted.

I wanted to die, to punish myself for Sammy's death. When the sword turned into my stick, I hopped on and flew away. I wanted to find the highest mountain and throw myself off. I held on, rested my cheek on the stick, and sobbed. I flew what seemed like hours. I don't remember drifting off.

When I opened my eyes, I was at the top of a mountain. I lay on a bed of grass, my clothes wet and muddy. I didn't know how much time had passed. It seemed like I'd been asleep for days. I heard my name on the wind in the distance. I thought it was a dream.

When my heart filled with anger, I knew it was James. How had he found me? How could he have possibly known I was here, wherever here was? I got to my feet and brushed myself off. I couldn't let him near me. I searched the area for a hiding place, but I was too high up, surrounded by rocks and seemingly little else. I spotted a lake with cabins and a sign that read *Closed for the Season*. I searched frantically for my father's wand. I had to get out of there. I held out my hand and called, but it didn't come to me.

James' voice drew closer. I started to panic. What was he thinking? He knew I'd try to kill him if he got close. I was still searching for the wand when he finally reached me, his eyes frantic. He held a piece of paper in his hand with what looked like a map drawn on it. My father had told him where I was.

I ran to the edge of a cliff. "Stay away from me!" I screamed.

"Thea, please," he said, extending his hands. "Get

away from there."

When I looked into his eyes, the monster rose within me. "You have to get out of here!"

"Sammy's death wasn't your fault," he said, stepping closer. "Don't do this to yourself."

I looked down over the cliff, and my stomach lurched. But there was no other way. I couldn't live with myself if I killed James. I had to end this spell, die, and set everyone free of the trouble I'd caused. I put up my hand when James was within inches. "I don't want to kill you."

"Please," he said. "Take my hand. I'll leave as soon as we get off this mountain."

I shook my head, fighting the urge to wave my hand at him. I inched closer to the edge.

"Thea, don't!"

I looked into his eyes. "I love you."

One of my feet slipped over the edge. James lurched forward and managed to seize my hand. His touch sent a surge of anger through me. I was breathless as I fought against the spell. "Let go of me!" I screamed.

"Never!"

He tried with all his strength to hold onto my hand, his eyes dark as the night. He was trying to fight the spell, to stop himself from letting go, but he would lose this battle. Any moment now the spell would win, and he would allow me to fall to my death. His heart wanted to save me, but his mind was poisoned by the spell. The desire to let me fall was winning.

James gasped as his grip loosened. He tried to pull me up, but I fought him. If I made it back up, I would kill him. I struggled to free my hand from his grip. It was time to cast Attor's spell.

"No, Thea," James cried. "Please don't."

I looked into his eyes one last time.

"Please don't do this to us," he said. "Don't cast that spell."

I wasn't surprised that he knew about the spell, but it didn't matter. Without it, he would die, and I couldn't allow that to happen.

"In the depths of hell," he said, "my heart will find you."

"With the power of the sun, and the force of the wind, I take out all the memories that made our life begin," I chanted.

James closed his eyes. "No, I beg you."

"Your heart has never known me, our lips have never met. Every memory of me inside your head, I now make you forget."

"No!" James screamed.

My hand slipped from his. I saw James grab his head as I fell. I closed my eyes and waited for death to embrace me. I smelled the heavens as tears streamed down my face. The fragrance of a beautiful garden surrounded me. The warmth of the sun kissed my face. I would soon be with my mother. I spread my fingers and felt grass under my hand.

I opened my eyes.

An animal-like man towered above me. "Who are you?" he asked.

I knew this much: I wasn't dead. I tried to stand, but the creature threw a net over me and kicked me down. I tried to make sense of my surroundings.

Where am I?

I noticed my father's ring on my finger. James must have slipped it onto my fingers before I let go of his hand. I tried to pull it off, to escape from this animal before he killed me, but the ring wouldn't budge. Three more creatures emerged from a nearby cave—Attor's cave. I was in Magia.

"The guards," I muttered to myself. They were about seven feet tall with alligator-like skin and blood-red eyes. Their heads resembled that of an owl. Their human-like hands stood out in direct contrast to their long, leathery tails.

They slipped two metal poles through the net and lifted me from the ground. I wanted to wave my hand, but suddenly thought better of it. They might be taking me to the wizards. This might be my chance to confront them. I grabbed the net tightly as they curled their legs around the staffs and took to the air.

From above, I spotted Attor and the other dragons trudging out of the forest.

Attor blew fire into the air and waved his wing, sending me a clear signal that he knew I was there. I breathed a sigh of relief.

The guards flew until several towers came into view ahead of us. They landed in front of a gate at the entrance to the structure. They dropped me on the ground and pushed open the massive wooden gate. Passing through was like going back in time. The towers looked nothing like the village beneath them. High, thick walls surrounded the village as far as the eye could see. I turned my head to the smell of burning wood and saw a woman stirring a large cauldron over a fire.

The woods beyond the gates were filled with cherry and jacaranda trees. Their white, pink, and purple blossoms permeated the area. Crepe myrtles cast a magnificent red glow across the entire forest. Lush, green grass covered the ground. The beauty of this place took my breath away.

The guards walked further into the village. I gazed dumbly in amazement. It reminded me of Salem's medieval fair, only bigger and more authentic. The village was made up of quaint old cottages. A blacksmith held up a sword as we passed. Two small children ran to his side and gaped at the spectacle. Another villager, a woman, gasped as the guards made their way with me through the dirt streets. Slowly the village square filled with curious eyes.

Another woman, adorned in velvet and silk, was obviously richer than most. She gasped when I eyed her as we passed. I must have looked like a monster to her, disheveled and covered in mud. From what I could see there were no phones or electricity. The clothes were of a distant era. I saw not a single hint of the modern world.

The guards carried me past the cottages and into some trees. I heard the sound of running water. My jaw dropped when what looked like a castle came into view. It was a few miles away, but I could see from here that it was stunning. It must have been two hundred stories, and its crystal walls gleamed like stars in the night.

Between the bodies of the guards, I spied the backs of several men gathering by a river. When we reached a giant oak tree, one of the men turned to face us. I was dropped to the ground, and landed with a thud.

They stood aside as a man approached. "What do you bring?" the man asked.

He was a tall, bearded man with dark eyes. Two others stood behind him wearing elaborate velvet robes. Their eyes sparkled like diamonds, and their hair was shiny and smooth.

The guards pulled the net away. "She is half wizard, your majesty."

The wizard laughed. "And what is her other half?" he asked.

"She is also half witch, sire."

The other wizards raised their hands, poised to kill me, no doubt.

I scrambled to my feet. "No, you have to help me!"

One of them waved his hand, but it only knocked me down.

He huffed. "A wizard shield."

"Who are you?" the first wizard asked.

"Wendell," another cut in, "she is truly half wizard."

Five more wizards arrived, two looking much younger than the others. They had short black hair and brown eyes. Their smooth skin was flawless, their bodies muscular and fit.

"Who is this girl?" one of the young wizards asked.

"Silence!" the one named Wendell shouted. "I will be the only one asking questions here."

The young wizard studied me curiously. His eyes grew wide when he spotted the ring on my hand. "She wears Xander's ring!"

Wendell looked down at my hand. "Impossible!"

A shred of hope grew inside me. "It's my father's ring," I exclaimed.

I heard gasps throughout the village. Wendell looked into my eyes. He waved his hand and sent me flying into the water. I flailed as his spell held me under.

After a few moments, I felt the spell break. I came to the surface, gasping for air. It took me a moment to realize: he was trying to wash the mud from my face. I stood in the shallows, noting the fear in

Wendell's eyes. He was almost shaking, but why?

The other wizards dropped to one knee and bowed their heads. "Your highness," they said in unison.

I stared at them, puzzled. I looked beyond the wizards to find the entire village bowing their heads.

"Do not bow to this witch," Wendell shouted. "She is the daughter of a traitor, the one who put all our lives in danger."

"She is the daughter of our true king," the young wizard said.

I couldn't believe what I was hearing. My father was a king?

"Silence, Martin," Wendell snapped. "You have no say here. I am now the king."

"You are the king because Xander is dead," Martin replied. "And you have done nothing but shelter us behind these gates. What do we wait for?"

"Xander told that human about the leaves," Wendell answered. "We can be killed now. You all know that."

Martin moved closer to him. "Xander would never give away that secret," Martin answered. "Someone betrayed him."

"What does that matter now?" Wendell asked. "Xander is dead, and I am now king."

"My father lives!"

The villagers buzzed with excitement. Whispers and gasps flooded the square.

Martin ran to the shore and lifted me out of the water. "Xander is alive?" he asked.

"Yes," I replied.

"She lies!" Wendell shouted. "She wants to bring the witch Simon to kill us all."

"Then how do you explain the wizard shield?"

Martin asked. "How do you explain the ring?"

"She is half witch," Wendell answered. "Perhaps she killed Xander."

The other young wizard ran to my side. "Is my father with him?" he asked. "Is he alive?"

I looked at him questioningly. "I'm sorry, I don't know who your father is."

Martin put his hand on the young wizard's shoulder. "Be well, Morgan," he said. "We will get to the bottom of this."

"This witch killed Xander," Wendell said. "She dies today."

I stepped forward into their circle. "My father is not dead. He's weak and needs your help. A black spell was cast on him. That's why he never came back."

"Who would dare cast a black spell on Xander?" Martin asked.

"Simon."

"But how would a half human know such a spell?" Martin asked.

"You see," Wendell continued. "She knows the witch Simon. She's helping him, I tell you."

Martin reached for my hand. "Come, I will give you some energy to take to Xander. We can clear all of this up when he gets here."

"You will give her nothing!" Wendell shouted. "Xander made his choice when he married that witch. He chose the other world."

"Xander was going to bring his family here," Martin shot back. "But he always knew they would be in danger from one of you." He looked around at the others. "That's why he stayed in the human world. He needed to first find out who was betraying him."

Wendell laughed. "Defend your friend all you

want, Martin," he said. "But Xander is no longer welcome here."

"You have no say in that now, Wendell," Martin replied. "Our true king still lives."

"I am your true king!" Wendell shouted.

"Then why is that ring not on your finger?" Martin asked, pointing to my hand. "Only the next in line for the throne can wear it."

"Perhaps she bewitched it," Wendell suggested.

"Wasn't it you who said Xander was dead?" Morgan asked. "How exactly did you come to find that out?"

Wendell's face reddened. "I answer to no one. How dare you question your king in such a way? I have never left you for a witch. I have never brought humans here. It was Xander who betrayed us. It was he who told Simon about the leaves."

One of the others spoke up. "He's right. It was Xander who brought Simon here. We would never be living in fear if he didn't bring that half human into our world." He looked at Martin. "You will give this witch nothing."

"We are wizards," Martin answered. "Fear does not grow in our hearts. Wendell filled you with that fear, not Xander."

The wizard continued. "Xander gave Simon a powerful weapon—one he hopes to use to kill us all. We are forced to live inside these walls because of it."

As they argued, I kept looking into Wendell's eyes. His soul was black, his heart greedy. Wendell did not have the wizards' best interests at heart. He almost reminded me of Simon.

"I'm giving her some white energy," Martin said.

"We must give Xander a chance to explain himself."

"You will give her nothing," Wendell shouted, the veins in his neck pulsing. "This witch dies now." He waved his hand at me.

Martin and Morgan waved Wendell's spell away. Martin held out his hand, and a crystal staff came flying into it. Before I knew what was happening, we were flying away together with Morgan close behind, and the other wizards in hot pursuit.

"Did Xander give you a capsule for the energy?" Martin asked.

"Yes, but Attor used it," I said, holding on tight.

"The dragons?"

"Yes."

As the wizards drew closer, Martin flew faster. "Hold on!"

"Fly into the forest near the dragons," I shouted.

"No, that forest will kill us."

"I can protect us. Just do it."

When the wizards realized we were flying toward the forest, they backed off. Only the guards continued the pursuit. I saw Attor and the other dragons take to the sky. They blew fire at the guards as Martin flew us straight into the heart of the forest. When Morgan arrived, I chanted hastily and a protective bubble enveloped us. Martin tried to run out, but hit the bubble wall. He fell to the ground and tried again.

"You're safe," I explained. "We can't hurt the leaves in here."

"Hurt the leaves?" he asked.

I told them everything I'd learned about the forest, why the leaves sapped the wizards' powers.

Morgan shook his head at Martin. "I can't believe we didn't figure this out ourselves."

The sound of raging flames redirected our attention. Attor and the others were fighting the guards. Attor had one of the guards in his mouth. He tore him to shreds and spit the pieces into the lake.

When the fighting was done, Attor motioned that it was safe to come out.

"How do we get out of this?" Martin asked.

I grabbed his hand and started walking. Martin and Morgan looked amazed as the bubble moved with every step we took. Attor motioned into the cave. Once inside, I waved my hand and broke the shield.

Martin hurried to Attor. "Why didn't you tell me Xander was alive?"

"Because the wizards would have killed you," Attor answered.

"How long have you known?" Martin asked.

"Is my father alive?" Morgan chimed in.

A loud noise boomed outside. Attor and I rushed to the entrance of the cave, and Martin and Morgan followed.

"Give us the girl, and we'll let you live."

Chapter 27
The King and I

Hundreds of guards gathered at the entrance of the cave. Attor turned to me. "Stay inside!"

I saw shadows above us as hundreds of dragons descended on the guards. Attor took to the sky, taking two guards with him. He tore them apart with his teeth and talons and swiftly grabbed another. The two wizards waved their hands, sending several guards into the path of the dragons. One guard tried to grab me as he flew at the entrance of the cave. Katu appeared out of nowhere and sliced him in two.

"Go inside, Princess!" Martin shouted. He waved his hand at the lake. The water rose up and swallowed half of the guards in one wave. Morgan waved his hand at the ground, and it started to rumble. Martin reached for me and threw me over his staff. He took to the sky, and Morgan followed us.

Morgan yelled to the dragons and pointed at the ground. The dragons whipped their tails in a circular motion and knocked the guards off their staffs. The ground was like a hungry monster as it swallowed the guards one by one. When the sky was free of guards, Morgan waved his hand, and the ground stopped rumbling. We looked around for the wizards, but they were all gone.

"Where did they go?" I asked.

"They left to protect the energy," Martin answered.

Attor motioned to the cave. "Get the princess back inside," he ordered. "She needs to get out of here before they send more guards."

Martin nodded and flew us into the cave. Once inside, he asked Attor about the capsule. "Do you have another one? I can try and get around the wizards and get her the energy to take Xander."

"We have no time for that now," Attor answered. "The princess needs to get out of here."

Princess. I couldn't get used to hearing that. I wondered why my father never told me. "Come back with me," I suggested to the wizards.

"We can't, your highness," Martin replied. "Not until Xander allows it."

I nodded. "Please don't tell the wizards about the leaves."

"I will tell them nothing," Martin said. "We will stay here and await Xander's orders."

Morgan stepped forward, his eyes intent. "Please ask him about my father."

Martin pulled a crystal from his robe and waved his hand. The crystal glowed, changing from green to blue and, finally, to white. He placed it in my hand and looked into my eyes. "Tell my friend I am with him."

I hugged him. "Thank you."

~ 339 ~

Attor stepped forward. "You must leave now. Xander is waiting."

"Wait, Martin," I said. "Can you break a spell for me?"

"What kind of spell?" he asked.

"Simon put a spell on me to make me kill my husband."

"We'll break it at once," Martin replied, raising his hand.

Attor blew fire our way. "You will kill the princess if you break that spell," he warned.

Martin looked at me, eyes wide. "He enchanted her?"

"Yes."

"How did he learn our wizard spells?" Morgan asked, stepping forward.

"You realize you must kill him here," Martin warned Attor. "She will die otherwise."

"Yes, I know," Attor replied. "The princess will bring him to us."

"What about his army?" Morgan asked. "They will use the leaves against us."

"No," Martin said. "We have a way to protect ourselves now." He smiled at me. "Thanks to the princess."

I stepped forward. "But the other wizards will figure it out. The dragons will have no defense against them if that happens. Besides, you don't have to worry about Simon's army. Simon won't have any help if his army is dead."

Martin smiled. "You truly are your father's daughter."

"Are you going to be okay?" I asked. "They'll try and kill you now."

"Morgan and I have a place to go. We'll be safe there."

"What about my father?" I asked. "He's very weak."

"Just give Xander that crystal," Martin instructed. "It will help. I've sent him some of my powers."

I smiled at Martin. "Thank you for believing in him."

"He is my friend, and the king. You have nothing to thank me for."

"I'll return as soon as I can."

"Tell Xander we are ready," Martin said. "Come back when he has orders for us."

"And please, ask him about my father," Morgan reminded me, smiling sheepishly.

I nodded and turned to Attor. "Are you going to be okay?"

"We can live in that forest for years, Princess. Do not worry about us."

I threw my arms around him. I had no words to thank him.

"Don't forget to find those leaves," Attor whispered. "You must find out how Simon is keeping them alive in the human world, and then destroy them. I will explain to your friends what you're doing."

"I'll find them," I said. "And I'll bring Simon to you."

He pulled away from me. "I did it, Attor," I said, my eyes filling. "I cast the spell."

"You did the right thing, Princess," Attor replied. "It was the only way to save him."

"Am I still going to feel like killing him?" I asked.

He sighed. "Drink the tea. It will help."

"But the leaves didn't work," I said. "I nearly killed him."

"They will work, your highness," he assured me. "The most you'll feel around him now is annoyed." He took two steps back. "Now, go. Your father is waiting."

I nodded and looked down at my trembling hand. The ring slipped off easily.

I was at the top of the mountain again. James was gone. It took me a minute to realize the ring would bring me back to the last spot I had used it. I searched for my father's wand. Before I could hold out my hand, the wand came to me, turning into my stick as it flew.

I held on and took off, not knowing where it was taking me. When it flew toward the mansion, I tried to stop and change direction. I couldn't bear the thought of seeing James. But the stick wouldn't be stopped; someone else was controlling it. When I flew into the house and through the kitchen door, my father stood— eyes closed, hand out. The stick came to a stop in front of him, and he collapsed.

I jumped off. "Father!"

He looked over a hundred years old, weaker than I'd ever seen him. He'd drained the last of his energy trying to get me back home.

"Father, hold on!" I pulled out the crystal Martin had given me and placed it in his palm. I wrapped his fingers around it and waved my hand. My father's body glowed with the energy.

"Father, wake up," I said, shaking him. "Please don't leave me."

His eyes fluttered as the powers in the crystal flowed into him. He began aging in reverse. His weak, thin, frame filled out and took on new life. The gray in his hair disappeared. He opened his eyes.

"Father, are you okay?"

When I helped him to his feet, he embraced me. "My child, I was going mad with worry."

"Father," I cried. "Why didn't you tell me?" I looked up at him, my eyes filled with tears. "It wasn't you, was it? You're not the fool who trusted Simon, are you?"

"No," he said, wiping my tears. "But I am the fool who allowed him into my world."

"It was Wendell, wasn't it?"

"Don't talk about it, Thea," he said. "It's still not safe."

"I know what you fear," I said. "But I want you to know that I'm not going to tell Simon anything. I won't let his spell do that to me."

He sighed. "I fear you will lose yourself to him."

"I can do it."

"I don't think you can. You have yet to find the strongest part of you." He touched my face. "Bring me the energy, and I will take care of things."

"No," I said, pulling away. "Attor told me. I know what you're trying to do."

A look of surprise washed over his face. "I see you have been plotting behind my back."

"I'm only trying to save you."

"And do you think I want to lose you?"

"I'm going to be okay, Father. I can survive this spell."

"Very well," he said. "I see I must change my plan."

It was obvious my father knew I didn't have the energy. Deep down inside, he always knew.

"Martin is still with you, Father. He knows it

wasn't you."

He sighed. "I never wanted to put his life in danger."

"Morgan was with him. He asked about his father."

"His father lives, but I can't talk about that now."

I saw my father in a whole new light. He was a king, a real king. "Can I ask you something, Father?"

"Is it about James?"

I nodded. "Yes. Does he know you're a king?"

"Why do you think he has so much money?" he asked. "Why do you think he owns homes all over New England? He acquired all that for you. He wanted to give you the life he felt was fit for a princess."

"He did it for me?"

"You must understand, Thea," my father explained. "He married a princess. He felt it was the only way to be equal with you somehow."

"He thought he wouldn't be good enough for me?" I asked.

"It sounds silly, but yes."

Everything about James suddenly made sense. He didn't care about the money, he cared about being my equal. How foolish could he be? All the money in the world couldn't give me what he did. If he were a poor man, I wouldn't love him any less. How could he think I would care about those things?

I looked into my father's eyes. "Father, you're a king. Why do you live as a butler?"

"This is my place now, Thea," he said. "I live in the only place I know I can always find you. The only place I know your heart will always lead you. No matter how lost you get, I know you will always end up here."

"You're wrong, Father," I said, bowing my head.

~ 344 ~

"I don't belong here anymore."

"You are my greatest love, Thea," my father said, smiling down at me. "If there is anything I am sure of, it's where you belong."

"Why did you leave your world?" I asked.

"Because being a father was more important."

"Will you ever go back?"

We turned our heads to the sound of the front door opening.

My father pushed me behind the kitchen counter. "Stay down," he whispered.

"William!" James' voice rang out through the foyer.

"In here, master."

"Ah, there you are," James said, walking in. "Look at you, William. You look very rested."

He gave James a quick nod. "I am, master."

"Good," James replied, nodding back. "Please prepare a picnic basket. I'm taking my sweetheart to Martha's Vineyard."

I closed my eyes, already filled with tears. He sounded so happy, so in love.

"I'll be gone until tomorrow, William," he added. "I have a very important question to ask Helena."

"Yes, master. I will prepare the basket at once."

"Make it special, William. It's not every day that a man asks the woman he loves to marry him."

"As you wish, master."

"Are you not happy for me, William?" James asked. "I've just told you I'm going to ask Helena to be my wife."

"I wish you all the happiness in the world, master."

"Thank you, William. Now, I'm off to buy the

ring. I'll pick up the basket in an hour."

"Yes, master."

James exited the kitchen. We listened as the front door opened and closed. I broke into a sob.

My father lowered himself to the floor and gathered me in his arms. "It was the only way, Thea."

"I can't take this," I cried. "I have to break Attor's spell."

My father shook his head. "That's not possible. A dragon spell cannot be broken."

"It's going to kill me, Father," I cried. "I can't watch him marry her."

He sighed and kissed my head. "You won't have to," he said. "I will not sit by and watch you suffer like this."

"What do you mean?"

"If he is to forget you," my father said, sighing, "I feel you should forget him as well."

"A spell?"

"Yes."

I looked away. Just to think of it caused me pain. It made sense. I couldn't survive watching James live his life with Helena. But should I allow my father to cast a spell like that? What if he was up to something?

I looked at him. "This isn't some kind of trick is it, Father?" I asked. "You're not going to fix it so I remember him someday, are you?"

"I give you my word of honor," my father replied. "After today, I will do nothing to trick you."

The kitchen door opened. My father quickly stood.

"We saw James leave," Cory said. "Is Thea back yet? We've been worried."

"Is she here?" Delia asked, storming in.

"What did William say?" Fish asked, coming in behind them.

My father helped me to my feet. I was too ashamed to look at them. They hated me, and with good reason.

"Thea," Cory said, stepping forward, "where have you been for three days? I was so worried."

I looked outside. Sammy was gone. Only ashes from the wood remained, scattered about the yard.

"I'm so sorry," I said, overcome by a choking sob.

They stepped around the counter and threw their arms around me. Joshua and Javier arrived and joined in the group embrace.

"Please forgive me," I said, over and over.

"Stop saying that," Cory said, tears in his eyes. "It wasn't your fault."

"We were so stupid," Fish added.

"I didn't get to say goodbye to him," I wailed, crying into my hands.

Delia squeezed me tighter. "Yes, you did," she soothed. "He knew you were there."

"I'll never forgive myself."

"Don't say that," Cory said, grabbing my face. "He died fighting, just as he would have wanted."

I threw my arms around him. "Don't hate me, Cory."

"Oh Thea," he said. "I could never hate you." He pushed back and smiled at me. "I love you."

"I love you, too, you stupid witch," Delia said, hugging me again.

"Save some for me," Fish said, wrapping his arms around both of us.

Joshua lifted all three of us off the ground. "I love

you guys," he cried.

"Put me down, Ginger," Fish said.

I turned to look at Javier. I extended my hand and he, too, joined the circle.

"I'm so sorry, Thea," he said.

We all sobbed together as we let the pain of losing Sammy wash over us. It was time to heal our wounds. I cried for Sammy, for James, and for all the pain I knew I still had to live through. But in the midst of my pain, there was happiness, because my friends had forgiven me. "I love you, all."

My father stepped forward. "You should get Thea out of here now," he said. "I fear James may return."

"You're coming with me, Father," I said, pulling away from the others.

"I've told you," my father replied. "My place is here."

"But you can't, how will I ever see you?"

"We will work that out later," he said, herding me toward the door. "Right now, you must leave this house."

"What about Attor and the others? I told them I'd come back and help them."

"You will, but first you have leaves to find and warlocks to kill."

"Maybe I can help?"

We all turned to see Jason, the police officer, in the doorway.

Kym was right behind him, pulling on his arm. "Don't do this, son," she begged.

"You can't hide me anymore, Mother." He gently peeled her fingers from his forearm.

"Please, Jason. I did it to save you," Kym

continued. "You're my only son. I did it out of love."

"I'm sorry, Mother, but I'm not a coward. Thank you for breaking the spell. It's time for me to be a man." He turned to look at me. "Count me in, I want to help."

"We're all with you, Thea," Cory said.

"No," I replied. "I've seen these warlocks fight. You're no match for them. Simon taught the last of these warlocks some extremely powerful wizard spells." I paused, breathing deep. "I will fight them alone."

"Perhaps it's time your friends learned them, as well," my father suggested.

I shot him a look. "No, Father, I don't need their help."

"It's not going to be that easy, Thea," he replied. "Simon has a very strong ally."

"Who?"

"You."

I couldn't help but notice the worried glances exchanged between my friends.

I exhaled, frustrated with my father's lack of faith. "I told you, I won't let the spell do that to me."

"I don't think you're strong enough to fight it."

"You're wrong. I can."

"Can you fight the urge to tell Simon everything?" he asked. "Will you stop yourself when Simon demands that you bond with him?"

"I would never bond with Simon!"

He grabbed my shoulders forcefully. "Do you know how my vision ends, Thea?"

"How could I? You never told me. You said it would change."

"That's why I'm going to tell you now." He drew a deep breath. "After you kill James, you bond with Simon. You then marry Simon and, together, the two of you kill all the wizards in Magia."

"No!" I said, pushing him away.

He seized my shoulders again. "Now it will change," he said. "Having told you, I've now given you control over it."

"How?" I asked. "I don't know what to do."

He looked at me intently. "Bring me the energy. I can help you."

"I'm not letting you die," I said.

"You can't do this without my help!"

"I'm not bringing you the energy, Father!"

He banged his fist on a counter, and a faraway look suddenly clouded his eyes. It was like a light bulb had gone on in his head.   What was he thinking about?

I reached for him. "Don't you believe in me, Father?"

It took him a moment before he finally looked at me. "I believe in my daughter, but I don't believe in you."

"William," Cory gasped.

My father looked down at his ring, still in my hand. "Tell Simon to use it well." He walked to the stove. "I'm sure you'll show him how."

Tears rolled down my cheeks. "I'm sorry you have no faith in me, Father."

"You dare call me 'Father'?" He began preparing tea. "You are no child of mine."

"William, what's gotten into you?" Cory asked.

"Get this woman out of here," he said. "I don't want to look at her another minute. Take her out the back door and put her out with the trash."

"Father?"

"Why are you acting like this?" Cory asked. "She's your daughter."

"My daughter is dead," he replied. "Soon, you will all die at her hand, as well."

"Shut up!" I shouted.

"It's a good thing you cast that spell on James," he said over his shoulder. "I can't imagine you would ever be able to make him happy. Helena will be a good wife."

"William, what are you doing?" Delia asked.

He ignored Delia's question. "I fear James will not be able to wait until the wedding," he said, looking at me. "They may very well bond tonight."

Rage surged through me. I wanted to hurt him.

He smiled and continued. "I should prepare your old room for them. I'm sure Helena will enjoy sleeping in your bed."

I grabbed a knife from the counter and came at him, my hand high in the air, ready to strike. I stood, panting, suddenly realizing what I was about to do. "No!" I screamed.

The others stepped in to intervene.

My father held up his hand to them and looked into my eyes. "That is how deeply you will need to search within yourself to fight this spell."

The look in his eyes woke up something inside me. At that moment, I knew what I had to do. I tapped into a part of me I'd never known before—the wizard part of me. My fears evaporated as I found my confidence, the same confidence my father exuded. My doubts disappeared.

Carefully, I set the knife down on the counter. "I can do this, Father."

He smiled. "Yes, I know."

I felt like a new person, as though I'd been reborn. I sensed things I never had before. I knew where

Simon was, and knew how many men were helping him. I pictured in my head exactly how I would kill each and every one of them. I knew exactly what my father would be doing ten minutes from now. I knew what he was going to cook for dinner, knew what clothes he would wear tomorrow.

I turned to my friends. I smiled, looking at Fish and Delia. They were going to have a happy marriage and four beautiful children. Javier was going to fall in love with a witch. Information flooded my head. I turned to my father, overwhelmed by the flood of visions.

He smiled knowingly. "The thoughts will slow down," he said. "You won't always see as much as you do now."

When I looked deep into his eyes, I could see all the secrets he wasn't ready to tell me yet. Not because he didn't want me knowing them, but because he feared I would share them with Simon. I would prove him wrong.

A plan formed in my head. I knew exactly what to do. It all seemed so simple now. I turned to look at the others. "Go to the apartment," I ordered. "I'll meet you there later. There is something I need to do."

"We'll go with you," Cory replied.

"No, I have to do this alone." I looked back at my father. "I'll find a way to see you, Father. I'll go back and tell Martin what's going on. I'll bring you the energy when Attor breaks Simon's spell."

"I'll give you instructions for them."

I slipped the ring into my pocket. "I'm taking your wand with me. I'll be back after I take care of something."

He nodded. "I'll be waiting."

I smiled at my father one last time and flew out of

the house.

Epilogue
You Filthy Animal

I flew high up into the clouds, out of view from the ground below. It was time to face my demon. I sensed that Simon was expecting me. I had to keep James safe. Simon could never get his hands on him again. I flew straight in through the closed door of the dingy blue house. Helena gasped and jumped to her feet.

Pam rushed into the living room from the kitchen. "Thea, what is it?"

I threw my stick to the side. "Get out," I ordered, "both of you."

Helena's eyes grew wide, then narrowed. "You can't have him back."

"Get out!" I shouted. I looked at Pam intensely, gesturing toward the door with my head.

She nodded, grabbed her cousin's hand, and fled.

Slowly, I searched each room of the house. "Face me, you coward!" As I carefully examined the wall in the living room, my heart began to race.

He was here.

A low, deep rumble shook the house. Cracks formed in the wall and broke apart the sheetrock, revealing a grinning Simon. Muddy sand oozed around his feet and onto the living room floor. The stench burned my eyes and nose. Behind him was a path, leading back to god knows where.

His dark eyes scrutinized every part of my body. A sense of unease crept in as I admired his dark hair and tall stature. His malevolent smile did little to detract from how handsome he was. I fought the urge to throw myself into his arms. I balled my fists and closed my eyes as he approached.

"Is my angel upset?" he asked, his hand on my cheek.

I ignited at the feel of his touch.

"Has Simon done something to upset you?"

His lips brushed mine as he spoke, sending waves of ecstasy through my body. I slid my tongue into his mouth and pulled him to me. His hands traveled my body as I ran my fingers through his hair.

"Leave us," he said.

I heard footsteps behind the wall, but didn't bother to look to see who Simon was talking to.

Simon whispered a spell, and the wall closed up.

"What has my little dove come to tell me?" he asked, planting delicate kisses on my neck.

Finally I found my voice. "I've come with good news, my lord."

"Then I shall reward you," he said, kissing me again.

My breathing accelerated as I fought to control the spell. He pulled away from my lips. "So tell me, my angel. What good news do you bring me?"

"I took the heart," I lied.

He kissed my neck, "So James is dead?"

"He is not, my lord."

"I see. And why didn't you kill him?"

"We have no further use for him," I said, closing my eyes.

"I don't recall giving you the authority to decide that," he said, tugging at my earlobe with his teeth. "I wanted him dead." He pulled away. "You have been a very bad witch." A wicked smile spread across his face. "Would you rather I torture you?"

I smiled back. "Would you rather I kill you?"

His smile disappeared. He glanced nervously at the wall, obviously kicking himself for sending his warlocks away. After a moment, he laughed.

"Is something funny?" I asked.

"Indeed there is," he said, pacing the room. "It seems you're aware of the spell I cast on you. Are you not?"

"I am."

"And do you know if you kill me, you will die with me?"

"I do. But I have a few secrets of my own. Perhaps you'd like me to share them with you."

He stopped and turned. "Please, amuse me."

His penetrating stare sent a shockwave through my body. I fought to compose myself. "If you so much as put a scratch on James, my spell will kill you."

"I see," he said, resuming his pacing. "It appears you have prepared yourself."

"I have, my lord."

He approached me. "Tell me, witch. Does my spell remain unbroken?"

"It does."

"Well then, we shall see. If my spell truly remains unbroken, then you can deny me nothing."

~ 356 ~

"I do not wish to, my lord. I only wanted to warn you."

"Then a test it shall be." He came closer, grabbed my hand, and placed it over his manhood. "What does this do to you?"

I closed my eyes. "It pleases me, my lord."

"Then touch it," he said, guiding my hand. "Show me how much you wish to please me."

"I cannot please you like that . . . yet."

He shoved me back. "This is why I ordered you to kill James!" Again, he paced the room.

"My lord, once James is married, my bond to him will be broken and I can give myself to you completely."

He glanced at me, clearly suspicious. "Then why did you put that spell on James if you wished it so?"

"I did so before I loved you, my lord," I replied. "I'm afraid it cannot be broken."

"And you say once he's married, your bond with him will be severed?"

"Yes," I lied. "I have even chosen a bride for him." I fought the urge to tell him the truth, that my bond with James was already broken.

He smiled. "And did you really take the heart?"

"Yes, I placed it in the crystal."

Simon stopped pacing, and turned. "And where is the crystal?"

I sensed his growing excitement. "In a very safe place, my lord."

He swiftly closed the gap between us and slapped my face. "Did I tell you to do that?"

I lifted my hand to my cheek. "I can take you to it."

"Where is it?" he shouted. "What are you hiding in it?"

"I was hiding this," I replied, pulling out my father's ring.

Simon's eyes widened.

"Wendell sends his regards, my lord."

He extended his hand toward me, his eyes transfixed on the ring. "Give it to me, my angel."

I placed the ring onto his open palm.

Simon wasted no time. He hastily slipped it onto his finger and closed his eyes.

I stifled a giggle. "I'm afraid it only works for me, my lord."

He slapped me again, and I fell back to the floor. Simon stood above me. He leaned over, grabbed a fistful of my hair, and pulled my face up to his. "Make it work for me."

"The ring only works when on my finger."

He seized my shoulders and threw me across the living room. "This will delay things. I wasn't counting on your little maneuver with the crystal."

"It was before I loved you, my lord."

"Yes, yes, so you say," he said, throwing up his hands. "How many can you take there with the ring?"

"As many as you wish, my lord."

"Excellent. A bit of good news for a change. And what did Wendell say?"

"He fears you, my lord," I replied. "He says you possess something that will kill them all."

Simon laughed. "The fool. How could he ever think I would trust him?"

I propped myself up on my elbows. "Did he send you to kill my father?"

"He sent me to kill both of you—the king and his heir." Simon sniffed. "Of course, I knew he would never keep his word."

"So you made your own plan, yes?"

"Wizards shouldn't share so many secrets," he said, smiling.

I tilted my head. "What exactly did he promise you?" I asked.

"Silence! I will deal with Wendell when I return to Magia." He extended his hand and pulled me to my feet. "And you're going to take me there, witch."

"I can take you there now, my lord."

I winced as he brushed his hand across my stinging cheek. "We will not be going alone, my dearest. And I'll need some time to plan—a few months." He pulled off the ring and held it between two fingers. "My tools are not yet ready."

I gazed down at the ring. I had an impulse to snatch it and take Simon to Magia right now, so Attor could kill him, but I knew that now was not the time. I thought about the leaves. I had to find them and destroy them, because I knew in my heart it would set my father free.

"When do we leave?" I asked.

Simon regarded me curiously for a moment. "Why did you hide the crystal in Magia?" he asked, pushing me back against the wall.

"Because I knew it would be safe there," I replied.

His eyes narrowed. "Why don't I trust you, witch?"

"I would rather die than betray you, my lord."

He exhaled loudly. "You're sure my spell remains unbroken?"

I reached for his face and drew him close, our lips inches apart. "If the spell were broken, I would have killed you the moment I saw you."

He slowly pulled away.

My stomach lurched. He seemed unconvinced.

"We'll see," he said, stepping back. He looked down at my blouse and back into my eyes. "Take off your clothes."

My heart thumped in my chest. I stood, frozen, staring back at him.

He tilted his head and smiled. "I gave you an order, witch."

My hands trembled as I slowly unbuttoned my blouse and allowed it to slip to the floor. I unzipped my pants and stepped out of them. I hesitated.

"Everything," he ordered.

I swallowed hard and obeyed.

He stepped close and lifted my chin with the tip of his finger. "Do you love me?"

My lips quivered. "No one could love you more."

He ran his hand over my breasts. "Does my touch please you?"

"It does, my lord."

He reached for my hand and placed it on his manhood again. "Touch it, witch. Show me how much you want me."

I did as he asked.

He moaned and slid his tongue into my mouth. "More," he whispered. "Feel me more."

When I did as he asked, he pushed me away and laughed. "Here," he said, tossing me the ring. "Look for me at the ship in a few days. I'll have another place for us to meet." He turned toward the wall. "Oh, and I expect you to speed up this wedding, witch. I'll be waiting, my little dove," he said as he disappeared down the path, the wall closing up behind him.

I hastily waved my hand, and my clothes flew

back onto my body. I slipped the ring into my pocket and grabbed my stick. I flew straight up into the clouds, screaming into the wind. I wiped my lips with the back of my hand. I felt dirty, tainted. "You filthy animal!"

My stomach churned as I flew. I fought the urge to vomit. Desperate to wash off his stench, I flew toward the lake and right into the water. I let out another scream as I disappeared under the surface.

Minutes later, I dragged myself out and spit onto the grass. I couldn't get Simon's taste out of my mouth. His touch didn't please me the way it had at the Halloween ball. Instead, it turned my stomach. But I had done the impossible: convinced him to leave James alone, and that his spell had control over me. He now believed I would do anything for him, even bond myself to him.

I commanded my stick out of the water and flew off. When I finally got back to James' house, I was surprised to see Cory through the kitchen window. When he spotted me outside, he shook his head. I immediately ducked and peeked in.

James was there, holding up a ring. The large diamond glinted under the kitchen lights. "I'm a happy man, William," James said. "By this time tomorrow, my dreams will have come true."

My father nodded politely. "I'm sure of it, master."

James turned to Cory. "And I'll be needing a best man."

Cory glanced my way and back to James. "I'd be honored, James."

"You know, it's funny," James said. "I woke up this morning feeling like all my problems were suddenly gone. The sun shined a little brighter, the flowers more fragrant than ever. It's like I've been given a whole new lease on life. I've never been happier."

My eyes filled as James shook Cory's hand, grabbed the picnic basket from the counter, and walked out. I dropped to my knees and cried into my hands, my heart shattered. James was happy now. His problems were behind him. I swallowed hard at the realization: the problems in his life had been caused by me. Without me, he was free to live the life he deserved.

As much as it hurt, I knew it was time to give myself the same chance, to rid my memory of our ill-fated love. I hurried inside, straight into my father's arms. "Just do it," I cried. "Do it now."

My father wrapped his arms around me and held me. I leaned back and looked at him. "Cast your spell, Father," I pleaded. "Take him out of my head."

A single tear escaped the corner of his eye. He touched my face and smiled kindly. "Do you have faith in me?" he asked.

"Yes, Father."

"Close your eyes," he said.

"Only James, Father," I said. "Only take out James."

"I give you my word," he assured me. "You will remember everything else."

I drew a deep breath and rested my head on his chest. He called Cory over. "Take her home when I am done," my father ordered. "She will lose certain memories, but I have already taken care of that."

"Is she still going to remember all that's going on?" Cory asked.

"Yes, but we will discuss that later." He took Cory's hand and placed it on my shoulder. "Take good care of her, son. Love her and make her happy."

Cory's voice trembled. "I will, William. I'll do everything you have asked of me."

My father waved his hand.

When I opened my eyes, the entire kitchen was aglow. My memories were spinning into a funnel in front of my eyes—James' face, our wedding, the first moment I laid eyes on him. One by one, the memories of our love spun and pulled away and, with them, went the pain in my heart. I closed my eyes again when the memory of his name began to fade.

"James," I whispered as I drifted into a deep sleep.

Made in the USA
Lexington, KY
24 September 2015